"You expect me to behave better than you, Miss Wells?"

Paris asked softly, a wry smile playing about his lips.

"Yes, I do," Clara answered, trying to sound determined, all her effort threatening to be undone by the pleasure his touch sent thrilling through her.

"You present me with an interesting dilemma. Most people believe me to be the epitome of wasted profligacy, yet you seem to think me to be an honorable nobleman. I wonder why, and which you would truly prefer?"

"I expect you to be honorable all the time," she said, her pulse throbbing in her ears, her breathing rushed and shallow. She felt like a moth trapped in the flame of his eyes. Suddenly, he blew out her candle, trapping her in the darkness.

"That would be your mistake," he murmured, and she felt his arms go around her and draw her to him....

Dear Reader,

The Wastrel, by Margaret Moore, introduces a new series of Victorian romance novels from this award-winning author, featuring a trio of "most unsuitable" heroes that she has aptly named MOST UNSUITABLE.... *The Wastrel* is the magical story of a disowned heiress and a devil-may-care bachelor who learn about love with the help of her colorful relatives. Don't miss it.

Longtime Harlequin Historicals author DeLoras Scott is back this month with *The Devil's Kiss*, a Western romantic comedy about two misfits who discover love, despite Indians, outlaws and themselves. And with her is talented newcomer Tori Phillips, whose new medieval novel *Silent Knight*, is the tale of a would-be monk and a French noblewoman who fall in love on a delightful journey across medieval England.

A Western from Rae Muir, another 1996 March Madness author, *The Trail to Temptation*, about a star-crossed couple who fight their attraction on a trail drive from Texas to Montana, rounds out this month's selection.

Whatever your taste in reading, we hope Harlequin Historicals will keep you coming back for more. Please keep a lookout for all four titles, available wherever books are sold.

Sincerely,

Tracy Farrell
Senior Editor

Please address questions and book requests to:
Harlequin Reader Service
U.S.: 3010 Walden Ave., P.O. Box 1325, Buffalo, NY 14269
Canadian: P.O. Box 609, Fort Erie, Ont. L2A 5X3

MARGARET MOORE

THE WASTREL

Harlequin Books

TORONTO • NEW YORK • LONDON
AMSTERDAM • PARIS • SYDNEY • HAMBURG
STOCKHOLM • ATHENS • TOKYO • MILAN
MADRID • WARSAW • BUDAPEST • AUCKLAND

ISBN 0-373-28944-8

THE WASTREL

Books by Margaret Moore

Harlequin Historicals

*_A Warrior's Heart_ #118
China Blossom #149
*_A Warrior's Quest_ #175
†_The Viking_ #200
*_A Warrior's Way_ #224
Vows #248
†_The Saxon_ #268
*_The Welshman's Way_ #295
*_The Norman's Heart_ #311
*_The Baron's Quest_ #328
‡_The Wastrel_ #344

Harlequin Books

Mistletoe Marriages
"Christmas in the Valley"

*Warrior Series
†The Viking Series
‡Most Unsuitable...

MARGARET MOORE

confesses that her first "crush" was Errol Flynn. The second was "Mr. Spock." She thinks that it explains why her heroes tend to be either charming rogues or lean, inscrutable tough guys.

Margaret lives in Scarborough, Ontario, with her husband, two children and two cats. She used to sew and read for reasons other than research.

To my brother, David,
who teased me.
You're forgiven.

Chapter One

England, 1862

"We should be there, should we not?" Aurora Wells demanded anxiously as she leaned toward the window on her niece's side of the hansom cab and peered out onto the foggy streets of London.

"We haven't been gone quite long enough, Aunt," Clara Wells replied patiently. She surreptitiously tried to extricate the skirt of her gown from beneath her aunt's ample hip before the expensive silk was hopelessly crushed.

Aunt Aurora's turban of cloth of gold perched on her henna-dyed hair tilted over one pale blue eye and threatened to tumble into Clara's lap. "It cannot be this far to Lord Pimblett's, surely," she insisted, this time addressing her husband, "not even in such fog. I do believe the cabbie intends to cheat us!"

"'Had we but world enough, and time,'" Uncle Byron quoted absently from his place on the opposite seat, his gaze fastened on the water-stained ceiling of the cab.

Despite his distracted manner, he was, Clara noted approvingly, dressed in very proper evening clothes, unlike Aunt Aurora. With his beatific expression and shoulder-length white hair, Uncle Byron looked kind, and even quite wise. Kind he certainly was, and wise he might have been, had his mother not made the fatal error of naming him Byron, for her son had come to believe that with such a name he *must* be a poet.

Her aunt, on the other hand, wore what might have been fashionable among the artistic set fifty years ago. Her gown was a Regency style, with the waistline beneath her substantial bosom and made of several layers of flowing white muslin, which was at least inexpensive, if not flattering. The style was intended to look Grecian. Over this, she wore a flowing stole of gold-colored taffeta that matched her usual exotic headdress.

Aunt Aurora blessedly shifted and Clara's dress was momentarily out of danger.

The gown had cost far more than Clara had been willing to pay. Unfortunately, her aunt had been embarrassingly insistent. After all, she had exclaimed several times, regardless of the other customers in the dressmaker's shop, Clara should dress as befitted her station. She *was* a duke's granddaughter, even if her mother had been disowned by the old reprobate, and this was to be her introduction into London society. It was only by using her knowledge of her aunt's mental processes that Clara had managed to avoid a garish gown of bright peacock blue or deep purple and a headdress that resembled an overgrown bouquet. Clara had convinced her aunt that she should appear demure, almost nunlike, in case word of her appearance should get back to her grandfather. Let there be nothing—*nothing*—about Clara's clothes or demeanor that anyone could fault. Fortunately, Aunt Aurora had agreed, so Clara had no cause to be concerned about her garments—provided they could escape being squashed.

"Perhaps Lord Mulholland will be there, too," Aunt Aurora said excitedly. "Wouldn't that be wonderful—the handsomest man in England, or so they say! What a triumph it would be to do *his* portrait!"

"I daresay he already has several, if he is the conceited wastrel people say he is," Clara replied. "He's probably a vain coxcomb without a brain inside his handsome head," she concluded, for she had indeed heard of the wealthy nobleman whose first name, Paris, seemed to have been chosen with predestination. Paris of Troy was the legendary seducer of Helen of Sparta, an act which caused the Trojan War.

No one possessed of such a combination of looks, wealth and title would pass unremarked in London. Unfortunately, Clara could easily imagine how such a man would respond to her aunt.

"I am absolutely *certain* the cabbie has gone out of his way," Aunt Aurora declared again, straining to see outside. "Is that not Rotten Row? We should *not* be in Hyde Park! I feel sure he is going to deceive us!"

"No, Aunt," Clara said calmly. "He is going the right route."

She kept a bemused smile from her face, for even if the cabbie *was* trying to cheat them, Aunt Aurora would never confront the man. It would be Clara's responsibility to pay the cabbie, just as she paid all the household bills for her guardians. She had done so from the time she had come to live with them after her parents' deaths when she was thirteen. Clara realized then that Aunt Aurora and Uncle Byron had minds above the daily practicalities, or so they honestly believed.

For her part, Clara was in no great hurry to get to the London mansion of Lord and Lady Pimblett, for the distance from their lodgings in Bloomsbury to this exclusive part of the city was much farther socially than it was geographically.

She wasn't even sure why or how they had been invited to this ball. She had been lingering over one of the mummies in the British Museum when she realized that her aunt had approached an extremely well-dressed, extremely poised older woman and engaged her in conversation.

Clara had immediately suspected the worst: that her aunt was asking if the lady wished to have her portrait painted.

No matter how many times her aunt approached complete strangers with the object of obtaining a commission, Clara never got used to it. This summer, her aunt had been worse than usual, and Clara knew it was all her fault. If she had not been over the age to be "out," her aunt would have been much less persistent. Clara sighed as she wished that she didn't have to grow up at all, if this...this *solicitation* were to be part of the price.

After the woman had moved on, her aunt had revealed, with her usual unbridled enthusiasm, that they were invited to this ball.

"Just think of it!" Aunt Aurora declared, returning Clara's thoughts to the present as she clasped together her plump hands bejeweled by rings of paste stones that she thought quite lovely. "An invitation to a social evening with Lord and Lady Pimblett! What a delight! What a pleasure! I *knew* it was no mistake to speak with her in the museum! Dear Lady Pimblett! What a form! What a figure!"

"What a corset," Clara remarked with a good-natured smile. "She swooned when she tried to catch her husband up at the museum. I suppose she spends most of the day on a sofa and considers herself sickly."

"Clara!" Aunt Aurora admonished, tapping Clara on the arm with her fan that was decorated with a hand-painted scene of half-naked nymphs and dryads that Clara was certain was going to cause some scandalized whispers at a Mayfair mansion. "She is a woman of great position, and we are deeply honored to be invited to her home. I must ask you to remember that."

Clara flushed and nodded, for it was not often that kindhearted Aunt Aurora rebuked her. She would simply have to be calm and patient, and try not to let Aunt Aurora's manner upset her, even though she knew exactly what was going to happen. Her aunt would wander about the ball asking anybody who glanced her way if they would care to have their portrait done.

Clara wondered for what seemed the thousandth time why she had let her aunt talk her into accompanying them to this vast house surely full of dull, uninteresting people who would snub her. Or worse, look at her as if she led some kind of vaguely dishonest life not much removed from those unfortunate women in the streets.

Aunt Aurora, however, seemed to neither fear nor notice other people's reactions, like that of the cabbie, who had stared with his mouth open as they approached his vehicle.

Aunt Aurora frowned. "Perhaps she needs such an undergarment. She may have a weak back, and not every woman is naturally blessed with a figure like yours, Clara."

"Nor has every woman such an amiable and forward-thinking aunt to ban the detestable undergarment from her home," Clara acknowledged.

"Hear, hear!" Uncle Byron cried, leaning forward suddenly and grasping his wife's hand while gazing at her adoringly. "My Amazon! My warrior queen, has ever been, so far seen...." Uncle Byron's brow wrinkled, his green eyes became serious and he began to rub his chin as his attention returned to the ceiling. "Now what?" he murmured. "Queen, been, seen, tangerine...?"

"The muse speaks!" Aunt Aurora whispered quite unnecessarily as she put her finger on her lips, obviously unable to remain silent despite the muse's unseen presence.

Clara turned to look out the window and hide her smile. When the muse spoke, she had best be quiet. It was the fastest way to achieve the end to one of Uncle Byron's poetic reveries.

A row of particularly fine town houses alight with blazing windows came into view. The tall white buildings seemed to glow in the moonlight, as if even the fog could be held at bay if one was rich enough.

"I believe we have arrived," Clara said softly, suddenly terrified.

She knew nothing of these people and little of the aristocratic world they inhabited, for her mother had been disowned before Clara was born. What did they know of hers—of watching how every tuppence was spent, of the small, stuffy flat they lived in, of the noise of the neighbors and the street? What would they make of *her,* a woman of no great beauty whose mother had had the effrontery and bad taste to fall in love with her dancing master, and worse manners to marry the fellow? How could her guardians have accepted this invitation? How could they be so willfully blind?

She looked at them again, her uncle thoughtfully surveying the town house, her aunt breathless with anticipation—and was ashamed of herself. Why *shouldn't* they be there? Aunt Aurora was the kindest, sweetest person Clara knew. Her uncle was an intelligent, well-read man who could have been a success in almost any field, if his mother had named him anything other than Byron. *She* was a lady's daughter, of higher rank than even Lord and Lady Pimblett. She would remember these things, and hold her head high.

After they disembarked, Clara reached into her reticule and brought out the exact amount necessary to pay the cabbie, leaving a similar amount for the journey home. The cabbie squinted at the coins in his palm, sniffed scornfully, then clicked his tongue to alert his horse and drove off.

"That poor man does not have the artistic sentiment, I fear," Aunt Aurora remarked sadly, as if the man suffered a grave deficiency.

Then, blissfully unaware that Clara was not enthused by this social engagement, Aunt Aurora and Uncle Byron proceeded toward the steps leading into the mansion while Clara followed slowly behind.

As they reached the bottom step, a private coach adorned with a family crest stopped where the cab had been moments before. Clara glanced back as the door opened and a top hat appeared, followed quickly by a broad-shouldered, well-dressed individual wearing an opera cape. The dark fabric swirled when the man leapt lightly onto the walk, revealing a brilliant scarlet lining.

As if this man needed anything extra to draw attention to himself, Clara thought, looking at his classically handsome profile in the lamplight.

Then she realized, without having to be told, that she must be looking at the handsomest man in England—Lord Paris Mulholland. There could not be two men in London with such a form and face.

He reached into his pocket and flipped a coin toward the driver. "Three hours, Jones," he announced in a languid, deep voice that bespoke wealth and education, and that also held a tinge of amused good humor in it. "Mind, I shall be most aggrieved if you are late, and I won't listen to any excuses! Then we'll be off to White's, for I've laid on a bet with poor, dim Boffington that I can make her ladyship swoon at least five times before I meet him there. Too easy, really. I should have made it ten."

The lighthearted command in the man's voice quite captivated Clara and she wished she had a part of that bet, which would surely be won, so much so that when Lord Mulholland suddenly turned and looked at her, she gasped with guilt. She attempted to mask her shame and surprise by effecting a cough—and wound up sounding as though she were in immediate danger of choking to death.

Aunt Aurora and Uncle Byron, who had also halted when the stranger arrived, hurried to her. "Are you quite all right, my dear?" Aunt Aurora asked.

Clara nodded, took a step toward the town house and unfortunately tripped on the hem of her lovely new gown. She hastily disentangled herself, but before she could move farther away, the stranger was beside her.

"Somebody expiring on the very steps?" he inquired politely, reaching out to take her arm in a grip that was surprising strong.

Seen so close, Clara realized he was *extremely* attractive, with eyes of such brilliant piercing blue beneath finely arched blond brows that she felt some kind of pure, invigorating energy blaze forth from them. He was smiling, and his chin had the merest hint of a dimple beneath full, sensual lips.

She had expected a man with his reputation to be a vain dandy, but she couldn't have been more wrong, for Paris Mulholland exuded a masculinity that needed no embellishment.

If there was any mercy under heaven, the ground would open up and swallow her.

"I tripped." Her embarrassment caused her to put on as severe an expression as she could muster as she pulled away from Lord Mulholland. "I am fine, thank you."

Clara could look very severe, yet that only seemed to amuse the man, who smiled most charmingly and ran his gaze over the three of them.

It was happening already, Clara thought with dismay. Impertinent appraisal. She knew what he would think when she discovered that her aunt was an artist and her uncle a poet—that she, living with such people, must be of lax morals.

Clara drew herself up and directed a steely gaze at him, remembering that she was most properly and demurely dressed, so there could be no good reason for his long assessment of *her*.

"Greetings, fellow bacchanal! Are you come to join the revels?" Uncle Byron asked by way of salutation.

To speak so to a stranger, and in Mayfair, too! Would Uncle Byron *never* learn to observe the social niceties?

The nobleman lifted his black silk top hat and bowed gracefully, and she noted his sleek, blond hair and long, slender fingers. "Allow me to present myself. I am Lord Paris Mulholland."

Aunt Aurora gave Clara what could only be described as an impressed and triumphant look, and Uncle Byron would have swept his hat from his head if he had worn one. Instead, he made a very low and flourishing bow such as Lord Mulholland might recently have witnessed on a theater stage. "Byron Bromblehampton Wells, sir," he announced. "My wife, Aurora, and our niece, Miss Clara Covington Wells. Charmed to make your acquaintance, my lord!"

"I've been hoping to meet you, my lord," Aunt Aurora gushed with equal enthusiasm. "I have heard it said you are a handsome man worthy of your legendary name, and it is most gratifying to see that your reputation is quite well-founded."

"Thank you, dear lady," the sleek and undoubtedly seductive Lord Mulholland replied as he took Aunt Aurora's plump hand and gallantly pressed a kiss upon it. "But I am named for the city, not the man."

He took Clara's hand in his. Even though they both wore gloves, his touch was astoundingly delightful—firm yet gentle, too. "Your servant, Miss Wells," he said, kissing the back of her hand lightly. He glanced up at her face with a roguish grin.

It occurred to Clara that it didn't much matter how Lord Mulholland came by his name, for it was all too fitting.

"Have you ever had your portrait done?" Aunt Aurora asked eagerly.

At that moment, it would have been a blessed relief if there had been a tornado, or an earthquake or any other cataclysm—anything other than to have to stand there and listen while Aunt Aurora said, "I'm an artist, my lord, and nothing would give me greater pleasure than to paint you."

"Indeed?" Lord Mulholland replied. "That is a most intriguing proposition." He faced Clara. "And does this delightful young creature also paint?"

"No, my lord. This *creature* does not," she answered firmly, moving away and telling herself that his roguish smile was probably nothing more than a habit with him. No doubt he considered any and every woman an object for an attempted seduction.

"A pity," he replied. "May I escort you inside?"

No! Clara wanted to shout. What would people think if they entered here together? Think! They would believe they *knew.* A female stranger of such dubious social heritage accompanying a man like Lord Paris Mulholland must be "under his protection." What little reputation she might have hoped to maintain with a demure manner and extremely plain and modest gown would fly away like a frightened sparrow. She should have insisted that she remain at home tonight!

He held out his arm, but toward Aunt Aurora, not her. It was the most impeccably correct thing to do, and Clara thought she must have been temporarily deranged to imagine that he would want to escort her.

"How perfectly delightful," Aunt Aurora said as she stepped ahead to take his proffered arm. "Now, about your portrait...."

"I shall have to give it some thought," Lord Mulholland said, and Clara could hear the laughter in his voice.

A man of his wealth could have any painter from the Royal Academy. He would never want to sit for Aunt Aurora, so why did he have to lead her on? Did he enjoy making sport of others or placing them in embarrassing positions? Probably. It would be in keeping with what she had heard of him from some of her aunt's friends: that Paris Mulholland's sole goal in life was to enjoy himself.

If he did decide to have Aunt Aurora paint his portrait—and Clara had to admit that they needed the money—and if he did come to her aunt's lodgings to sit, she would ensure that she was out of the house. Or perhaps, finances notwithstanding, it would be better to discourage any talk of a portrait entirely. Although Clara loved her aunt dearly, there was no escaping the fact that every portrait her aunt painted bore a marked resemblance to the Duke of Wellington. She could almost hear the cutting criticism Lord Mulholland would make of the picture, and the way he would regale his equally ne'er-do-well friends with tales of her relatives' eccentricities.

"A fine fellow!" Uncle Byron whispered in her ear as they followed him into the well-appointed house.

Clara didn't answer. Instead, she concentrated on the large, ornately decorated foyer, which was nearly the size of their entire flat. The floor was Italian marble, and the wallpaper was of intricate design, obviously costly. "So noble, so charming," Uncle Byron continued. "Worthy of his name, wouldn't you say? I can believe a man like that could seduce the most beautiful woman in the world."

"And I can believe he wouldn't care that such a selfish act would start a war," Clara said, reminding her uncle that the name Paris was not one a man should be particularly proud of.

Lord Mulholland, having handed his flamboyant cape and hat to a footman, suddenly whirled around to face her. There was a smile on his good-looking face but also something that looked suspiciously like criticism in his brilliantly blue eyes. "I believe I mentioned that I am *not* named for the man who seduced Helen of Troy. My mother, in a flight of fancy, named me for the City of Light, where I was apparently conceived.

"Now, if you will all excuse me, I see an old friend inside," he concluded coldly. He made a slight, polite bow before striding away.

Clara flushed again, and told herself she had been a fool to speak her thoughts out loud. She had been rude, too. Of all people, she should know how it felt to be judged by a name or an occupation.

"We must speak later, my lord, about the portrait!" Aunt Aurora called after him, waving gaily. "My dear, just think!" she exclaimed rapturously, clasping her plump hands together and ignoring the footman who waited to take their wraps. "Lord Paris Mulholland! If he agrees to sit for me, I shall be quite famous!"

Clara kept quiet, but she would rather walk barefoot to Dover in the middle of winter than have a man like Paris Mulholland in the studio.

She told herself that her reservations had absolutely *nothing* to do with his provocative manner and handsome face, or that the evening dress of pristine white shirt, white cravat and black tails seemed to have been designed with him specifically in mind. After all, her guardians' bohemian friends had been trying to seduce her for years, with no success. She could fend off Lord Mulholland, too.

Even if he was the most tempting man she had ever met.

Chapter Two

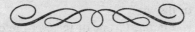

"Don't you agree, Mulholland?" Lord Pimblett demanded, smacking his palm on the marble mantle of the drawing room, which was decorated with all the embellishments currently in vogue. "Give 'em a bit, and they only want more! Workhouses and the Poor Law Amendment Act are the best things that ever happened to this country, sir!"

Paris was quite sure Lord Pimblett was adding, "You young muttonhead!" in his mind, even though the man clearly cherished hopes of having his eldest daughter wed to the Mulholland name and fortune, if not the physical embodiment of those things. He was also very well aware that he had an audience of young female admirers gathered about him like so many colorful butterflies, so he waved his wineglass in a shallow salute.

"I myself have never lived in one of their hovels," he replied to the indignant nobleman, whose face flushed with irritation, "worn filthy, flea-infested clothing or eaten one of their pitiful meals. Since I do not possess the imagination of your lordship, so necessary to pass judgment when one lacks experience, I must bow to your superior knowledge of the lives of the lower classes.''

Lord Pimblett's face turned scarlet, which made an interesting contrast with his white muttonchop whiskers. Paris knew he had made his point and gone quite far enough in exposing the shortcomings of his host's opinion. Therefore, he smiled graciously and took a sip of his wine.

"Fancy *you* in rags!'' one of the ever-present young women said with a shocked gasp and a giggle.

"None of you would ever look at me again,'' Paris said sorrowfully and waited for the young women to protest. As they immediately did.

It amused him to watch their reactions—one of the few things in London that *did* amuse him anymore. Some bored young men turned to drink, or gambling or more sordid vices when life palled; Paris Mulholland amused himself by playing the charming wastrel, with the additional benefit of being the center of attention for such delightful bevies of carefully bred young ladies.

Not that he had any desire to seduce even one of the eager women, although it pleased his vanity to make them swarm around him. They were too innocent and unworldly, most of them, and despite his name and not completely unearned reputation, he would not take advantage of their naiveté. Trying to maintain their adulation simply made the interminable Season pass.

He turned away to hide his satisfied smile, and encountered the watchful eyes of the young woman he had met outside, the artist's niece, Clara. She sat in the farthest corner of a window seat, nearly hidden behind a large potted fern, as if she were afraid to be seen.

She looked like a nun in a cloister, and a strict one at that, with her dark brown hair pulled back plainly in a hard little knot of a bun, her dark brows slightly too thick to be conventionally pretty, and her full lips pressed together repressively. She wore an abominable gray dress with an absurdly high neckline and tight sleeves. A hair shirt would be more comfortable than that garment, he thought, which did nothing to flatter its wearer. Perhaps she enjoyed the mortification of the flesh.

As he caught her eye, her mouth frowned as grimly as the sternest of nannies catching a young charge in some mischief, and in her eyes was contempt rather than admiration.

So he winked at her.

She didn't do anything. Didn't blush, didn't glare, didn't smile, didn't frown. She simply looked at him as if . . . as if he weren't there.

Paris Mulholland was not used to being ignored, and he found it an intensely unpleasant experience.

Telling himself one young woman's lack of response was unimportant, he looked away and saw Lady Pimblett slowly advancing toward him, nodding graciously at the assembly. Her presence, along with the nearly overpowering scent of perfume that pervaded the air around her, reminded him of his bet. He didn't need Boffington's money, of course; he simply found betting on such things harmless sport.

And if certain young females thought him nothing but a complete waste of breath and life, he didn't care.

"I was reading a book by that chap Dickens," he drawled, bestowing a warm smile on his hostess.

"*Oliver Twist*. He's rather too good at describing things we shouldn't have to think about, wouldn't you agree, my lady? Poorhouses and starving children and thieves. And that part about beating a young woman to death...."

"Oh, my," her ladyship murmured.

Paris then had the immense satisfaction of seeing Lady Pimblett sink onto a sofa and fan herself violently. Four times in less than two hours! Too easy, really, indeed!

"That Dickens fellow should be horsewhipped!" Lord Pimblett blustered. "Stirring up all kinds of trouble. Thinks we should all give up our money to buy mansions and sweet cakes for the poor, I suppose! Stupid fool!"

"He's a wonderful chap to have at parties," Paris remarked, recalling well the only time he had met the writer, whose works he had never actually read. Dickens enjoyed the theater, and had been almost a whole play in himself as he acted out parts of *Oliver Twist*. It was a never-to-be-forgotten experience.

"If I ever meet him, I'll...I'll... He'll be sorry!" Lord Pimblett continued. "The poor are lazy, sir, *lazy*, and if they won't work, they should starve!"

Paris's fingers tightened around the delicate crystal glass that cost more than many a man earned in a year. He never ceased to be amazed at the way the men of his class were all too quick to ascribe certain characteristics to the lower classes when he could think of several of them who would starve to death if they didn't have family fortunes to sustain them.

Lady Pimblett recovered sufficiently to rise slightly, her action causing him to note yet again the opulent ostentation of the woman's garments, as well as the fraudulent air of weak ill health that she enjoyed to the utmost.

One more swoon and he would win his bet. Telling himself not to fret about any disapproval a gray-gowned young lady might express, he quite remorselessly applied himself to the task.

"But the bodies, my lord," he said plaintively. "What would we do with the piles of bodies that would be left in the street? The stench—"

He won his bet, and in the process it looked as if he had succeeded in causing Lady Pimblett to truly faint. His audience of young ladies emitted politely shocked squeals of alarm, and their fans moved rapidly.

His glance was drawn once more to the window seat, now empty. Just as well. The gray nun would only be looking daggers at him anyway.

"Don't just stand there!" Lord Pimblett rumbled to nobody in particular. "Water!"

Paris obliged by yanking some huge and exceedingly ugly chrysanthemums out of a vase standing on a spindly-legged table, dipping his fingers in the water, and sprinkling his hostess's face.

Lady Pimblett came to with startling abruptness as her cheeks changed color before their very eyes, going from a fashionable paleness to a far more healthy rose. The young ladies, whose mothers would never permit any application of cosmetics and acquainted that practice with the oldest profession, drew back in stunned horror as Lady Pimblett swiftly covered her face with her lace fan.

Lord Pimblett was staring as hard as any of them, and it occurred to Paris that perhaps he had never seen his wife without certain cosmetic additions. Poor man—and poor, deluded Lady Pimblett, for her natural color was far more pleasing to Paris's eye than the white of her powder.

Then, out of the corner of his eye, Paris saw a beautiful and haughty young woman at the far end of the room, wearing a very expensive, fashionable, low-cut gown of pink silk that exposed her considerable personal charms. Lady Helena Pimblett, the woman he was supposed to marry—or so Helena firmly believed, although he himself had said nothing about such a thing—hurried toward him, a questioning look on her fair and arrogant face.

A precipitous flight was clearly called for. Paris muttered another apology and strode toward the door.

As he passed by a gaggle of different young women, each one perfumed and overdressed in the latest fashions, which meant that they resembled nothing so much as large bells, he smiled and nodded and wondered what the severe Miss Wells would make of the way they eyed him. Each one, he knew, was sizing him up as marriage material; each one would probably take him, if he offered.

Not Miss Wells, he ventured, recalling her indifferent expression.

He kept walking, since it would be a little time yet before Jones returned with his carriage. People were everywhere, it seemed, and the air was warm and stuffy. He spied the entrance to the library, and decided to see if that dark, mahogany-paneled room was any emptier. He opened the door, then paused.

A man was sitting on the floor, surrounded by a pile of books, mumbling. Paris recognized Byron Wells by his unusually long, white hair. A scholar, probably—something guaranteed to make Paris flee his presence. The young man slipped out again unnoticed.

He was about to continue on his way when he saw the edge of a now-familiar gray gown just inside the door of the music room and heard the artistic Mrs. Wells, her voice enthusiastically issuing forth from inside.

"I quite *dote* on flowers," Aurora Wells said. "They make such pretty still lifes, don't you think?"

Hester Pimblett, Helena's younger sister, moved into view. Unlike her elder sister, Hester dressed in a simple manner. Her ball gown was made of blue velvet, which looked well with her brown hair and managed to bring out the blue in her large eyes. For embellishment, she wore only a simple pearl necklace and white elbow-length gloves. She would no doubt find the stern Miss Wells something of a kindred spirit, at least as far as simplicity of clothing went. Nevertheless, compared to Clara Wells, Hester—indeed, all the young ladies of Paris's acquaintance—seemed distinctly lacking in some vital energy.

The prospect of seeing the rather straitlaced middle Pimblett sister, who was a sweet young woman with about as much personality as a bowl of porridge, encounter any kind of artist would be entertaining, and even more so if the artist were the vivacious Mrs. Wells. There was also the added inducement of watching Clara Wells when she was with other women to make Paris choose to linger.

Not that he cared if she was dour only when he was nearby, indicating a disapproval of him personally. She was nobody, and so it was completely irrelevant what she thought of him.

However, Paris also realized that Hester would become as silent as a stone if she knew he was listening, so he hid in an alcove behind a large Oriental vase on an ornate wooden stand.

"People are so much more interesting than a bowl of fruit!" Mrs. Wells continued. "And the fresh fruit attracts flies, especially in the summer months! I assure you, I thought I would go mad the last time I did such a painting. I *much* prefer portraits. So much more scope for expression!"

"Do you have models?" he heard Hester ask timidly.

"Of course I do," Mrs. Wells replied. "Painting the human figure is not easy."

Paris shifted behind the vase, wanting to catch a glimpse of Clara Wells' face for no reason he wished to acknowledge. He was rewarded for his efforts by encountering a type of expression that he had never seen before, but had often felt upon his own visage when his mother had been in one of her gayer moods: a sort of patient forbearance, embarrassment and defiance all rolled into one. His mother, much as he had loved her, had frequently scandalized a dinner party with her comments.

"What of the classical scenes you do, such as your lovely fan," Hester asked, "when your subjects are . . . that is, when they aren't . . . ?"

"When they're nude?" Mrs. Wells demanded.

Paris had to shove his hand in his mouth to avoid laughing out loud at poor Hester's blushing yet avidly curious face—and he thought Clara Wells not incapable of plotting a murder, judging by the look in her eyes as she regarded her aunt and crossed her slender arms.

Hester nodded once and looked around guiltily, causing Paris to move as far back into the alcove as possible. He had no idea that Hester would ever express curiosity on such a subject.

"Nudes are all very well, but I can so rarely find a decent body."

"Aunt Aurora!" Miss Wells admonished helplessly.

Paris's heart went out to the blushing, appalled Miss Wells. He well remembered how easily upset a young person could be by a parent's behavior.

"It's all right," Hester said in her warm, friendly way. "I asked her about it. And I appreciate her honesty. It's quite refreshing."

Clara Wells relaxed visibly, and smiled.

She really wasn't homely, with her frank hazel eyes, pointed elfin chin, perfect complexion and widow's peak. Indeed, she seemed quite a different person altogether when she smiled, and one he would like to know better.

"What would you consider a decent body?" Hester asked, a studious expression on her face.

Mrs. Wells played with her absurdly delightful turban, which had slipped slightly askew. "Michelangelo's David, for one. And I daresay that under Lord Mulholland's clothing there's a body worth painting."

"Or else he has a magician for a tailor," Clara Wells said. The expression in her hazel eyes could only be called devilish.

Paris was not exceptionally vain; however, he did not appreciate hearing that *anyone* would think he had need of special tailoring to render his form attractive.

"Oh, that's all natural," Hester said, laughing softly.

"Really?" Mrs. Wells demanded. "How do you know?"

Paris waited for her answer with acute curiosity.

"My sister Helena told me."

It took a great deal of self-control for Paris to remain where he was instead of demanding to know what the devil Helena knew about it. But Hester would never answer such a query if he were to ask it bluntly.

Fortunately, Hester saw the almost equally curious expression on Clara Wells' face. "She saw him without his shirt one day when she was walking past his bedroom," Hester explained.

Gad! Paris thought angrily. He would keep his door bolted from now on, especially given that the Pimbletts were due to visit his country home when the Season ended.

"Well, then, I *must* do a portrait of him," Mrs. Wells replied decisively. "I shall have to improve upon the acquaintance first, of course, and show him samples of my work. If only the Season were not nearly over! I shall have to wait until it resumes, I suppose."

"Yes," Hester agreed. "He is leaving soon for his house in the country." She gave Mrs. Wells a smile. "My family is to visit him there later." She flushed a bright red. "I don't know how I shall ever look him in the face now!"

Mrs. Wells laughed genially and winked. "The man is so perfectly charming, I'm sure you'll find a way."

"Oh, no! Not at all! I have no interest in him *that* way," Hester protested sincerely, blushing again. "My sister..." Her words trailed off, but there could be no mistaking the significance of her look.

Paris frowned. He had never given Helena much encouragement; she had never needed any. And he had supposed that if he had to marry, he could do worse. Helena was a beautiful and wealthy young woman from a fine, old family. She was also spoiled, vain and had a voice that could grate like a squeaking wheel, but he had thought he would have to make some compromises when he eventually married. Nevertheless, he did not enjoy having this match presented as a fait accompli, not even by the harmless Hester.

"I envy you your invitation, Lady Hester," Mrs. Wells said with a sigh. "Being poor and struggling artists," she continued, not without a certain obvious pride in the virtuosity of her sacrifice, "we must remain in the dirt and congestion of the city."

When Paris heard that, he knew there was only one thing to do, and he did it.

Chapter Three

With the suddenness of an apparition, Lord Paris Mulholland appeared in the music room, a wry grin on his handsome face.

Startled and embarrassed, Clara unfortunately said the first thing that entered her head. "What are *you* doing here?"

Hester Pimblett gasped and Aunt Aurora gaped. *Rightly so,* Clara thought helplessly as the full realization of the rudeness of her demand came to her. She flushed hotly, thinking of all the times she had secretly condemned her aunt for doing the same thing.

But where had he come from? How much had he heard? She surveyed the room, desperately seeking some avenue of escape. There wasn't any, for his muscular body blocked the door.

"The general answer is fulfilling a social obligation," his lordship replied as if there were nothing untoward in her unorthodox greeting. His lack of affronted shock did not assuage Clara's embarrassment, and she wished she had stayed in the drawing room. Being bored was infinitely better than her current state of flustered feelings.

"As for my presence here," he went on smoothly with a graceful wave of his aristocratic hand, "I am merely being decorative."

Coming from any other handsome man, such words might have been taken as outrageous vanity; in his case, there was enough evidence of self-mockery in his tone and his blue eyes to lead her to believe he was trying to be amusing.

Clara told herself that she didn't find his efforts charming, or his way of playing the droll comedian humorous. He was an intelligent man and, judging by his conversation in the drawing room with the pompous and ignorant Lord Pimblett, one with at least a particle of social conscience. Why did he hide those qualities? Or was it simply that it was so much easier to play the lighthearted gadabout?

Why should she care?

"If you think I'm intruding, I shall take myself off," he finished.

Before Clara could speak, Aunt Aurora recovered. "Oh, dear me, no! We are so glad to see you!" she cried happily. "We were just discussing you."

"I hope you were only saying *good* things of me," Lord Mulholland said genially, looking at Lady Hester.

Although Hester Pimblett's smile lighted her good-natured face, Clara couldn't help noticing that she did not meet his gaze. "I believe I hear the music for dancing," she said softly, moving toward the door. "So if you will excuse me, I shall look forward to meeting you again at Mulholland House, my lord."

She hurried out of the room, and Clara fought the urge to follow.

"I have been reconsidering your offer," Lord Mulholland said.

"*Really?*" Aunt Aurora cried, clapping her hands like an excited child. "How delightful! How wonderful! I do think you owe it to posterity, Lord Mulholland."

"That shall be for posterity to decide," he answered. "I only know I should be honored to sit for you."

He sounded so sincere, Clara could almost believe he meant it. Nevertheless, she kept her attention firmly fastened on Aunt Aurora, who was apparently perfectly content, and further, quite delighted to think she had achieved so much so soon.

Then he frowned slightly. "However, I am leaving London tomorrow, so it occurs to me that you must come to my house in Lincolnshire to do the picture, if you are able."

"Oh, my lord! How marvelous! Of course we shall be only too delighted to go! Clara, isn't he just too kind?"

"Too kind, indeed," Clara replied flatly. Her mind was full of suspicions. Why would this rich, titled man want Aunt Aurora to do his portrait?

"I will happily pay your travel expenses," he offered.

"Well, my dear man, this is so sudden—so unexpected. I shall have to finish one or two small commissions—a matter of mere days—and a few trifling bills to pay... then the house must be shut up."

"Aunt, we cannot abandon the household," Clara protested.

"Bring the household along, by all means," Lord Mulholland said languidly. "Or perhaps your niece would prefer to remain in London?"

To her great chagrin, the idea that he could so easily leave her behind disturbed Clara immensely. Had she somehow imbibed far more wine than she realized?

Fortunately, Aunt Aurora looked as if he had proposed doing away with her niece. "I certainly could not! She cannot remain alone in London, Lord Mulholland. It would not be proper."

There! Clara thought triumphantly. This man had best understand that she belonged to a family every bit as moral as his own. Or, considering what she knew of the upper classes, considerably more so.

"Very well," he acquiesced graciously. "Then she must come, too, by all means."

Damn him! She didn't *want* to find him gracious, or charming or handsome. Nor did she want to go to his house in the country, even if it meant getting out of London for a while.

Had Aunt Aurora forgotten everything they had heard about Lord Mulholland? The flippant bets, the mistress who had made a bonfire of all his clothes when she thought he was dallying with another woman who was said to be married, the money he wasted on frivolous entertainment? Surely Aunt Aurora wouldn't wish to expose her niece to such a man, not even for the sake of a major commission.

"Perhaps we should settle the details of our arrangement at once," Lord Mulholland said, his deep voice persuasively soft as he gazed at Clara. "Then your niece will believe that my desire is a serious one."

Clara had read of women's knees weakening at certain romantic moments, but she had always considered it an invention of fiction, until Paris Mulholland said, "desire." Now she knew that it could indeed happen. Nevertheless, she would die before she would let him know that his words or tone had any effect on her at all.

"You are too gracious, my lord!" Aunt Aurora cried, obviously completely oblivious to the undercurrent of anxiety her niece was experiencing.

"Don't you wish to see examples of my aunt's work?" Clara asked, a hint of desperation creeping into her voice.

"Not at all," he said. "I'm sure I will be completely satisfied."

She risked a glance at the noble wastrel, and saw the laughter lurking in Lord Mulholland's eyes. So, he found them amusing, as if they were clowns he could hire? Perhaps, while having her guardians for jesters, he thought to practice his seductive skills on their surely easily-wooed niece.

Anger built inside Clara. Aunt Aurora could be absurd, but she was a kind, generous woman who truly thought of herself as an artist. Despite his lack of skill, Uncle Byron took his writing career seriously. As for seducing *her,* she was no easy prey for any man, not even the famous Paris Mulholland, as he would inevitably learn.

She summoned every reserve of calm she had, so that when she faced him, her countenance was bland and her voice controlled. "Don't you want to know my aunt's usual commission?"

"I must go tell Byron about your proposal, my lord!" Aunt Aurora said excitedly, obviously believing that only the details remained to be settled.

"Aunt!" Clara said swiftly. "You can't—!"

"Oh, never fear. I'll find him somehow. And you know I never like talking about money!" With a dismissive wave of her hand, Aunt Aurora trotted off in search of her husband, leaving Clara alone and *unchaperoned* with the most notorious wastrel in London.

"I won't bite," Lord Mulholland remarked coolly.

"This is most improper, my lord, as you well know," Clara said, wanting to run out the door, but just as determined not to seem frightened or flustered.

"Then you can afford to pick and choose who your aunt will paint?"

Like the Paris of the myth who shot and killed Achilles, he had found her weakest spot. They *did* need the money, and badly, too, a weakness she hesitatingly acknowledged.

"Very well. Let us do our haggling and rejoin the others before there can be any hint of impropriety."

"Oh, yes, we wouldn't want *your* reputation to suffer," Clara replied sardonically.

He tugged the cuff of his jacket into perfect alignment with his shirt. "I was thinking of yours."

To her surprise, he sounded absolutely sincere. But then, he had sounded the perfect fop in the drawing room. She decided it would be better to settle the price at once, and get away from such a chameleon.

When she met his interrogative gaze, she thought it might be better just to get away. She would run and fight another day. "The hour is late," she said abruptly.

"Not very," he said, glancing down the hall with his mocking little smile, as if he knew very well why she was sidling toward the doorway, and found her concern amusing. "You seem less than delighted by the prospect of your aunt rendering me."

Since he spoke the truth, she did not deign to reply.

"Don't you want your aunt to paint me?" he asked.

"What shade did you have in mind?" she retorted.

"What color would you suggest?" he countered. "Perhaps something to bring out the color of my eyes?"

His response made Clara look at his eyes, which were a shade of deep blue like the sky in springtime. Then she realized he was laughing at her. She could see it in those merry, mocking, sky blue eyes, and detect it in the slight upturn of his sensual lips. He reminded her of a sardonic satyr.

She was no plaything for his amusement, and it was time he learned that. She wouldn't have fled from him now if he pulled out a pistol.

Instead, she thought of a reasonable sum for the portrait, and quadrupled it. Then she doubled that. "Four hundred pounds," she announced gravely.

"Very well." Lord Mulholland reached into the breast pocket of his jacket with his long, slender fingers whose warmth she well recalled, and drew out his wallet. "Will a check do, or would you prefer the cash?"

In spite of her anger and resolution to remain cool and calm, she gasped. "Surely you…you don't carry such a sum on your person?"

He simply smiled.

Good heavens, he was a fool. Rich, but a fool!

"Since I have never paid for my portrait before, I will have to trust that this is an honest rate."

Clara's gaze faltered. She was ashamed of herself, despite her reasoning. For an instant, honor and a desire to hoodwink him battled in her breast; honor quickly triumphed. "No, Lord Mulholland. It is not," she said quietly. "I inflated the sum."

"Why? Did I strike you as an easy mark?" He did not look angry at her admission, which she rather wished he would. He made another calm, inquisitive smile.

She straightened her slim shoulders and gazed at him staunchly. "I thought you were making sport of us."

"Ah!" His eyes grew serious.

"You would not be the first."

"I give you my most solemn assurances that I truly want your aunt to do my portrait, and I have no ulterior motive beyond that."

He was so unmistakably earnest that she felt some of the anxiety flee her body. Nevertheless, she did not relax. She couldn't, not when she was alone with him.

She nodded stiffly. "Then we shall accept your commission."

"That makes me very happy," he said softly as he reached out to take her hand. "I am suddenly all aflame to have my portrait done." She held her breath as he bent down and kissed her fingers gallantly.

She yanked her hand from his. It had to be the unexpectedness of his action that took her breath away and made her heart race.

"The real price is fifty pounds," she said huskily, hoping he was in no mood to haggle. She had discovered that some of her aunt's wealthiest patrons were the ones most unwilling to part with a penny. "Twenty-five before she begins, twenty-five when she is finished."

His expression mercifully returned to languid normality. "That much?"

"It will be a large picture," she said quickly. "My aunt does them life size."

"I see. So I will be certain of getting my money's worth. Perhaps I could use it as a substitute for myself in the House of Lords when the debates get too boring." He opened his slender wallet and drew out twenty-five pounds.

Clara took the offered money, then chewed her lip as she considered where she should keep it. Her reticule was too small, being made with the idea that a woman need only carry a delicate lace handkerchief and smelling salts to be prepared for any emergency. After another moment's consideration, she turned away from Lord Mulholland and swiftly tucked the folded bills into her bodice.

"I envy my money," he remarked with a gleam in his sparkling eyes, all his indifference gone.

This man was indeed seduction personified! "As well you should, since it is safely where you will never venture," she answered defensively.

He sighed melodramatically. "Hard-hearted wench!"

He drew out his watch with such a knowing smile that she cursed herself for a fool and a ninny. She was reacting like some green schoolgirl! But he was surely a master of seduction. She must be on her guard.

He glanced at the timepiece. "I perceive that it is time for me to leave, and as much as I would dearly enjoy chatting with you, I have friends awaiting me. If you will excuse me, Miss Wells, I look forward to meeting you again in Lincolnshire."

She watched him stroll away unconcerned, as though nothing of any import had happened. *She* felt as if one of the Greek gods had suddenly appeared before her in mortal form and invited her to Olympus.

Most surprising of all, she wanted to go.

Paris leaned back against the cushions of his carriage, oblivious to the sounds of London as Jones took him to White's.

Paris knew he *should* have been feeling quite pleased with himself, for he was going to get a considerable sum from old Boffington, and could probably dine out on the tale of this wager for the rest of the year.

However, there could be no denying, even to himself—and Paris Mulholland was a past master at denying any troubling twinges of emotion—that his little interview with the artist's niece upset him far more than it should. By rights, he should be quite immune to the opinions of others, and especially those of a very serious, disdainful young lady whose social station was so below his own, even if she did proclaim them in a delightful voice, her eyes shining with indignant passion. When was the last time he had seen authentic passion, even of an angry sort? He couldn't remember—and he shouldn't be trying to.

What did it matter if her shrewd observation that he was planning to get some amusement from her aunt's foibles had been correct, at first? She said it had happened before; she should be used to it. Indeed, he told himself, if she were *really* clever, she would have been exploiting her aunt and uncle's eccentric ways as a means of living. They could easily be a traveling circus.

He wrapped his cape tighter against the damp chill. No, he didn't mean that. He knew how it felt to have the adult in one's life make embarrassing remarks. He, too, would have bristled at such treatment, had he been in her place.

Paris Mulholland suddenly had the distinct sensation that this perfect stranger, this hazel-eyed embodiment of outraged familial loyalty and pride, had not just upset the equanimity of his life. She had managed to touch his heart and set it strumming in understanding sympathy.

He didn't want his life disturbed, or any sympathetic feelings roused. He didn't want to feel very much of anything. Life was much safer and so much more pleasant that way.

He wished he had never extended the invitation to her aunt that they all come to Lincolnshire. Perhaps he could undo it . . . but then, he would miss the pleasure of her guardian's company.

They *were* amusing and interesting, and would certainly liven up his dull days. What was so very wrong with taking advantage of that?

Chapter Four

The Wells heard nothing further from the infamous Paris Mulholland during the few days immediately after Lord Pimblett's ball. Clara decided he had changed his mind about the portrait and told herself she was glad of it. No matter how her aunt fretted— and dear Aunt Aurora *could* fret—Clara couldn't help feeling it would be a blessing if they never saw the man again. It would be awkward to return the money, yet that might be far preferable to dealing with Lord Mulholland for any length of time.

There was also another reason Clara did not wish to spend more time in such company. What might her guardians say or do at Mulholland House? They were so...so *enthusiastic* about their passions! She was not ashamed of them exactly, but more than once their unbridled remarks had caused Clara to wish to bury her head in the proverbial sand. A man like Paris Mulholland would have stories to tell for years—and he would tell them, too, in that seductive, utterly captivating voice of his.

Then, a fortnight after the Pimbletts' ball, they received a note from a Mr. Mycroft, Lord Mulholland's man of business in the city, detailing the travel arrangements and providing the funds. They were to go to Folkingham in Lincolnshire and disembark at the Greyhound Inn, where they would be met by a coachman from Mulholland House who would drive them to the manor.

There was no doubt, from that moment, that they would go.

Although preparing for the journey to Lincolnshire severely taxed Clara's patience, she dared not protest. Aunt Aurora and Uncle Byron now believed that Lord Paris Mulholland was something of a saint, and they would not listen to any attempt to persuade them otherwise.

Aunt Aurora, who considered her commission to paint Lord Mulholland as the beginning of a new and important phase of her career, simply could not be made to see the troubles this journey entailed. She quite cheerfully entrusted all the arrangements to Clara, with the single exception of the preparation of her painting materials.

Uncle Byron concerned himself with composing a farewell ode to the Thames and outfitting himself with what he considered the proper garb of a country gentleman, which meant tweeds and gaiters. Under no circumstances did he wish to hear that they could not afford new clothes, and Clara finally gave up trying.

The landlady of their shabby and meager lodgings proved to be completely unreasonable. She insisted that if they were going to vacate the rooms, vacate them they must, which meant packing up *all* their belongings and paying rent for the cellar, where they were graciously allowed to store the few pieces of furniture they owned outright.

There was also the matter of Zeus, the family cat, a large and dignified black feline. Clara wasn't sure what to do about him, until Aunt Aurora suggested turning him over to the tender mercies of one of her artistic friends, a young woman who kept decidedly odd hours and rarely managed to feed *herself,* let alone a cat. Clara refused, and finally decided that since Lord Mulholland had invited "the whole household," he would get the whole household.

Clara's anxiety over their imminent departure was not assisted by her deep-seated dread that they would all have a terrible time in the country. For one thing, their host, who was said to be completely at the mercy of his whims, might take it into his head not to have his portrait painted at all once they arrived, and they would be left with no lodgings and perhaps having to return the twenty-five pounds, already gone to the purchase of new paints, canvas and Uncle Byron's clothes.

That was bad enough, but the idea of living in the same house as the handsome and charming Lord Mulholland who could make her knees weak with a look was worse yet. She knew the visit was going to prove a great strain, especially if he exerted himself to seduce her. Not that she thought he could succeed, of course; she knew all the games and stratagems, even if they had not been practiced by such an attractive man. She finally decided she would simply avoid him and hope that Aunt Aurora painted quickly.

At last the day they were to leave for Lincolnshire arrived. Clara greeted it with great trepidation and considerable anxiety, and all too soon found herself wedged inside the coach for the journey north, with her aunt on one side and the basket holding Zeus on

her own lap. Her uncle sat across from them with his
feet sticking out into the middle of the compartment.
He fell into a doze the moment the coach, with several other passengers perched on the top, lurched into
motion.

Despite her misgivings, as the coach left the sub-
urbs of London and entered the countryside, Clara
found herself pleased and excited to be out of the city.
She had forgotten how green and pleasant rural England could be, and how much sweeter smelling. The
day was a fine one, and although the road was dusty,
it was still better than London.

If only they were not going to the country home of
Lord Paris Mulholland!

"Folkingham!" the coachman bellowed as the
coach began rattling over the cobblestones of a village street.

Clara woke with a start and a jerk. She had fallen
asleep during the last stretch of their journey. Mercifully, this final part of the ride was brief, or Clara
doubted that her internal organs would ever be set
right again. The jostling also managed to awaken her
aunt, whose bonnet was more than slightly askew.

"We're at Folkingham," Clara said, grabbing
Zeus's basket with a tighter grip.

"Folkingham?" Aunt Aurora repeated, confused.
As she struggled to a more upright position, she
looked like a caterpillar making its way out of a co-
coon, for she was encumbered by petticoats, a heavy
skirt, a cloak and three shawls, having decided there
was an unseasonable chill in the air that morning after they had stopped for the night. "Heaven forbid I
should have the ague!" she had declared.

She had also wrapped a large scarf round her head, which was topped with a bonnet of her own design generously covered with artificial flowers. It looked more like a centerpiece than a hat. "Folkingham?" she said again.

"Yes, Aunt. We are to meet Lord Mulholland's carriage here, remember?"

"Oh, indeed. *Byron!*" Aunt Aurora gave her husband a gentle kick.

"Hail, my nymph!" he muttered sleepily, blinking. He looked not unlike a turtle whose slumber has been disturbed. "Where the devil are we?"

"Folkingham," Clara reiterated as the coach came to a stop. They felt the conveyance sway as the driver and some of the passengers climbed down. "I daresay this is the yard of the Greyhound Inn."

She looked out the window at the large, pale orange brick building, and saw a confirming sign of that name. "I wonder if we shall have to wait long for Lord Mulholland's carriage."

"It matters not!" Uncle Byron exclaimed. "Such a beautiful day in the heart of a bucolic paradise! It will be a pleasure to wait here!"

He opened the door and stepped forth like a conquering hero surveying his recently acquired domain. Such was his natural grace and bearing that nobody, either from the top of the coach or the stables nearby, made any comment, and for that, Clara was grateful. She put her hand in his outstretched one and stepped down.

Folkingham was a delightful village, small but utterly charming. The large green was surrounded by prosperous-looking houses, and the contented bleating of sheep reached them from the surrounding low hills.

Then Clara noticed several poorly dressed people being handed a small loaf of bread by a couple, neatly and plainly dressed and standing behind a table upon which other loaves were piled. The ragged wanderers gratefully accepted this apparent gift. Munching on their bread, they trudged toward the southern end of town.

Looking their way, to the south and between the houses, Clara saw a tall, all-too-familiar wall. Either it was a workhouse or a prison. She surmised the tattered and threadbare group were on their way to visit the inmates, and those two kind souls were doing their best to relieve some of their poverty.

Clara sighed. Even here, poverty and want reared its ugly head. Perhaps she had been foolish to think it would be otherwise.

"Ah, Arcadian delights abound!" Aunt Aurora cried as she grappled her way down from the carriage, quite oblivious to the straggling walkers. Unfortunately, her appearance seemed to unleash the impertinent snickers of the other passengers.

"The horses'll eat that hat!" one wag called out.

Her aunt didn't seem to hear the comment as she happily surveyed the street and green. "How absolutely delightful! How picturesque! How truly rustic!" she enthused.

"Indeed, my Ceres!" Then Uncle Byron realized he had stepped into something he should not have, wrinkled his nose in distaste, scraped his boot on the wheel rim and held out his arm for his wife to take, all his actions accompanied by hoots of laughter from the other passengers of the coach.

Clara flushed to the roots of her hair, straightened her shoulders and tightened her grip on Zeus's basket as she tried to lift her fast-muddying skirts a little higher. She, wearing a very severe, plain traveling gown of dark brown, and a most demure bonnet, feared no censure from anyone regarding *her* clothing. She glanced over her shoulder and gave the passengers a black, chastising look. She had been practicing that look for many years now, and had it to such an art that it was far more effective than any mere words could have been. Not surprisingly, the rabble fell silent.

"Come, Clara!" her aunt said, grabbing Clara's arm and strolling toward the inn.

With Zeus's basket bumping against her leg, Clara allowed herself to be thus escorted, Uncle Byron following majestically behind.

The inside of the Greyhound Inn was dim, the oak wainscoting dark and the rest of the walls and ceiling smoke stained.

A middle-aged man in spotless blue livery and hat in hand approached them, his gaze fastened on Aunt Aurora's distinctive bonnet. "Mrs. Wells?" he asked, making a small bow.

"Yes," Aunt Aurora replied.

"I'm from Mulholland House, Mrs. Wells. I was sent to bring you in the carriage."

"Just as Lord Mulholland promised!" Aunt Aurora cried triumphantly.

Clara did not point out that if Lord Mulholland had not sent his carriage, they would have had few alternative means of getting to his estate.

"Byron, my own!" Aunt Aurora said to her husband. "See here! This is the driver to take us to Mulholland House."

Uncle Byron regally nodded his understanding.

"It's not a long drive," the driver said deferentially. "Perhaps you'd care to refresh yourself first?"

"A simple drink of spring water, a crust of bread and the delightful air of the countryside will be enough for me," Uncle Byron announced. "Under yon towering oak on the charming village green would be the perfect spot for an alfresco repast, don't you agree, my dear?"

Clara had an instant vision of the spectacle of her aunt and uncle lunching on the village green. "It is the middle of the afternoon," she pointed out. "I think it would be better if we were to get to Mulholland House without further delay."

The innkeeper's rosy-cheeked wife appeared. "Ale, sir? Coffee, ladies?" she asked with a pleasant smile.

"Ah, *salve,* prophetess!" Uncle Byron declared. "Ale, indeed—something smooth and dark. And tea for the ladies."

"I don't believe there will be time before we must be on our way," Clara said firmly. "Thank you all the same."

"You're going to Mulholland House?" the innkeeper's wife inquired cordially. "Ah, a lovely place!"

Before Clara could steer Aunt Aurora outside, her aunt said, "Who are all those poor unfortunates on the other side of the green?" Proving that she had, perhaps, not been as oblivious to the other attributes of Folkingham as Clara had assumed.

"Visiting the House of Correction, ma'am," the woman replied cheerfully.

Aunt Aurora was horrified. "A jail? Dear me! A jail! Aren't you afraid to sleep in your bed at night?"

Clara gave her aunt a fierce look. Supposing the woman *was*—it didn't do to remind her.

"Oh, no. It's not that *kind* of jail, really. Mostly vagrants, disorderlies." The woman lifted her chin with a touch of pride. "Takes them from all of Kesteven, they does."

"I suppose the building keeps them warm and dry," Clara offered doubtfully.

Uncle Byron shielded his eyes with his hand and sighed loudly. "Deprived of the open air, shut up in a dungeon! It is monstrous! It is *cruel!*"

"Don't upset yourself, my own!" Aunt Aurora cried, putting her arms around him and laying her forehead on his shoulder.

The driver and innkeeper's wife exchanged looks over Aunt Aurora and Uncle Byron's heads. "I believe I heard his lordship's going to wait tea for you," the driver murmured.

"There, you see!" Clara said with some desperation. "We had best be on our way."

"Very well, my good man," Uncle Byron said, suddenly brisk. "You will find our baggage on the coach, clearly marked."

Clara thought of the trunks her aunt had decorated in her own inimitable way one afternoon and decided the driver would have no trouble deciding which articles of baggage were theirs. Not many traveling bags would have pictures of scenes from the Arabian Nights on them. Nevertheless, Clara thought being outside would be preferable to staying inside the inn, so she said, "I will show you which ones they are. There is also an easel and a large package of canvases."

The driver nodded and led the way outside. The coachman was seeing to the changing of the horses, and some of the passengers milled about in the yard. Clara ignored their speculative looks as she showed the driver the appropriate baggage, then followed him to Lord Mulholland's gleaming black landau that was at the far side of the yard. A pair of very fine horses had their noses in feed bags.

The driver glanced at her as he loaded the largest piece of baggage. "Quite a pair, those two, miss."

"My aunt is an artist and my uncle is a poet," Clara explained matter-of-factly. "They are both very... emotional."

The driver chuckled companionably. "Oh, we've had lots of emotional people at Mulholland House," he said. "And some were just plain crazy, if you ask me."

Clara wondered peevishly which category the driver thought Aunt Aurora and Uncle Byron would occupy. Perhaps Lord Mulholland didn't invite people to his country home only for his own amusement; perhaps he tried to keep his servants laughing, too. She should have refused the invitation, and let Aunt Aurora complain....

"Our dear mistress, the late Lady Mulholland, that was, liked lots o' different sorts of people," the driver continued, chuckling. "Her son's just the same. Why, one time, this Italian count we had a' stayin' here—walked about in somethin' looked like a baby's nappy most o' the time. Been to India or some such." The driver reached down for the canvases. "'Nother time, these singers came. Sounded like a bunch of cats in a bag, we all thought." He sighed for happy days gone by. "There, all stowed. We can go now."

At least Aunt Aurora and Uncle Byron wouldn't be the most unusual people to stay at Mulholland House, Clara thought as she nodded absently. Nevertheless, her dread was not lessened by that notion. If anything, the closer she got to Mulholland House, the tenser she became.

She reminded herself that she would simply evade the sleek and seductive Lord Mulholland. The painting would be done soon, and then they would be gone. "I shall fetch my aunt and uncle," she said.

As she made her way toward the inn, the coach, with its passengers restored, rattled on its way. Clara was not sorry to see it, or its noisy passengers, leave.

Uncle Byron spotted Clara in the doorway and sprang to his feet. "Come, my dear!" he called to his wife. "Our chariot awaits!"

Chapter Five

Paris sat in his study in a large, comfortable wing chair, with his dog, Jupiter, at his feet. The yellow-haired beast of dubious parentage lay as still as one of the statues in the garden as he slumbered. His master was likewise motionless as he deciphered two letters, one from Tommy Taddington and the other from Reverend Jonas Clark, both of whom had been Paris's friends at Oxford. Tommy's letter informed Paris that Tommy was once again experiencing familial troubles, and unless he heard otherwise from Paris, would arrive sooner than planned. Jonas, to whom Paris was gladly giving the living in one of the nearby parishes, was expected to arrive at Mulholland House shortly, there to stay until the vicarage of St. Andrew's had been repaired and prepared for the new pastor.

Paris's attention was drawn from the letters by Jupiter, who lumbered to his feet just as the study door opened to reveal the presence of the butler, Witherspoon. At present, the white-haired Witherspoon looked decidedly icy.

"Yes?" Paris asked.

"My lord, the Wells have arrived." By a process that Paris had yet to figure out, even though Witherspoon had been butler at Mulholland House for twenty years, Witherspoon managed to convey the impression that it would have been better if the Wells had never been born.

"Oh, come now, Witherspoon!" Paris chided. "They're not as bad as all that! Granted, the niece is rather severe, but the aunt is delightful and her husband most amusing." Grinning, Paris rose and tugged down his waistcoat. "I thought we needed some livening up around here, Witherspoon. I shall die of ennui otherwise."

"Indeed, my lord." The butler's eyebrow rose a fraction and Paris saw a telltale twinkle of amusement in the man's dark eyes. "That cause of death would at least be *tasteful,* my lord, unlike your guest's bonnet."

Paris chuckled amicably as he clapped a familiar hand on the retainer's narrow shoulder. "Mrs. Wells is an artist," he explained patiently. "She's going to paint my portrait."

"If you say so, my lord."

Paris drew back and examined Witherspoon suspiciously. "You look as if I were up to no good, Witherspoon!" he exclaimed.

Witherspoon thawed a little, as he always did.

"I assure you, I will treat them royally," Paris continued. "Speaking of which, where have you put them?"

"Since the hour is so close to tea," Witherspoon said, miraculously conveying the impression that the late arrival of the Wells was somehow their fault, "I told Mrs. Dibble to escort them to their rooms." He nearly smiled. "I must say the older lady was most fulsome in her praise of Mulholland House."

Paris grinned. "I daresay she was. I believe Mrs. Dibble, our jewel among housekeepers, may finally—"

He was going to say that Mrs. Dibble may finally have encountered someone even more vivacious than herself, when there was a loud crash from the vicinity of the kitchen, followed by the sight of a black shape streaking past the study door as a lamenting female voice wailed, "Zeus, come back!"

With a bark and a bound, Jupiter shoved his way past the butler and his master and was out the door, his progress impeded by the freshly waxed floor. His huge paws slipped on the polished surface as he tried to give chase toward the foyer. After a moment of desperate scrambling, he found his footing and bounded away.

"Call off your dog!" Miss Wells cried, appearing in the corridor with a very flushed face and attired in the most ugly brown traveling dress Paris had ever seen. "Call him off!"

"Zounds and gadzooks," Byron Wells cried from somewhere nearby, "what's afoot? Tallyho!"

Mr. and Mrs. Wells appeared at the top of the staircase, by their appearance having interrupted their toilette. Byron Wells wore a finely tailored tweed suit that owed more to town than country, and Mrs. Wells' dressing gown simply defied description.

Before Paris could answer, Clara Wells darted past him at the same time the black cat reappeared, this time returning toward its mistress and the kitchen wing. Before Paris could step back inside the sanctuary of his study, Jupiter tore down the corridor and crashed into his master, sending him reeling. Paris slipped on the polished floor and collided with Miss Wells. Stumbling over her skirts, he managed to right himself, then lost his footing again and finally fell to the ground, one foot shooting out and inadvertently kicking Miss Wells.

She lost her balance and landed on top of him in a pile of skirts and righteous indignation. "Get up!" she cried, putting her slender hands on Paris's chest and pushing. "Get up!"

Paris could easily imagine how ridiculous they looked, him flat on his back in the middle of the hall with a young lady, red of face and glaring of eye, sprawled on top of him and telling *him* to get up. However, he wasn't so startled that he didn't notice that although her eyes blazed with indignation and despite her ugly brown dress, Clara Wells was really *very* pretty.

"I should point out that task would be much simpler if you were to rise first," he said, hard-pressed not to laugh out loud as he put his hands about her slim waist to lift her up.

She wore no corset, for he felt only soft flesh beneath her gown, not whalebone. She was breathing hard. A few wisps of hair had escaped her tight bun and her mouth was partly opened. He had but to raise himself a few inches and he could capture those lips with his own....

Miss Wells' face turned even redder as she realized her position. "Take your hands off me, sir!"

"May I be of assistance, miss?" Witherspoon intoned.

"Yes, please," Miss Wells said, scuttling backward in a crablike manner that imparted to Paris new and fascinating sensations.

With great dignity, Witherspoon inclined and took Clara Wells' hand in his to help her stand.

"Lord Mulholland, are you hurt?" Aurora Wells asked, bustling toward him solicitously, her ringlets quivering with concern.

"Only my pride," he replied, standing and bestowing a gracious smile on his guests, especially the youngest of them.

Then Jupiter started to bay.

"He's trapped Zeus!" Clara Wells cried anxiously as she turned once more toward the corridor leading to the kitchen. "Poor thing!"

"Jupiter won't hurt your cat," Paris said, hurrying after her. "He's very gentle."

Miss Wells shot him a withering glance. "I was thinking of your foolish dog," she said. "Zeus can take care of himself."

Before Paris could formulate an answer, Jupiter gave a great long howl, and in the next instant, came careening around the corner, Zeus clinging to his back and yowling. Jupiter looked as if he had Satan himself for a rider, and this cat could have been a familiar, for it held on with demonic determination as they rushed past the startled onlookers who pressed themselves back against the wall. Jupiter, with another wild yelp, spun around in the foyer and dashed back past them.

"I believe they are returning to the kitchen, my lord," Witherspoon remarked unnecessarily.

A shocked screech—Mrs. Macurdy, the cook's, no doubt—and a clash of pots confirmed Witherspoon's assumption.

Paris ran to the kitchen followed by the Wells and halted abruptly on the threshold. Mrs. Macurdy, surrounded by fragments of pastry and pieces of tea sandwiches, was leaning against the table in the middle of the large room as if she had had the fright of her life. A kitchen maid stood in the corner with a ladle clutched in her hand, Jupiter was in the corner by the coal box whimpering and a black cat not nearly as huge as it had looked on Jupiter's back sat on the windowsill calmly licking its paw.

Mrs. Macurdy turned her shocked visage toward him. "What in the name of heaven happened, my lord?" she asked in a stunned whisper. "Is that cat possessed?"

"No, he isn't," Miss Wells said as she pushed her way past him. "Your maid dropped a pan." The scullery maid flushed guiltily and slowly lowered her ladle. "That scared poor Zeus, so he ran." She glanced over her shoulder with a scathing look. "And then your brute of a dog chased him."

She went to the windowsill and picked up the cat, nestling it to her chest and crooning, "Did he try to hurt you, Zeus, that nasty, stupid dog?"

Paris felt contrite until he saw the bloody scratches on Jupiter's back. "That cat is a menace!" he said through clenched teeth as he went toward his wounded pet. "Poor Jupe," he murmured. He crouched down and stroked the dog's head. "Did that nasty, stupid cat attack you?"

Jupiter looked at him as if to ask what he had ever done to deserve such a punishment, and Paris had to agree.

"Since there is nothing for me to do here, I believe I shall decamp," Aurora Wells announced grandly. She gathered her brightly colored wrapper around her ample frame. "Come, Byron!"

Byron was in the process of sampling one of the remaining intact pastries when his wife's command interrupted. While continuing to unashamedly hold on to the cream puff, he bid everyone an airy adieu and ambled after her retreating figure, taking great care not to step on any fragments of food.

"I assume, my lord, that tea will be indefinitely postponed?" the ever-unflappable Witherspoon remarked.

Miss Wells paused in her crooning and, for the first time since this whole episode began, looked contrite. "Oh, dear me," she said, and Paris noticed she spoke more to Mrs. Macurdy than to him. "Please, don't make any more on our account. We can wait for dinner."

"Good," Paris said rather ungraciously. He was discovering that he detested being ignored, especially in his own home. "Mrs. Macurdy, don't bother with tea."

The cook nodded, turning a murderous eye onto Miss Wells and her cat triumphant. Witherspoon nodded his understanding and drifted out of the room.

"He's usually no trouble at all," Miss Wells said defensively. She brushed back one of the stray wisps of hair from her flushed face with the back of her hand. "I don't think he'll bother Jupiter again."

"I should hope not."

She frowned, making a furrow of worry appear between her shapely brows. So, she was not completely immune to his opinion.

Suddenly all was forgiven. Until she spoke again. "Such a large dog should be kept outside, shouldn't it?"

"I like having him in the house," Paris replied. "I didn't realize you were bringing a cat."

"You did say to bring *all* the household."

"And is this *all,* or have you a mynah bird, a bear or an elephant somewhere hereabouts?"

"No, my lord. Only Zeus." Clara Wells' lips twitched as if she were trying to suppress a smile.

Paris did not remark that "only Zeus" had reduced his kitchen to a shambles and possibly upset Mrs. Macurdy's delicate nervous system. He didn't speak because the knowledge that she found his sarcastic comment amusing affected him strangely. On the one hand, he was pleased to think he could make her smile. On the other, he had never before wanted a young woman to take him seriously, as he did Clara Wells.

She glanced at the door leading to the kitchen garden and buttery and went toward it, opening it and setting her cat down. The beast walked majestically away, as one would expect any pet of the senior Wells to do.

"Sending your familiar to fend for himself?" Paris inquired.

Clara Wells rose and turned to face him. Rather unexpectedly, she did not meet his gaze. "I will see that he stays outside, my lord."

Paris was suddenly aware that Mrs. Macurdy and the scullery maid were listening attentively as they made desultory motions of cleaning up.

He moved into the corridor. Miss Wells followed him, albeit a few paces behind. Once they were out of earshot of the kitchen, he looked at her and smiled. "If you keep your cat outside, who will guard your potions and spells?" he asked softly.

Chapter Six

Clara was now convinced by Lord Mulholland's mischievous eyes and friendly smile that he wasn't angry, which pleased her. It would not do to upset their host. Unfortunately, she suspected that other emotions were now coming into play, at least on her part. In self-defense, she forced herself to meet shallow levity with a similar nonchalance. "I left all my brews behind in London," she answered.

"There is no need to banish the cat."

"You won't mind him in the house? What about your dog?"

"Jupe will recover, I'm sure," he said, "although his primary caretaker is an irresponsible lout." He frowned with what looked like genuine dismay.

"If he is, surely you have several people who could care for the dog."

"I was referring, my dear Miss Wells, to myself."

"Oh." Clara fell silent. She was no longer in any humor to play games, nor did she wish to remember that he had called her "my dear" in that sinfully wicked voice of his.

"I daresay he'll avoid your pet the next time," Lord Mulholland said, "so all should be well."

"I'm sorry. But you did say the household," she repeated, trying to avoid looking at his face, which she felt was far too close to her own.

"I meant your servants."

Clara bit her lip and blushed. "We don't have any servants."

"Who keeps your household organized?" he asked. "Your aunt, worthy woman though she may be, hardly seems the type. And your uncle—I cannot see him shopping in a market."

"We are not of your class, my lord," Clara pointedly observed.

"I daresay there are plenty of people who would say I'm not worthy to belong to any class," he replied flippantly. "I suspect, Miss Wells, that it is you who sees to the orderly running of your household, the cat included."

"Someone has to, and since I am not a gifted painter, nor can I write, much to my uncle's chagrin, those tasks fall to me," she admitted.

His expression softened and his blue eyes were full of sympathy. "That must be very difficult."

"No more than trying to keep a large dog under control," she replied, attempting to sound matter-of-fact. She was determined not to let herself get weak and silly in his presence. "I must say, my lord, I would have expected you to have a purebred hunting dog. I would not have thought a mongrel elegant enough for a man of your distinction."

Then something happened that Clara would not have expected in a hundred years. Lord Paris Mulholland blushed. "I caught a fellow trying to drown a bag of puppies. Jupe was one of them," he explained.

Clara took a step back. She should get away from this man at once. She was proof against his foolish-wastrel persona; against this sincere and handsome man who had saved drowning puppies, she had fewer defenses.

His gaze met hers and he paused, then straightened his shoulders as if attempting to resume his usual languid attitude—with some success, Clara noted regretfully. "I tried to give him away once he was recovered, but the poor chap looks upon me as his savior apparently. If I give him away, he keeps coming back. Foolish, isn't it, but there it is."

"I don't consider loyalty a foolish characteristic, my lord," she replied. "I hope you will forgive Zeus. And me."

"Since the destruction of the kitchen was also the fault of my dog, I could hardly hold you responsible, could I?" He stepped in front of her, so that she had to look at his face. "Quite frankly, I'm relieved to be spared the social necessity of teatime. Besides, I detest the beverage, and Mrs. Macurdy, while a dear old soul and the maker of the finest pies in Christendom, is utterly defeated when it comes to sandwiches."

There was something so winning in the way he said this that Clara had to smile.

"I'm delighted to know I can make the iron maiden laugh," he remarked, with a truly warm smile that, had Clara known him better, she would have realized was very rare indeed.

Unfortunately, she did not know him better, and it did not please her to be called "the iron maiden" by anyone.

"Clara, my dear!" Aunt Aurora called out from upstairs, just as if they were at home. This time, her aunt's lack of social polish didn't trouble Clara. She was far too glad of an excuse to get away.

"If you will excuse me, my lord," she said coldly. "I must see if my aunt requires assistance."

This time, his smile was charming and completely devoid of meaning. "Of course, Miss Wells."

With her slim back as straight as Witherspoon's, and her chin high, she walked past him and up the stairs.

She marched along the upper corridor. She could tell from her aunt's rather loud tones which room had been given to her, and headed toward it.

Iron maiden, indeed! Was she supposed to be flattered by his attention? Did Lord Paris Mulholland think, in his smug, bold way, that he could *make* her laugh?

If she seemed hard or cold, it was because *somebody* in her family had to be, or her poor aunt and uncle would be at the mercy of every tradesman, merchant, landlord and swindler in London.

What would this lazy, selfish man know of her troubles? What gave him the right to call her names?

She suddenly realized a short, thin man stood at the other end of the corridor staring at her. He had thick, dark, wavy hair brushed back and oiled, a thin mustache, well-tailored clothes in the latest fashion and a very shrewd expression in his beady black eyes. "Greetings, *mademoiselle*," he said in a French accent as he came toward her. He stopped and made a gentlemanly bow. "Permit me to introduce myself. Jean Claude Beaumaris, valet de chambre to Lord Mulholland."

"*Enchanté de faire votre connaissance, Monsieur Beaumaris,*" Clara replied in French.

"Ah, mademoiselle!" he cried with pleasure. "*Votre accent est excellent.*"

"*Merci, monsieur. Excusez-moi, s'il vous plaît. Ma tante a besoin de ma présence.*"

"*Certainement,*" he replied with another bow as he backed away, a wide grin on his face that made him resemble the mask of comedy.

She rapped once on Aunt Aurora's door. *What a strange fellow,* she thought as she heard Aunt Aurora respond. Almost as strange, she supposed, as one would consider her guardians.

She entered the bedroom. Aunt Aurora was sitting in front of a large gilt mirror wearing her brightly patterned dressing gown and attempting to arrange her heavy, hennaed hair. The furniture was Oriental in design, with beautiful gold inlays in the dark lacquer. The bed had an ornately scrolled, gilded partial canopy. The bed curtains, of a light chintz pattern, matched the embroidered satin coverlet and the Oriental wallpaper.

Clara could think of no room in the world that would appeal to Aunt Aurora more, because of her love of all things exotic, except perhaps one in a sultan's palace.

The moment she saw Clara, Aunt Aurora swiveled on the chair and looked at her niece worriedly. "What on earth happened below?" she asked. "I hope his lordship isn't too upset!"

"No, he didn't seem to be," Clara replied. "I was letting Zeus out of his basket when the kitchen maid dropped a pot. Zeus was frightened, so he ran. Then Lord Mulholland's dog gave chase."

"Oh, dear, I *knew* bringing Zeus was not a wise idea."

"It was the dog's fault, too."

Aunt Aurora continued to look concerned. "I don't want to anger Lord Mulholland and have to leave," she said. "I didn't want to alarm you before, Clara, but we have not the funds we should and this commission is rather important."

Clara was surprised that Aunt Aurora suspected the perilous nature of their financial situation; nevertheless, she hastened to reassure her. "He wasn't so very angry," she said placatingly. "More annoyed, I believe, and he was soon over that."

"I should have known you would make things right," Aunt Aurora said with satisfaction as she turned back to regard her reflection. "He is a most delightful young man. Just think, my dear, if your foolish grandfather was not so stubborn, you would be enjoying such society as a matter of course."

Clara said nothing as she began to unpack her aunt's gowns. What was there to say?

"Lord Mulholland is perfectly charming," Aunt Aurora went on enthusiastically. "And so handsome! Paris, indeed!" She glanced at Clara. "He looks so much better in these bucolic surroundings, don't you think?"

"He *is* handsome," Clara agreed.

Who could disagree, she thought, recalling his casual attire of an open-necked white shirt, his surprisingly broad shoulders that were certainly not the result of the tailor's art and his fawn-colored riding breeches that emphasized the muscularity of his thighs.

Aunt Aurora tried another arrangement of her front hair. "He's a perfect gentleman, too, I'm certain."

"I hope so," Clara replied absently, staring at the brilliant colors of her aunt's wardrobe and mentally contrasting them with the muted tones of the wallpaper.

"Not like some of those other young men who've come to my studio."

Clara slowly turned to look at her aunt. Until this moment, she had assumed Aunt Aurora had no inkling of the antics of some of her male customers and models.

"Why, you needn't stare so, Clara, although I'm sure a girl of your moral fiber didn't even notice their cruder behavior."

Clara certainly had; the wonder of it was that Aunt Aurora had not been oblivious. "You...you never sent anyone away," she said slowly.

"Why should I? They were harmless enough, and I certainly had no fear that you would not see them for the vain puppies they were!"

Clara didn't know whether she should frown or smile. It was good to think her aunt had faith in her perception, but was it not her guardian's place to *guard* Clara from her customers' attentions?

There was a soft knock on the door, and Clara opened it to find a pretty, smiling young woman in a maid's uniform who dipped a curtsy. "Good day, miss," she said nervously. "I'm to be your maid while you're here."

Clara was about to protest that they didn't need a maid when Aunt Aurora rose as majestically as any queen and gave Clara a most triumphant look. "How *thoughtful* of Lord Mulholland! *I* am Aurora Wells, and this is my niece, Clara."

The maid dipped another curtsy. The young woman looked so keen and anxious, Clara didn't have the heart to send her away, and on second thought, it occurred to her that it might be a pleasant break not to have to help Aunt Aurora for a little while.

Nor should she make too much out of Lord Mulholland's generosity. Providing a maid for their assistance was surely to be expected of any gentleman.

Of course, it still remained to be seen if Lord Mulholland was worthy of such an appellation.

Paris opened the door of his bedchamber at the far end of the corridor to discover that his valet was in a state of such excitement, the fellow could barely stand still. He looked not unlike one of the drunken revelers depicted in the medieval harvest tapestry hanging in the small drawing room.

"My lord!" Jean Claude exclaimed with true Gallic enthusiasm. "At last you bring home a young woman worthy of your attention!"

"What are you talking about?" Paris demanded as he closed the door, although he thought he could guess what Jean Claude was talking about. "The only young woman new in the house is Miss Wells," he said coolly, shooting the bolt home when he recalled Hester's tale about another young lady spying on him. "And she's no beauty. Pretty, perhaps, but surely not worth your fulsome praise. Now where's my dress shirt?"

He went over toward the large canopied mahogany bed and began to undress, still wondering why the laughter in Clara Wells' beautiful hazel eyes had died and her mouth had become a hard, grim line.

Because he had teased her a little?

Then, when her aunt had shouted for her, she had started and looked around as if she expected to see a bevy of Robert Peel's bobbies waiting to arrest her. Because her aunt was a little boisterous?

Perhaps he would regret his hasty decision to have Aurora Wells paint his portrait, he thought grimly as he unbuttoned his shirt. It was not going to be a blissful experience, having such a stern, censorious miss in his household.

He could send them away, he supposed, and he had to admit that the thought was tempting. However, he couldn't deny that Clara Wells was rather tempting, too, in a challenging sort of way. Besides, the family could use the money this commission would provide.

Jean Claude frowned darkly as he brought forth a fresh white shirt while Paris divested himself of the one he had been wearing. *"Ce n'est pas possible!* Am I in the presence of a dolt? A fool? A simpleton? Have I not taught you better than that, you . . . you Englishman! Anyone of any breeding and discernment would see that she is *une jeune fille très magnifique!"* He handed the shirt to a half-naked Paris and crossed his arms, daring his employer to disagree.

Which naturally Paris did, for it appeared that Jean Claude was going to outdo himself in defending Miss Wells—and his own judgment, of course. "I think she's a prim-and-proper bourgeois prude," he said.

"Are you *blind?"* Jean Claude demanded as Paris changed his trousers. "That woman is a powder keg waiting for a match!"

"Why don't you try lighting her up then?"

"Because she is not French," Jean Claude announced huffily.

"I'll agree she's explosive," Paris replied, lifting an aristocratic eyebrow as he tied his white cravat. Jean

Claude impatiently adjusted it before providing Paris with his white satin vest. "However, that is not a quality guaranteed to recommend her to me."

"It should be," Jean Claude retorted while Paris put on his tails.

The valet picked up a clothes brush and attacked Paris's jacket furiously, nearly knocking Paris backward with the violence of his strokes.

"Besides, she is not of my social class," his lordship said.

Jean Claude's brush strokes became even more aggressive. "You are not such a pigheaded cabbage to think that way," the Frenchman admonished. "And even a pigheaded cabbage could see that she must have royal blood in her veins."

"Really?" Paris drawled skeptically, moving away before Jean Claude did serious bodily harm with the brush. "How can you tell?" He combed his hair and studied Jean Claude's reflection in the mirror.

"By the carriage of her head, the posture of her body—a hundred little things. Trust me, my lord, there is blue blood in her background, or I will shoot myself!"

Paris gave his valet an amused and sardonic look. Jean Claude threatened to shoot himself at least once a week. Yet Paris was secretly delighted that anyone thought Clara Wells was not too far beneath him socially.

Not that Clara Wells' social status was any concern of his. "It doesn't matter to me if she's the true heir to the throne," he said with a dismissive laugh before strolling out of the room.

Jean Claude contemplated his absent employer as he put away the comb and brush with a disgruntled frown on his angular face.

"L'anglais!" he muttered, and the word was not a compliment.

Chapter Seven

After a fine and sumptuous dinner, Clara sat on a chair in the farthest corner of the main drawing room, spread her brown skirts and opened a book. She had taken it from the library, which she had discovered while trailing after an enraptured Aunt Aurora, who had exclaimed about the beauty of the design of the hall's wall coverings as she led the way from the formal dining room to the main drawing room. Clara had taken a moment to duck into the library, grab the first book she could see and rejoin her aunt without her absence being noticed. Now it was her intention to read until the gentlemen joined them after their brandy and cigars. She also planned to be too studiously occupied for the wealthy wastrel to make any attempts at conversing with her.

Aunt Aurora, having dined well, reclined on one of the brocade sofas and promptly dozed off.

Clara tried to concentrate on the book, which was, rather unhappily, a treatise on the care and feeding of sheep.

It was no use. She kept remembering how handsome Lord Mulholland looked at dinner, and how perfectly at ease among the shining candles, pristine linen and gleaming silver. She had felt completely out of place in her plain, high-necked brown sateen gown, wearing the fingerless mittens she had crocheted herself, and with her hair in its usual plain style.

At least the dinner had proceeded better than she had dared to hope. In fact, she had managed to get through the whole meal without being embarrassed by her guardians once, for the conversation had been kept to the most harmless of subjects. She could not take the credit for that, as much as she wished she could. Lord Mulholland had led the conversation, which had been primarily concerning the sorry state of the Thames.

Somewhat more disturbing was the realization that she had hardly paid attention to anything anyone said, and had spent far too much time watching Lord Mulholland's attractive face and graceful gestures.

Clara shut the book abruptly. Where were the men? What was taking them so long? What was Uncle Byron saying? Was he regaling Lord Mulholland with stanza after stanza of his epic poem, *Childe Roland,* which was modeled after Byron's *Childe Harold?* Was Lord Mulholland managing to keep a straight face? Did it matter what Lord Paris Mulholland thought of Uncle Byron, or any of them?

She rose impatiently and wandered around the finely appointed room. The furniture was extremely well made, and the seats upholstered in a rich brocade patterned in green and gold. The mantel was made of carved Italian marble. Over this was a portrait of a very lovely young woman with blond hair and blue eyes. As she regarded it, Clara didn't doubt that she was looking at Lord Mulholland's mother, for there was not only similarity of feature, but similarity of expression, from the twinkle in the woman's merry eyes to the slightly amused lift of the lips. The painting had been done by a master, and Clara couldn't help stifling a sigh as she glanced at the recumbent form of Aunt Aurora, who couldn't have painted such a representation if she tried for a hundred years.

She strolled toward the door leading to the corridor and opened it a crack. She could hear Uncle Byron declaiming something about the glory that was Greece. At least he wasn't reciting his poem!

Then she realized the men were not in the dining room. They were in the library. They were coming!

Quickly she ducked back inside the drawing room, hurried to her chair, swiftly arranged her skirts and picked up the book just as the men entered.

Uncle Byron ambled in as if he were the lord of the manor, followed by Lord Mulholland, whose gaze swept the room before coming to rest on Aunt Aurora.

Clara was glad he wasn't looking at her. Yes, she was.

Aunt Aurora awoke with something between a snore and a snort. "Dear me! Have I been asleep?"

Clara forced herself to stop staring at Lord Mulholland.

"Having dined upon ambrosia, my own," Uncle Byron said, "it is not surprising to find you in the lap of Morpheus. Begone, cares! Begone, woe! Tranquil rest enfolds us into its soft bosom."

Clara happened to catch Lord Mulholland's eye at that moment. His gaze flicked to *her* bosom, the impertinent rogue, and she quickly looked at the book in her hands, unseeing, all her efforts going into trying not to blush.

"Your niece is most accomplished, sir," Lord Mulholland remarked, sauntering closer. "Not many people can read a book upside down."

To her horror, Clara realized she was indeed holding the book incorrectly. But admit her error to this smirking, supercilious nobleman she would not. "I am practicing for reading Japanese," she remarked coolly, lying outrageously with very little compunction. "It is my belief that although they have no desire to trade with the outside world, they will one day. I intend to be prepared."

She didn't know if he believed her or not, because she wouldn't look at his face. She did note, however, that he moved away.

"Our Clara is quite a student of the world, isn't she, Byron?" Aunt Aurora boasted.

"Indeed," Uncle Byron replied. "An untiring scholar, ever seeking in the quest for knowledge! Our own Minerva."

"I was never one for scholastic achievements myself," Lord Mulholland said, and Clara could well believe it. "What subject does Minerva prefer to study?"

Since the question was so obviously aimed at her, Clara had to answer. "Human nature," she answered, giving him a sly smile intended to show him that she understood *him* well enough.

"Then you will have plenty of examples to study soon. Two of my friends from my Oxford days are arriving tomorrow."

"I thought you were not one for scholastic achievements," Clara remarked.

"Oh, I never said I graduated."

Clara surmised, from the slight flush that appeared on his face, that he had been expelled. At least he was capable of feeling some sense of shame for such a wasted opportunity!

"After them, I expect Lord and Lady Pimblett and their charming daughters."

Clara couldn't quite tell by his tone what he thought of the daughters, and his expression remained placid. For her part, she was pleased to think she might see Hester Pimblett again, but she entertained no such pleasure in the thoughts of Lady Helena, whom she remembered as a vain and beautiful young woman wearing the most extravagant of gowns.

Nor did she particularly care to watch Lady Helena snaring her Paris.

"I hope you will have time to pose for your portrait," Clara remarked.

"Indeed, yes," Aunt Aurora cried worriedly. "You mustn't forget about that!"

"I shall be at your disposal whenever you like, Mrs. Wells. I have set aside a room near the billiard room for a studio," Lord Mulholland said with a gallant bow.

"What a delightfully accommodating young man you are!" Aunt Aurora replied.

"I always do my best to accommodate ladies," was the lord's gallant response. "Even serious, studious ones. You must make yourself free with my library, Miss Wells, as I see you already have."

Clara couldn't have felt more guilty if she had stolen one of his books. Then he smiled, with his lips and with his eyes, and she saw that he was not annoyed, or upset. He was teasing her.

She frowned and he turned his attention to Uncle Byron.

"You, too, sir," he said.

The older man raised his glass in a pleased salute. Was it possible for anyone to remain immune to Paris Mulholland's combination of charm and friendship? Clara thought.

No wonder women turned into empty-headed ninnies in his presence. In another moment, and if she wasn't careful, she would probably start babbling, too. She rose. "If you will excuse me, Lord Mulholland, Aunt Aurora, Uncle Byron, I feel fatigued. I believe I shall retire."

"Good night, dear," Aunt Aurora said, presenting her cheek for a kiss, which Clara bestowed.

"Good night," Uncle Byron said, taking hold of her shoulders and saluting her with a hearty smack on her ear when she turned to him.

Lord Mulholland stepped between Clara and the door. "Would that I could take such liberties," he said softly, bowing and taking her hand in his. "For now, I can merely wish you a good-night."

He kissed her mittened hand, and even through the fabric she felt the warmth of his lips. Her pulse started throbbing in her ears and heat surged through her body.

Clara hurried out of the room as fast as she could without breaking into a run, and didn't stop until she reached her bedroom.

It was a very pretty, feminine room that had delighted her when she had first entered. Every piece of dark cherry furniture was polished to perfection. The rugs were thick and patterned in roses, the same flower that adorned the lovely wallpaper. A vase filled with fresh tea roses scented the room, and the moonlight streamed in the wide windows draped in plain pink curtains.

Now Clara took no notice as she tried to make her mind return to its normal state. She felt as if somebody had inverted her and shaken hard, and she didn't enjoy the sensation.

She would not allow herself to be charmed by any wastrel, however handsome and alluring. She knew exactly what she wanted, and it wasn't Lord Paris Mulholland, who frittered away his time devoting himself to nothing more serious than balls and parties and visiting.

She wanted a husband. She wanted a sincere young man who would take his family and his responsibilities seriously. She wanted children, and the type of home she had had when her parents were still alive.

Perhaps more than that, she wanted to show her grandfather that her parents had done nothing shameful or sinful by marrying against his wishes, and that their offspring was as moral and upright as any woman.

Lord Mulholland wouldn't understand her or her needs in a thousand years. Indeed, he was the epitome of the type of man she most despised: one with wealth and little sense of social responsibility. He had probably only said those things to Lord Pimblett to get attention. He was a rake, a wastrel. He had surely seduced several women with his nearly irresistible combination of looks, charm and wit, and they probably represented nothing to him beyond a gratification of his lust and an increase in his vanity.

Well, *she* would never fall under such a man's spell. *She* was proof against such things as a smile and expressive eyes. *She* was...

She was so attracted to the man, she felt as if she were going mad with unfulfilled desire.

"Move your hand up a little higher, Lord Mulholland," Mrs. Wells said, peering at Paris over her upright thumb as if he were a particularly odious insect. "Oh, dear me, this will *never* do! Witherspoon, adjust those curtains a little to the left, if you please."

While the butler complied with suitable dignity, Jean Claude hurried up and removed a stray blond hair from Paris's shoulder. "*Exactement!* You must be perfect, my lord," he whispered before returning to his former post of observation.

Paris tried not to sigh with exasperation. He was truly beginning to regret his impulsive decision to have Mrs. Wells paint his portrait. Not only did he feel like some kind of objet d'art on display in a gallery, he had been standing in front of the red velvet curtains for over two hours, in a variety of poses. No sooner was Mrs. Wells certain she had found the proper stance for his picture than she frowned and suggested something else. At present, he was standing in a distinctly Napoleonic attitude, one hand at his side, the other against his breast.

Well, Napoleon or a wounded felon, he thought discontentedly, gazing at the woman wearing a huge smock over her voluminous gown. The smock had been worn many times, for many paintings, judging by the quantity of spatters and colors on it. Scattered about the room were various canvases—all large—paints, varnishes, oils, brushes and turpentine, which combined to make a smell that was unpleasantly reminiscent of house decoration.

Witherspoon had been pressed into service, and Paris could tell he was not the only person getting fatigued. Mrs. Dibble kept bustling past the room like a rampaging general, shooting looks at them like so much artillery. Unfortunately, Aurora Wells and the indefatigable Jean Claude seemed as fresh as they had hours before.

"Maybe we should go for a studious attitude," Mrs. Wells murmured thoughtfully. "Reading a book perhaps."

"I think that would not be considered in character, Mrs. Wells," Paris demurred, lowering his hand and thankfully feeling the blood return. "How would it be if I sat in a chair?"

He hauled over a small gilt chair with red velvet upholstery and sank down gratefully. "Where is your niece?" he asked, reminded of Clara by mention of a book.

How surprised she had been last night when he had caught her holding that book upside down—and how telling a sign that had been! She could not ignore him, try as she might, and he had been rather absurdly pleased.

Just because she was a challenge, of course. Nothing else.

"Oh, out walking, I suppose. She mentioned wanting to see the garden."

"Had I known," he said, "I would have been happy to show it to her."

"She will be fine on her own," Mrs. Wells said absently. "She knows all about flora and fauna."

Paris wondered if Clara Wells' aunt was always so dismissive of her niece, or only when she was working. It troubled him to imagine even so self-possessed a young lady as Clara Wells left too much on her own.

Her life must get rather lonely at times, he thought sympathetically. He certainly knew how terrible loneliness could be. How forlorn one could feel when left bereft.

Better to avoid any entanglements at all, to find happiness without love and to have plenty of company, so you didn't have to consider your feelings at all.

"My lord!" Mrs. Wells said with exasperation. "Please! Not so serious. You *wrinkle!*"

"Heaven forfend!" her model replied and assumed a more impassive air.

"Now, if Witherspoon would move the curtains a little more to the right, please," the artist commanded.

Witherspoon obeyed.

"Place your hands on your lap, Lord Mulholland. Loosely. No tension in the fingers, if you please. Witherspoon, can you adjust the drapery a bit better? We don't want a huge gather right behind his lordship's head. Yes, that's right."

"I shall look off into the distance, shall I?" Paris suggested, "like the clever, cunning fellow I am, beholding my many acres." He shifted a little, so that he was angled to look out the window.

An unexpected sight greeted him. Clara Wells, with her dark brown hair uncharacteristically unbound, was walking through the garden with a delightful half smile on her face. Because the day was warm, she wore a light frock in a somber shade of brown—far too somber for that smile, he thought. Yellow would have been much better. She would look like a buttercup, a small wildflower among the formal flowers, and putting them all to shame.

Why did she wear such plain and dreary gowns of brown or that horrible shade of gray she had worn at Lord Pimblett's? With her coloring, she should be in delicate shades of blue, or green.

He had not noticed the many hues in her hair, now shining in the sun. She wasn't conventionally beautiful, but wholesomely pretty, and her lips were definitely a woman's lips that deserved to be kissed.

It was also obvious she had a figure she should be proud of. He didn't doubt that her breasts were perfect, just large enough to nestle in the palm of his hand. He could easily imagine clasping her about that slender waist. Then he would pull her gently to him and capture that rosebud mouth of hers with his own until she moaned with pleasure. A powder keg indeed, he thought, recalling her passionate temper. His lips and hands would be the match to ignite her other passions.

She bent down and straightened with that blasted cat in her arms, smiling benignly, and rubbed the top of the beast's head. The cat closed its eyes contentedly, as well it should, with such delicate fingers stroking it. . . .

"Per-*fect!*" Mrs. Wells cried, nearly stopping his heart with surprise. He had quite forgotten the existence of anyone except Clara.

"That is perfect! You must remain in just that pose, with that delightful little smile on your lips. You look like a man who has just seen a vision!"

Good God, he was breathing like a man who had just run a mile. And that damn fool of a Frenchman was looking like a cat after a saucerful of cream, his gaze shifting from Paris to the garden beyond.

Clara Wells thankfully passed out of sight.

"Would you care for a glass of sherry, my lord?" Witherspoon inquired.

"I think his lordship has no need for additional stimulation," Jean Claude said, his face a mask of seriousness.

Paris directed a condemning glance at both of them. "No, thank you, Witherspoon." He spoke to Mrs. Wells. "Are the curtains arranged to your satisfaction?"

"I believe so...perhaps...yes."

"You may leave, Witherspoon," Paris said, and he detected some slight relief on Witherspoon's part. "Call me when Taddington and Clark arrive. You may go, too, Jean Claude. I think my clothing doesn't need your personal supervision any longer."

Witherspoon glided noiselessly out of the room. Jean Claude frowned, but he obeyed.

"I'm not sure about the position of those hands," Mrs. Wells murmured thoughtfully. "Perhaps they should be crossed. Or holding something. Or one on the chin, pensive."

Paris realized it was going to be a very long morning.

Chapter Eight

By mid-afternoon Clara had rambled through the lovely garden that was filled with delightfully old-fashioned flowers, gotten lost in the shrubbery, discovered the stables, seen the dairy, met most of the maids and been taken on a tour by the housekeeper, Mrs. Dibble. She had learned enough to know that reports of Lord Mulholland's wealth were not exaggerated.

The original Mulholland House had been built on the site of a Norman castle. Only the moat remained, for that structure had been pulled down to make way for a Tudor manor. Part of the Tudor hall still existed and was now the dark, oak-paneled library.

Later additions had apparently sampled every major architectural style that had ever been popular among the nobility, a testament not only to the Mulhollands' wealth, but to their ability to weather any political storm. As Mrs. Dibble pointed to portraits and explained how the Mulhollands had managed to straddle the proverbial fence during the Wars of the Roses and the English Civil War, Clara thought all one needed to comprehend the longevity of the family was to note the likeness many of the portraits bore to Paris

Mulholland. No doubt his predecessors also owed much to handsome faces and charming personalities.

After her tour with the loquacious housekeeper, Clara had eaten a delectable lunch all by herself. Her uncle made no appearance and Witherspoon reported that his lordship had taken light refreshment in the "studio," as had her aunt. Clara suspected Witherspoon found the whole business of portrait painting somewhat dubious, but was too well-bred to say so.

If he had ever seen one of her aunt's completed portraits, he would be even more convinced, Clara thought mournfully. She wished her aunt's dedication could be turned to a more worthy cause. Sadly, Clara believed that to try to persuade Aunt Aurora to pursue any other calling would be utterly hopeless. However, her landscapes were not bad, her still lifes sometimes quite good. If only Aunt Aurora was not more interested in people than bowls of fruit!

Usually Clara could content herself that the subjects of Aunt Aurora's efforts were vain or foolish, and so deserved a painting that was not particularly flattering. That did not explain why she wished to spare Lord Paris Mulholland, whom she had originally dismissed as both.

She finally headed for the library, thinking she might find something interesting to read, and opened the door on the vast, musty, book-lined room. There were rows and rows of leather-bound volumes of various sizes, a large fireplace and several thickly-cushioned, brocade-covered chairs. Heavy madras draperies in dark green covered the shuttered windows. Like the other rooms on this side of the house, double doors opened out onto the terrace, but the shutters were closed tight, making the room seem like the bottom of a deep well. Carpets that would muffle any footstep were on the floor. Nevertheless, she thought she could hear someone muttering.

Her first thought was that perhaps Mulholland House was haunted.

The second was that it was Uncle Byron's deep, sonorous tones.

She spotted him in one the corners, surrounded by piles of books. He appeared to have constructed himself a fortress of books; unfortunately, he had managed to shut himself in it as if expecting a siege.

"Uncle Byron?" she asked, going to the window and opening the curtains a little to let in the sunlight. "What are you doing?"

"Close that! The sun has done enough damage in here already!" he cried, turning around and sending a pile of books cascading onto the worn Aubusson carpet. "Oh, my! There go all the geographies!"

Clara obeyed and began to pile the books. "What is all this?"

"His lordship has the most marvelous library, my child. Absolutely first-rate! But the chaos—absolutely mythical in proportion. A great shame! However, like Hercules, I have asked to be allowed to labor here to correct the shambles. To clean out the Stygian stables of dust and decay and worm. To restore order. To bestride these books like a modern Colossus!"

Clara saw through her uncle's classical allusions. "You mean you're cleaning it up?" she asked incredulously.

Uncle Byron rubbed his head so that his hair looked like the straw from the Stygian stables. "I am restoring these books to their proper order," he said, quite convinced, she could see, that he considered this a noble calling.

She really should not be surprised. She often suspected he wanted to be a poet only because he loved literature so much. As a poet, he was not talented. But as she surveyed the piles before her and saw how he was ordering the works, and how reverently he handled books, it suddenly occurred to her that in taking care of a vast library, Uncle Byron might feel as if he had found heaven on earth.

"I was coming to select a book," she explained.

Uncle Byron's returning smile was angelic and childishly delighted at the same time. "Look at this, then! A folio edition of Shakespeare." He reached down and carefully lifted an immense book. "Almost mildewed, but not quite. The spine's quite faded, though. Most unfortunate." Despite his earlier joy, Uncle Byron looked about to weep. "I don't know what Lord Mulholland must have been thinking to let such a beautiful thing be almost ruined by neglect."

"I daresay Lord Mulholland has very little regard for anything except his own pleasure," Clara condemned. Of all the rooms in the house, this one apparently saw the least use. Indeed, she suspected Mrs. Dibble would have bypassed it entirely if it was not the original Tudor hall.

Setting down the book as carefully as another man might set a toddler down on unsteady little legs, Uncle Byron said, "It's rather heavy. How about this? *The History of Tom Jones, A Foundling.*"

Clara had already read that book. Then she noticed Uncle Byron's gaze wandering over the rest of the shelves. No doubt he would prefer to be alone with his work, so she accepted his offer. "Have you had lunch, Uncle?"

"No. I have been feeding my soul here instead."

Clara tried not to betray her frustration. Uncle Byron could never seem to think of the practicalities, even when it came to his own meals, unless he was forcefully reminded by the growling of his stomach. Then he would eat like a man who had been stranded on a desert isle for quite some time. She considered persuading him to go with her, but she was sure the luncheon was already cleared away. "I shall ask Mrs. Dibble to have a maid bring you a tray," she offered.

"Oh, no!" he cried, his tone one of panic. "No food here! The mice will come in legions! Or insects!" He shook his head several times. "No, no, no, it simply isn't to be thought of. I can wait for tea."

Clara reflected that although the day was proving interminable to her, it really wasn't that long until teatime. "Very well, Uncle," she conceded, promising herself she would make sure Uncle Byron participated if she had to drag him out of the library herself. A nice spectacle that would make for the servants! Still, she would do it, for Uncle Byron's sake. "Till teatime, then."

He nodded absently and reached up for another book. Already forgotten, Clara took *Tom Jones* and left the library. While it didn't please her to see her uncle so diligently at work for a man who would likely never appreciate it, she thought it was a better use of her uncle's abilities than poetry writing. He seemed happier, too. It would probably be some time before more was added to *Childe Roland*.

Then she smiled wryly. By the time Uncle Byron was finished in the library, Lord Mulholland would not be able to find anything, supposing he ever looked.

Her smile became a disgruntled frown. Not that Lord Mulholland would care one iota. What a pity a man like him, with all the advantages of wealth, power and prestige, spent his time so unwisely!

Well, Paris Mulholland was not her worry—thank goodness! And at least she needn't feel that they were taking advantage of the man's generosity. Uncle Byron would do a fine job, which would more than make up for any expenses while they were here.

Indeed, the only person who didn't seem to have a purpose here was herself, unless that would be to make certain Uncle Byron ate a proper meal and her aunt didn't keep Lord Mulholland too long in the studio. She had no household to oversee, no bills to consider. While that was something of a relief, she was also very bored.

As she wandered through the vast house seeking a suitable place to read, it occurred to her that if her grandfather had not disowned her mother, she might have spent days without any useful occupation.

How dreadful! As aggravating as living with her aunt and uncle could be, it was rarely dull. Surely the occasional embarrassment was little enough to endure compared to endless boredom!

No wonder so many of the young women she saw at parties were such determined flirts. Maybe that was the only thing they had to look forward to. Maybe that was why Lord Mulholland paid any attention to her at all: simply to relieve a state of ennui.

That was not a flattering notion. She went into the dining room and surveyed her reflection in the vast

mirror over the mantel. What she saw was a plain
young woman of serious mien gazing at her through
frank hazel eyes, one who saw things as they were—
not as she wished they might be—and who was dressed
in a simple, austere gown. A man like Paris Mulholland could never be interested in her.

Disgruntled and angry with herself for succumbing
to the weakness to even consider such things for a
moment, Clara clutched *Tom Jones* tightly and
marched out of the dining room into the foyer, where
she halted in some dismay. Two unknown young gentlemen were handing their hats to Witherspoon, and
by the baggage footmen were bringing into the house,
obviously intended to visit for some time.

Her first thought was that they did not bear comparison to Lord Mulholland either for looks or build.
The second was that she should run and tell Aunt Aurora to let her model go. The third, as they both turned
toward her and she made a hasty curtsy, was that she
should not have unbound her hair. What would they
think of her?

"Miss Wells, may I present Mr. Thomas Taddington and the Reverend Jonas Clark," Witherspoon
announced.

It was easy to tell which was the reverend by his
clerical collar. Above that was a firm, resolute chin,
lean, hawklike nose and intelligent gray eyes topped by
thick dark brows and even thicker dark hair. He made
a solemn bow as Clara hastily pulled back her hair and
desperately wondered where the ribbon had gone.

Mr. Thomas Taddington had a plump, pale face
rather like a pudding, round blue eyes similar to a
frog's, neatly trimmed sandy-colored hair and a wan
smile. His clothes were expensive and fashionably cut,

but they couldn't disguise the fact that the young man, whom she guessed to be no more than twenty-six, was going to be fat.

"Gentlemen, Miss Clara Wells, who is currently a guest of his lordship."

"Charmed, my dear, charmed!" Mr. Taddington exclaimed in a deep voice and with a significant look at the inscrutable Witherspoon. "What a delightful surprise, I must say. Friend of Paris, eh? Good friend, I expect, eh, what?"

The Reverend Clark, perhaps sensing Clara's discomfort at the implications in Mr. Taddington's tone and expression, stepped forward. "I am always delighted to meet a friend of Lord Mulholland. Have you come to teach at the new school?"

Clara wasn't sure what to make of this last remark. What school, and why would a teacher be a guest of Lord Mulholland? It was extremely difficult to equate Lord Mulholland and any kind of educational institution; still, that was much better than being mistaken for something else, as Mr. Taddington so obviously had.

Did Lord Mulholland often bring women of a certain type here? she wondered as she acknowledged their greeting. She found it hard to believe that Lord Mulholland had to resort to paid companionship of any kind. "My aunt is painting Lord Mulholland's portrait."

"Good God, can she get him to stand still long enough?" Mr. Taddington asked, quite serious.

"I hope so," Clara answered.

"It would be just like Paris to indulge in such frivolity," the reverend said sternly.

"Frivolity? I don't think so," Mr. Taddington exclaimed, winking at Clara most impertinently. "He needs to leave his likeness for future generations." He frowned as his gaze ran over her, and she sensed disappointment. "I say, I've never actually met an artist myself, Miss Wells."

"I do not paint," she said firmly. No doubt he would find Aunt Aurora more to his expectation.

"I shall summon his lordship at once," Witherspoon said gravely, looking at Mr. Taddington as if he were a very small, very naughty boy.

There was no need. A voice suddenly cried out, "Tommy, you old stick! And you've got the patriarch with you, have you?"

Lord Mulholland strode into the foyer and shook his friends' hands with enthusiasm. "I should have known you would arrive at teatime, Tommy. You've both met Miss Wells, I see."

Paris realized that the aforementioned Miss Wells was attempting to sidle away, and immediately wondered how he could get her to stay, until he saw the disgustingly speculative look in Tommy's eyes.

The man had all the subtlety of a slap in the face. Paris could well guess what kind of construction his friend would put on any obvious attention he paid to Miss Wells, and he would spare her such speculation.

So when she said, "If you will excuse me, gentlemen," in her starchiest manner, he merely nodded his acquiescence.

And tried very hard not to feel disappointed when she went away.

Chapter Nine

"I say, Paris, old chap," Tommy said a few moments later when he was refreshing himself with a glass of sherry as the young men stood together in Paris's study, "she's not your usual sort, is she? I mean, no beauty to recommend her at all. Not even friendly, I don't think."

Jonas looked as severe as a newly ordained minister could. "You are getting too old for such sinful activities, Paris."

"Having my portrait done is sinful? If so, someone should definitely write the *Times* to inform the world," Paris said before turning a quizzical gaze onto Tommy. "Surely you couldn't have been speaking of Miss Wells?"

Tommy caught the none-too-subtle tone of warning in Paris's voice, and swallowed hard. "No offense meant, old boy."

Paris cursed himself for not being more nonchalant, and swiftly assumed his customary levity of manner. "I should hope you would credit me with better taste! She came with her aunt, who's doing my portrait. Besides, you know I've been very chaste recently. And I've *never* brought my mistresses here."

Tommy and Jonas knew all about Paris's early infatuations, including his very first love affair. Lisette's conflagration of his clothing on the High at Oxford had passed into legend, ensuring Paris of some fame and not a little sympathy for many months, so there was no point dissembling.

His friends had also probably heard about his later liaisons—matters of the flesh and never the heart—but he had never bothered to try to explain that to them. Tommy always believed that every woman he— Tommy—dallied with was the love of his life and would never understand Paris's sense of detachment; Jonas was as yet a virgin who ostensibly felt pity for other men's sinful weakness.

"Chaste is obviously a relative term," Tommy noted good-naturedly. "How long has it been since that little nightingale from the opera? Six months?"

"I was her patron for a time, and that's all. She has a marvelous voice, as she is proving all on her own in Vienna."

"Oh, yes, of course. How foolish of me to forget you admired her *voice*."

"It's time you married and settled down, Paris," Jonas said sternly.

Paris grinned good-naturedly. "I don't plan to settle down for at least another twenty years, when I shall find myself a giddy young creature with no brains and enormous breasts who will appreciate my money, if not me, and produce the requisite heir. I assure you I am quite adamant about this, so you might as well save your breath."

Jonas shook his head. Although he was inclined to sermonize and he clearly considered Paris something of a black sheep, he knew when it was wise to stop. He also knew when Paris was not being serious.

"Why don't you ask Tommy why *he's* not married?" Paris asked.

He faced Tommy, who shook his head sadly. "I'll probably die an old bachelor with nobody near me except some ancient housekeeper with no teeth—if I don't set my house on fire, or drown or blow myself up first."

"What have you done now?"

Tommy's forlorn sigh seemed to come from the depths of despair. "I don't mind saying, my friend, that your invitation couldn't have come at a better time. I thought my father was going to throttle me on the spot." He frowned mournfully. "It would be a terrible thing to be murdered."

"What on earth are you talking about?" Jonas demanded, although, like Paris, he could make a very good guess.

"Well, I was simply standing in the factory, supervising and generally trying not to make a nuisance of myself while keeping out of my father's way, when I noticed this thingummy dangling from one of the machines. Just a loose thread, or so I thought. Deciding I'd be helpful, I pulled it." He shrugged his beefy shoulders. "Broke the whole damn machine. Don't ask me how. I *still* don't understand it. Something about tension and balance and warps and woofs. Anyway, I thought my father would have an apoplectic fit right there. My mother was all for sending me to Europe for a year or two until he calmed down. Fortunately, I got your welcome missive, and so here I am."

Paris shook his head in mock dismay. Tommy Taddington's father was a rich wool merchant who was firmly convinced that Tommy should learn the business from the ground floor, despite the fact that Tommy had set the factory offices on fire with the careless toss of a lit match, lost the company several hundred pounds by the improper placement of a decimal in the quotation price of a shipment of cloth, nearly been blackmailed when one of the spinners enticed him behind the factory and now, apparently, he had broken one of the machines. "Why didn't you ask one of the men to take a look?"

"I didn't think of that until later." Tommy looked sorrowful for another minute, then he brightened and said to Jonas, "I've got Father thinking about a school for the village, though."

It was Jonas's mission in life to promote schooling, especially among the lower classes.

"Thus blow the breezes, while Zephyr sneezes, and Jupiter wheezes," a deep baritone voice bellowed outside the study windows. Suddenly there was a loud, long mournful wail. "Alas, the muse has left me!"

"What the devil's that?" Tommy demanded while Jonas hurried to look outside. "Have you decided to turn this place into an asylum?"

"There's a strange man on the terrace with Miss Wells," Jonas said, giving Paris a quizzical look that would seem to indicate he agreed with Tommy that a madman was on the premises.

Paris joined him at the window and saw Byron Wells sitting on the terrace balustrade, deep in thought. Clara sat beside him, her arm tenderly around his shoulders while she whispered into his ear, her look earnest but not frightened.

It must be a delightful thing to have comfort of that young woman, Paris mused. An intelligent, shrewd young woman who had the courage to look at life straight on.

How long had it been since he had been so comforted? Perhaps never, considering his mother's fervent but indulgent affection. She loved not wisely, but too well, always choosing to overlook her son's faults, and always unwilling to admit that he could possibly have any problems. Was it any wonder, then, that he had grown so adept at hiding his embarrassing ignorance, and to pretend that he was never lonely?

Tommy pushed against him, trying to get a better look.

"He's not insane," Paris explained. "He's a poet—the husband of the artist doing my portrait."

"The uncle of the charming Miss Wells?" Tommy asked.

"Yes."

Suddenly Byron Wells sat bolt upright. "Very well, my dear. To the tea table!" he cried. Then he dashed into the house through one of the terrace doors, Clara hurrying along behind.

Paris couldn't help but be impressed by the young woman's maternal solicitude. Hers must be a difficult life.

A difficult, lonely life.

"Is he...is he *quite* well?" Jonas asked doubtfully.

"He seems to be," Paris said as he turned back to his friends. It wouldn't do to think too much about Miss Wells. "You'll be happy to hear that he says my library is in disastrous order and he has undertaken to fix it."

Jonas smiled, and clearly Byron Wells had risen in his favor. For his part, Paris didn't care what Byron Wells did to his library, for he never used the room.

Then it occurred to Paris that, for a clergyman, Jonas wasn't bad looking. He wondered if Clara Wells, who could surely match Jonas for seriousness and likely a passion for schooling, would find him attractive.

He never should have invited Clark.

He was being utterly foolish. What did it matter what Clara Wells thought of Jonas Clark? What if she married him?

Paris meant what he had said before. He was going to follow in his father's footsteps and not marry until he was at least forty-five. His mother had been over twenty years his father's junior, yet they had been very much in love, and very happy together. If they had had any regrets at all, it was that they had only one child. And if his mother had been somewhat immature and giddy, and if she had been rather helpless when his father had died, it didn't matter. By then, he had been of an age to help her. For his mother's part, she had been devoted to her son, and he had loved her very much. He missed her often, especially when he was here.

She probably would have been afraid to be in the same room with Clara Wells. She had had an absolute horror of what she called "booky" women, and he could understand why. Miss Wells was rather intimidating and far too serious.

Unless, perhaps, she was strolling in a garden on a sunny summer day.

"Paris!"

He came back to the present with a start. "Yes, Jonas?"

"I said, are you going to attend church with me tomorrow?"

Paris shook his head. "You know I never go to morning prayer."

"What about your other guests? Do you think they would care to accompany me?"

"I don't know," he said with a shrug. "I'll ask them at dinner."

"Oh, Byron! Byron!"

Paris was glad to be distracted from the idea of Jonas sitting beside Clara Wells at any time, even in the confines of a church pew, by the voice of Aurora Wells. In another moment, that worthy woman came charging across the terrace like a bull in a ring in Madrid. She still wore her spotted painting smock and turban. "I believe you'll find him in the drawing room," Paris called out.

Mrs. Wells' response was a quick nod with no pause in her progress.

"That must be the artist," Jonas remarked. "I'd like to see the picture."

"I'm afraid, gentleman, that Mrs. Wells has a rule she insists be kept. No one is to see the portrait until it is finished."

"I can hardly wait to see what she makes of you, old man!" Tommy said with a snort of a laugh.

Paris smiled and wondered what they would think if they knew he was far more interested in what the *niece* made of him.

Paris realized something unusual was afoot when he spied Clara Wells gliding down the staircase with roses in her hair. Any kind of adornment was so unusual that if it hadn't been for the severe snuff-colored gown, he would have been tempted to think a changeling had taken her place.

Did he say changeling? A goddess, more like, as he recalled the vision of her in the garden. She was like Diana, goddess of the hunt, free and beautiful with her frank hazel eyes.

He couldn't help noticing that this sudden impulse to womanly vanity had coincided with the arrival of two *other* gentlemen. He knew women well enough to be sure that Tommy was not the kind of man a woman like Clara would desire. That left the educated, well-spoken, socially responsible Jonas Clark.

Paris moved to the bottom of the stairs, determined to escort her to the drawing room before dinner. She looked a little taken aback when he approached, but she said nothing. Instead, she lowered her eyelids with demure modesty, her dusky lashes fanning upon her satin cheeks. Her fingers trembled as she placed them on his forearm, and he could not recall when such a touch had moved him so.

She, apparently, felt no such stunning reaction, for when they entered the drawing room, she pulled away from him and approached Jonas, who was smiling with more delight than Paris had ever seen him display before. Even Tommy was grinning like a damn idiot.

"Reverend Clark, good evening," she said sweetly. "Mr. Taddington."

They exchanged pleasantries for a few minutes, while Paris tried to calm his rapidly fraying nerves.

What had happened to the severe little nun—and why was he so upset by the change? It shouldn't matter to him at all that she had turned into this...this captivating creature.

As for Jonas, he was a man first, and a man of the cloth second. Nobody should blame him for smiling at her...and nobody should be angry with her for smiling back. After all, *he* couldn't marry her. She was not of his class.

Or rather, he, the charming, the blithe, the *ignorant* Paris Mulholland, was not of hers.

"Don't you agree, Lord Mulholland?" she said in her musical voice that was all too easy to imagine whispering endearments.

"I beg your pardon?"

"I was saying," she replied, looking at him with a speculative expression that was quite new to him, "that I shall have to convince Mr. Taddington and Reverend Clark to tell me all about your days at Oxford. I confess I envy you the opportunity to attend. It has never struck me as fair that women should be barred from attending such institutions."

That, at least, sounded more like the familiar Clara Wells. He relaxed, and slipped into the comfortable mask of unruffled gentleman easily, before the horrified Tommy could respond or the profoundly shocked Jonas speak. "I don't recall much of the days, but the nights, my dear Miss Wells, the nights!"

Her eyes narrowed slightly. She did not approve. Good. He didn't approve of the way she had looked at Jonas. "Of course, Jonas won't be able to tell you anything about that," he added with more sarcasm than the comment warranted. "He spent all his time studying."

"As a scholar should," Miss Wells retorted. "I would give anything to be allowed to study at Oxford."

"*Anything*, Miss Wells?" Paris asked with a significant look.

Chapter Ten

Clara knew she should giggle and blush and act as if his comments astounded her. Poor Paris Mulholland! She had heard double entendres from her aunt's acquaintances determined to seduce her that would probably shock him to his worldly toes.

Besides, he was trying to change the subject. She straightened her shoulders. "I would give my attention to the teachers, from whom any person could learn much. I would give my mind to my studies, for anything less would be a waste of precious time. I would give my heart to learn, intending to profit from the wisdom of those who have gone before me."

"Hear, hear!" the Reverend Clark said approvingly.

Clara ignored the well-meant interruption. "What did *you* give, Lord Mulholland?"

She had hoped to make him feel ashamed of his previous levity, or to force him into an admission that there was more to him than a merry gadabout, but she might just as well have tried to control the sun.

He smiled coolly and said with easy, arrogant pride, "The glory of my name, and the money they required, which seemed to satisfy all concerned."

"For shame," Jonas Clark said, his expression suddenly as reproachful as that of a biblical prophet.

"Oh, that's too harsh, Jonas!" Tommy Taddington protested. "We all know Paris would have graduated eventually, and he had to leave in the middle of his last term."

"Why did you have to do that?" Clara demanded. "Surely the studies could not have been so difficult for a man of your talents, even if you were functioning deprived of sleep."

"My mother died."

When Clara saw the flash of pain in those unusually blue eyes, she realized she had spoken as rashly as Aunt Aurora ever had, and she was full of shame. "I'm sorry."

Then Paris Mulholland smiled, a smile that was forgiving and sincere. "No need to look so upset, Miss Wells. She was sitting at dinner one night with three lords, an earl, a viscount and two bishops. She was laughing, so they tell me, and suddenly fell into a swoon. By the time I got here, she had died, without ever waking. We should all have such quick, painless deaths, doing what we enjoy the most."

"Here, here!" Mr. Taddington echoed. "I want to go in my sleep, too." His face fell. "I'll probably get blown to bits, knowing my luck."

Fortunately, or unfortunately when she saw the gaudy gown her aunt had chosen, Aunt Aurora sailed into the room at that moment.

Her dress was such an incredible combination of red, green and blue stripes that it looked like it had been made from the awning of a gypsy caravan. As for her headdress, some poor bird had sacrificed its plumes all for naught.

Clearly, however, Aunt Aurora considered her attire eminently suitable as she made her way toward the men, who, with the exception of Lord Mulholland, looked as if they had never seen anything quite like Aunt Aurora before.

They probably hadn't. Clara couldn't help feeling that Lord Mulholland's polite smile of welcome was all the more congenial because of his friends' reactions.

"The morning sun is the best, Lord Mulholland," Aunt Aurora announced. "Absolutely. There can be no question about it. I trust that you will always be able to sit then?"

"If there is no question about it, I shall endeavor to make myself available, at least until my other guests arrive."

"Other guests?" Tommy Taddington asked.

"The Pimbletts," he replied.

Clara stared at the lovely carpet. She had forgotten about them, when she should have certainly remembered Hester, and the lovely Helena.

It was a good thing they were coming. Really, it was. She would find it much easier to avoid Lord Mulholland if there were other people in the house—and that was what she wanted to do.

"You are so congenial, Lord Mulholland," Aunt Aurora gushed.

"I try," he replied with what Clara was certain was false modesty.

"Hail, glorious Paris!"

Clara did not have to look at the door to know that Uncle Byron had arrived, and she cringed at his familiar use of Lord Mulholland's name, which was entirely inappropriate. Still, *he* could be counted on to be wearing appropriate dinner dress, and he was.

"I really must compliment you, my lord, on your library! Such bounty! Such variety!"

"The work of my father and grandfather," Lord Mulholland said with a smile. "I had nothing to do with it."

Clara could well believe that, and yet she was surprisingly disappointed. It seemed a great pity that he was willing to let his library go to rot, as well as wasting his life.

"Miss Wells looks far too serious, doesn't she, gentlemen?" Lord Mulholland observed. "We had better exert ourselves to amuse her."

He made her sound like a child—and she didn't want Paris Mulholland to think of her as a child. "I do not require to be amused," she said, bristling. She went on before she could begin to consider how she *did* want Paris Mulholland to think of her. "I gather you approve of education in general, Lord Mulholland. Reverend Clark thought I might be a teacher for the village school."

Lord Mulholland waved his hand in an airily dismissive gesture. "Jonas wanted to start one in the village and I thought it would be as good a way as any to part with my money, so I agreed to supply the building. Simple enough."

"And the books, slates, pencils and desks. As well as pay the teacher's wages and provide her with a cottage," the Reverend Clark said. "Would that more men of influence thought as you did, Paris."

"Indeed!" Clara added with enough enthusiasm that, had she thought about it, she would have realized was remarkably similar to one of Aunt Aurora's outbursts.

"Yes, but what's the point, really?" Tommy Taddington asked. "Why teach people of that class to read when they don't have to? What are they going to do with an education? It will only make them discontented. They'll read about things, and then they'll want them, when they cannot possibly afford them."

"You would have them remain in blissful ignorance, is that it?" Clara asked.

"Exactly!" Mr. Taddington cried triumphantly.

"A cow is blissfully ignorant, Mr. Taddington," Clara said, "but a human being is not a dumb beast. We are rational, intelligent creatures. Besides, who gives you or anyone the right to decide what is appropriate for the public to know? If they become discontented, perhaps they will strive to overcome their fetters."

"Oh, I say, Miss Wells!" Mr. Taddington protested. "That's a bit harsh, don't you think? They're not chained up, you know."

"Is not ignorance the greatest chain of all?" she demanded passionately. "Is it right to deny any person the opportunity to learn how to read?" She looked at Lord Mulholland, half expecting him to make a joke. "Is it?"

Instead, he was quite uncharacteristically grave. "I cannot disagree," he said before strolling toward the windows.

"We must educate the people so that they will not be led astray by the temptations of the flesh!" Reverend Clark said fervently.

Clara gave the minister a puzzled look. She did not quite see the logic of his argument.

"Dinner is served," Witherspoon intoned, appearing in the doorway.

"Mrs. Wells, if I may?" Lord Mulholland said, holding out his arm to escort Aunt Aurora to dinner.

His serious expression had disappeared, and Clara was sorry for it. Although his smile was pleasant, there was a depth of intelligence in his mien when he was serious that thrilled her.

Aunt Aurora hurried to take his arm. "Mrs. Macurdy is a most excellent cook, my lord," she said. "Such soup! Such sauces! And her way with a pig is most exceptional!"

Clara took her uncle's arm and followed behind, wondering why Paris Mulholland persisted in being the court jester.

The other two gentlemen came last, one thinking that red roses looked charming on a woman of Clara Wells' coloring and he could quite admire her passionate defense of education, the other trying to decide just what kind of people these bohemians were. The niece was a pretty little thing, but what the devil was Paris thinking when he invited them here?

Clara turned away from the contemplation of her meager wardrobe, still not sure she had made the appropriate choice for church, and more importantly, trying desperately to rid her mind of the remnants of last night's dream.

It had been a startlingly vivid one, which no doubt accounted for its persistence. She had been in the drawing room, alone, it seemed, until Lord Mulholland materialized—and that could be the only word for his sudden appearance behind her. His voice saying her name had made her turn around.

He had been naked, save for a short white toga of the type seen in ancient Greek drawings of the gods. He repeated her name, and she went to him, knowing he was going to embrace her, and she was willing—nay, anxious—to be in his arms. He had enfolded her in his strong embrace and his lips had met hers in a searing, passionate kiss.

At that moment she had awakened, fully and quite cognizant of her excitement and delightful anticipation.

She told herself again that her dream was simply a reaction to Uncle Byron and Aunt Aurora's classical allusions. The after-dinner conversation had roved over many subjects, enabling Uncle Byron to display the extent of his knowledge on several subjects. Aunt Aurora had participated with her usual enthusiasm. Clara had been content to observe and speak only when addressed. The Reverend Clark had been most attentive to her, and Lord Mulholland his usual blithely charming self.

This morning, she was both pleased and dismayed that Lord Mulholland was not going to church with them. His absence confirmed that his was a wasted life, lacking in the truly important things. Nevertheless, she couldn't help wishing it were not so.

There was another reason she didn't want to see Paris Mulholland this morning, and that was the Reverend Jonas Clark. The clerical young gentleman was precisely the kind of stable, respectable young man she had so often thought she should meet. Marriageable to a fault. No wife of his would ever be lacking for a secure home.

He was already in possession of a good living, as he had made clear last night, and he had the friendship of a nobleman. However, compared to that most handsome, charming nobleman...

The Reverend Jonas Clark was good-looking, too, she reminded herself, and he appeared to have a sense of humor, albeit a rather stunted one. Lord Mulholland had related some harmless pranks in which the reverend gentleman had participated that showed he wasn't always solemn and serious.

She was ruled by her head, not her heart, and her head told her if she paid attention to any man at Mulholland House, it should be Reverend Clark. If she dreamed of a man, it should be any man but Paris Mulholland.

Determined to do as she silently vowed, Clara made her way to the drawing room to await the others. It seemed she was the first one ready, for there was no one in the room.

Yes, there was. Seated in the farthest corner by the terrace door, a man was reading a book. Thinking it was probably Reverend Clark, she went boldly forward, prepared to make some remark about the beauty of the August day.

Until she saw the strong, slender hand holding the treatise on sheep raising. Before she could move away, the book lowered... and Clara found herself looking at Paris Mulholland.

He was wearing a plain frock coat of dark blue, with a simple white shirt, black cravat, subdued checked waistcoat and dark brown trousers. He had on shoes, not boots, so she didn't think it likely he was planning a morning ride.

Was it any wonder she dreamed of him? No woman could be immune to the dangerous combination of charm, gallantry, masculinity and pure animal grace that comprised Paris Mulholland, not even a young woman adamant about maintaining her virtuous good name. Even now, Clara felt her pulse warm in her body and the blood rush to her face.

"Good morning," he said, surveying her with what she thought was a critical eye.

She contemplated her simple bonnet and modest gown, and quite ludicrously wished she had something more fine, which was worldly vanity, pure and simple, and therefore silly. "Are you going to the service with us, after all?" she asked, thinking there could be no other explanation for his presence there.

"No, I never attend this service," he answered lightly. He didn't elaborate, and once again she found herself disappointed. He probably only made a ceremonial appearance at the village church at Christmas and Easter, and perhaps Harvest Sunday, and only then if the mood came upon him.

"You're rather early. Won't you sit down?" He gestured languorously toward a chair. "I'm sure your aunt and uncle will be here shortly."

When she hesitated a moment, wondering at the propriety of being alone with a man in his drawing room, he smiled mockingly. "The church pews are made of oak, very strong, and very hard on the softer portions of one's anatomy. I suggest you enjoy a more comfortable seat while you may. No point in martyring yourself ahead of time."

Aghast at his mentioning any part of the body, let alone that particular one, she nevertheless appreciated the probable truth of his words. She decided that as long as she was far away from him, there was no harm in taking a seat, so she sat upon the sofa.

"Jonas will appreciate your company," he said.

Despite her best efforts, she could not tell if he was mocking her, or Reverend Clark or just making conversation. She remained silent.

"He quite likes you, I think."

What was Lord Mulholland up to? Why did he look so serious? Why was her heart beating so fast? "Does he?" she inquired, and her words sounded weak even to herself.

Lord Mulholland slowly stood and walked toward the window, his hands clasped behind his back.

Good heavens, he was a well-made man! How could she ever have suggested that a tailor was responsible for the breadth of his shoulders or the muscles of his thighs?

She had no business thinking this way! For once in her life, Clara wished Aunt Aurora and Uncle Byron would interrupt.

"I'm quite certain he does," Lord Mulholland remarked. "He would make a fine husband."

"I'm not husband hunting," she replied sharply.

"No?" He finally faced her and smiled.

Gracious heavens, he was a master of the smile! That, and his mocking eyes, seemed to make her heart turn over in spite of all her efforts to remain cool and calm.

"You are not setting a very good example for your tenants, not going to church," she remarked reproachfully, determined not to be distracted by his expressions or looks or the intensity of his steadfast gaze.

His mouth assumed its customary droll mockery. "Do you honestly believe my presence in the sacred edifice will inspire religious sentiments in their breasts?"

"At the very least, they would respect you for it."

"You do not think they respect me now?"

"It is your *duty* to set a good example. I am surprised Reverend Clark has not persuaded you to attend."

"Jonas knows better."

"It would seem he gives up too easily."

Lord Mulholland put his hand to his chest and assumed a wounded air. "My dear Miss Wells, you quite shock me."

"Why?" she demanded, annoyed at his cool disregard of a social responsibility and determined to attach no importance whatsoever to the fact that he had called her "my dear Miss Wells" again.

"Are you advocating hypocrisy? Would you wish me to be a mere Pharisee, praying only that I may be seen to be praying?"

It was difficult not to squirm under his shrewd gaze, because she knew that he was quite correct. On the other hand, it was not a good example to the tenants for Lord Mulholland to remain at home on the Sabbath. "I am sorry you do not believe it to be good for your soul, my lord," she answered at last.

His expression softened, and he looked genuinely interested in her opinion. "Why are you sorry?"

"Because I would have hoped for better from you," she replied. "As I would for anyone in a position of authority," she added quickly.

"Ah, well, there we come to the root of the problem, then," he said with a return to his cavalier manner. "If you are expecting me to be an example of anything except sloth and irresponsibility, you will be sorely disappointed. Besides, somebody has to keep an eye on Tommy."

He strode toward the door, then paused on the threshold. "I have ordered the carriage to take you all to church." He nodded politely. Distantly. As if she were a complete stranger. "So you see, I am not completely lacking in Christian charity."

Then he strolled from the room, whistling a jaunty air.

Chapter Eleven

Some minutes later, Clara took her place in the small country church between a relatively subdued Aunt Aurora, whose gown was all one shade, if that a vivid green, and the serious Reverend Clark, who stood as still as one of the stone angels depicted over the altar. The vicar, a kindly-looking, elderly man, was momentarily struck dumb at the end of the opening hymn by the vision of Aunt Aurora being escorted by Uncle Byron. Fortunately, the vicar recovered quickly and began the service.

His curate, a thin, anxious-looking young man, continued to stare, his mouth open like a carp seeking crumbs.

The Reverend Clark was not an agreeable companion with which to share a pew, Clara rapidly discovered. He was rather loud in his responses, and quick, as if to point out to the rest of the congregation that they had a divine prodigy in their midst. His singing voice was not pleasant, either, when one stood as close as Clara did. Nor did he seem aware that when he held the prayer book out the full length of his arm, she was quite unable to see the words. She made sure she commandeered the prayer book as soon as she was able, and then held it for him. He attempted to take it during the psalm, but she kept a firm grip and pretended she didn't notice his gallant efforts.

The church itself was a very old one of worn yellow stone, well maintained. This was not so surprising, when she glanced around the congregation. The service was well attended, with representatives from town and farm and manor. Witherspoon and several of the footmen filled one pew; Mrs. Dibble, Mrs. Macurdy and many of the maids sat directly in front of them. On the other side of the church, Lord Mulholland's valet sat alone, occasionally winking at one young lady in the choir who blushed furiously.

Perhaps Lord Mulholland truly believed his neighbors had no need of his example.

The vicar mounted the steps to the pulpit and began his softly spoken sermon about a rather obscure text. A sidelong glance proved that Reverend Clark was listening as intently as if the vicar were delivering the Sermon on the Mount. Uncle Byron was half-asleep, and Aunt Aurora stared at the angels, probably envisioning a picture of them.

Clara subdued a sigh. How much different it would be if Lord Mulholland were sitting beside her, speaking in her ear with his decidedly attractive voice, as he had in her dream last night. She could also imagine him looking about at the congregation with that combination of amusement and tolerance he so often sported. No doubt Jean Claude Beaumaris wouldn't be winking at the flustered chorister if his master were here.

What was the meaning of that change in his usual manner when he had seemed so interested in her reaction to his remarks about attending church, as if her opinion mattered a great deal to him?

Surely she was just imagining his sudden intensity. Why, to think that a man of his ilk would care one bit about her response to anything was...was just vanity. Or idiocy. Or ludicrously wishful thinking.

Why wishful? she asked herself. Because he was an attractive man, was the obvious answer. Handsome, well-bred, with an innate, lithe, almost animal grace that made him manly despite his lackadaisical air, which sometimes disappeared. As it had this morning, when they had been alone together.

Alone. Together.

The prayer book she had been holding slipped to the floor with a bang. Startled, she realized everyone else was standing up, for the sermon had ended. Blushing furiously, she sank down with all the decorum she could muster and retrieved her book, then stood. She opened the book to hide her red face, and as she did so, she noticed a bookplate pasted in the front: "Presented by Paris Mulholland, in loving memory of his parents."

She was surprised for two reasons. First, that he had not used his title, for she thought him a proud man. Secondly, that he had chosen to donate books to the church when he did not attend. It seemed an odd thing to do.

Or perhaps not. It could be that the vicar had suggested it, and Lord Mulholland had not seen any reason to protest. Still, it was a gesture that touched her, and she found herself hoping that it indicated a modesty, a discretion and a loving heart that was more the true character of the man than the mocking, superficial attitude he customarily displayed.

The service ended soon after. As Clara and her party made their way to the porch where the two clergymen practiced the subtle religious art of delaying the fleeing congregation with a handclasp and a smile, she was tempted to ask the vicar about Lord Mulholland, but quickly decided that would not be a wise or discreet thing to do.

"I enjoyed your sermon," Reverend Clark said as he took firm hold of the vicar's hand. "However, I thought you might have drawn upon Marcus Aurelius." He directed a sharp, arrogant glance at Clara that plainly said, *I have more education than this man, and am infinitely smarter into the bargain.*

She did not like or approve of his glance, especially since the kindly vicar was not deserving of such impertinence from a younger man. She was sure the vicar could tell the Reverend Mr. Clark a thing or two about human nature.

"A lovely sermon, Vicar!" Aunt Aurora cried. "A most unusual text. So different. So obscure! I was really *quite* edified." She paused and regarded him thoughtfully. "Have you ever thought of having your portrait done?"

The vicar's pleasant smile froze, so that he looked not unlike one of the monuments in the churchyard.

"Have you?" Aunt Aurora pressed, gazing at him earnestly.

"Why, no, ma'am, I have not," the vicar said, and Clara noticed that he let go of her aunt's hand with startling alacrity and reached for the next person.

"A great pity," Aunt Aurora declared. She would have confronted the young curate with a similar question, had not Clara rather forcefully drawn her away.

"Look, Aunt," she said, nodding toward the church-yard.

"Now *that* is an artistic scene if ever I saw one!" Aunt Aurora cried, all thoughts of portraits momentarily subdued. "Such melancholy! Such moss!"

Clara followed her guardians, her attention attracted to the statue of a beautiful angel. It seemed a pity that it was in such a sorrowful place. Placed upon the grave was a bouquet of flowers so fresh, they had to have been put there that morning.

By whom? A former servant? A friend?

I never attend this service. That was what Lord Mulholland had said. Not "I never attend services," or "I never go to church" or "Only on special holidays."

Which did not mean that he had not gone to the earlier service.

If he had, it would explain why he was already dressed and reading a book when she came upon him in the drawing room.

Fool! She now understood the subtle mockery in his eyes that morning. She had been upbraiding him when there was no true cause.

Her embarrassment quickly gave way to annoyance. Why hadn't he said anything? Did he enjoy listening to her chastise him?

If that was so, why had he become so seriously intent? Was there a more confusing man in all of England—and was there any point trying to decipher him?

"Clara, my dear! The carriage comes!"

Clara glanced over her shoulder to see Uncle Byron beckoning. With a last look at the well-tended grave and the beautiful angel, Clara hurried toward him before he shouted for her again.

Two nights later, Clara sat up in her bed, listening. For some reason, Zeus wasn't at her feet, as he usually was, but that wasn't important. She was listening to the footsteps, *his* footsteps, as they came up the stairs and drew closer to her bedchamber. And closer. And closer.

He stopped, right outside her door. Clara waited, wondering if Paris was going to knock, or simply pass by.

She suddenly realized she was naked. How did she get naked? What had happened to her nightgown? Frantically she pulled the covers up, only to discover that the sensation of the silk against her breasts added to her sense of heated anticipation.

The door opened slowly, and Paris Mulholland stood there—lean, muscular and temptingly attractive. He wore no jacket and his pristine white shirt was open at the neck, exposing his chest. Below that, he had on riding breeches and boots. Tight riding breeches.

He came inside the room and closed the door. She tried to speak, to order him to leave, but the words wouldn't come out of her mouth.

Her body tensed, still anxiously waiting.

Then he was beside the bed. His eyes burned with passion as he looked at her and his lips curved up into his seductive smile.

She no longer cared that he didn't speak. There were no words for the feelings coursing through her. She wanted him. And she knew, from the fiery hunger in his blue eyes, that he wanted her, too.

So it did not surprise her when he bent down and kissed her, his mouth moving slowly and possessively over hers as she moaned with desire. She felt the bed dip with his weight when he lowered himself to sit beside her as she responded willingly. His hands traveled up her arms to capture her shoulders, her own hands feeling the taut muscles of his back, while she thrust the shirt from his body.

His kiss deepened. His tongue touched hers tentatively, then with more craving passion. His hands stroked her. Caressed her. Aroused her like nothing she had ever known or imagined.

Slowly, he pushed her back and at last his body covered hers. She undulated beneath him, alive with a burning need that only he could assuage. With more frantic movements she undid the buttons of his trousers.

Then he, too, was naked, his flesh against hers. She brazenly spread her legs, anticipating the moment he would join with her and end her impatient yearning.

"Paris," she whispered. "Paris..."

She was waking up. She knew it and fought against it, struggling to stay in her dream.

It was no use. She was awake. Aroused, panting, unfulfilled and longing for her lover.

She opened her eyes and looked around the room. Paris Mulholland was most definitely not there, and Zeus was sleeping on the far side of the bed. She shifted, trying to make the cat move, but it was like trying to move a pile of bricks. He took up as much space as a cat possibly could, and he snored into the bargain.

She gave up with a sigh, the texture of her cotton nightgown unwelcome against her own body. Another dream. Another astonishingly vivid dream. An astonishingly vivid, *sinful* dream! Whatever was she doing, having such dreams?

She rolled over onto her side and stared at the curtains moving slightly in the summer breeze. The air was warm, but that did not fully explain why her body felt so very hot.

She rolled onto the other side, where the mirror was. If she needed anything to remind her that a man like Paris Mulholland would not want her, she had only to look at her reflection.

Unfortunately, this did not change the fact that she wished it could be otherwise. She could dare to admit that here, when she was alone in the dark, even though she truly wished it wasn't so.

Why did he have to be so handsome? And so charming? And so considerate? He constantly managed to steer conversation to the mundane when Aunt Aurora and Uncle Byron were participants, thereby sparing her considerable embarrassment. Clara felt her face burning a few times from their pronouncements, but only a few. If he had truly sought their company to create an amusing diversion, he would not have done that.

And what about those other signs that he was not the selfish wastrel he was reputed to be: the school and his early attendance at church? What of all those people receiving free bread on the village green? Did he have a hand in that, too?

But why pretend to be an irresponsible gadabout? Why donate books to church and school, and ignore his own library? It didn't make sense.

If only she had had more opportunities to formulate a better idea of the contradictions apparent in

Lord Paris Mulholland! Regrettably, sitting for his portrait kept him closeted in the makeshift studio with Aunt Aurora every morning. On Monday afternoon, he and Tommy Taddington had gone hunting for grouse and pheasant. On Tuesday, Lord Mulholland had managed to lure Uncle Byron out of the library to go fishing in his trout stream.

At least she had not been forced to keep the Reverend Jonas Clark company very often. He had spent the past two days seeing to the preparations for his future home and parish.

He was a keen and kind minister, and a genuinely good man, but there was nothing in him to inspire Clara to love or passion. She had finally given up trying to force her feelings where they would not be led— a wise decision, given the turn her dreams had insisted upon taking.

So, when Reverend Clark had suggested that Clara come to view the vicarage, her first reaction had been to refuse. However, since she lacked any other demands on her time, and could come up with no good excuse, she had gone.

The vicarage proved to be an eminently suitable one—a large house of old gray stone overgrown with ivy, with a very pretty garden and excellent rooms. She tried to be enthusiastic. She would have been, had she not found the reverend watching her reactions rather too closely.

Sometimes, she thought Lord Mulholland was watching her closely, too, but that was surely only a flattering imagination.... She mustn't think about him.

She would think about Tommy Taddington, who was at best a simpleton, at worst an ignorant fool.

Besides having no comprehension of the struggles of the poor, he was clumsy and insensitive. In the course of only two days he had spilled water in his room and stained the ceiling below, burnt a hole in an Aubusson carpet and enraged Lord Mulholland's valet by saying the French were all effeminate imbeciles. Fortunately, Lord Mulholland seemed a born conciliator, and things were soon smoothed over.

What a pity Paris Mulholland wasn't employed in some diplomatic capacity. He could be a great success there, even if it meant depriving some people of his company.

She *must* stop thinking about Lord Paris Mulholland.

Her stomach growled—and she told herself that she had found the main reason for her wakefulness. She was hungry. A little snack would allow her to fall into a deep, untroubled sleep. She would just sneak down to the kitchen and get a roll.

Clara threw off the oppressive covers, which were indeed silk, although she tried not to remember anything about silk, and put on her slippers. She had no idea what time it was, except that it was very late. Surely *everyone* would be in bed by now.

Feeling quite safe and having convinced herself that her hunger was only in her stomach, Clara lit a candle, drew on her robe and ventured into the hall.

Chapter Twelve

Frustrated, Paris ran his fingers through his hair and, holding his head in his hands, slumped forward with his elbows on the desk in front of him. Gad, he hated this sort of work, going through accounts and deeds and letters and lists. Unfortunately, his estate and business interests didn't run themselves, and although Mycroft generally manned the tiller of Paris's investments, there was but one captain.

Jupiter, who had been sleeping contentedly at his feet, opened one eye and looked at him. "I wish I had your life, Jupe," Paris muttered. "No worries, no responsibilities."

It seemed Jupe blinked in agreement, then he lumbered to his feet and gave his tail a brief wag.

"Want to go out?" Paris asked.

He got up from behind his desk and opened the door of his study. Jupe stood still on the threshold for a moment, then sauntered along the dark hall toward the kitchen. "Watch out for the devil cat," Paris warned.

He left the door partly open in case Jupiter should decide to return to keep him company, then went to the small table against the wall. He poured himself a brandy and swirled it around for a meditative moment before downing it in a gulp.

It warmed him, and he leaned back against the paneling, staring at his desk covered with papers. It was very tempting to make a small bonfire of them in the empty grate.

But that would be useless. There would be more tomorrow or the next day. He might as well get the business over with, however long it took.

Sighing, he returned to his seat, then smiled sardonically. If only the censorious Miss Wells could see him now. His hair was sticking out at all angles because he had the most confounded habit of taking out his frustrations upon it. His jacket was off and his shirt half-unbuttoned as if he had shoveled a mountain of coal because he found this sort of work more difficult than physical exertion. She would know he was not a complete wastrel.

Nevertheless, he would not have her see him this way, not for all the money his family possessed. Better she should not know how hard he struggled and how late into the night. Far better to act the lax fool than for her to learn the truth.

Which was that Lord Paris Mulholland could read no better than a child. It took him ages to get through one of Mycroft's letters, and a legal document seemed to require an eternity.

Clara Wells would think him a complete dunce, worse than even Tommy, who could read better, if not reason better. He had even resorted to the childish trick of grabbing a book and pretending to read when she had surprised him in the drawing room on Sunday.

"Damn!" he mumbled, setting the glass down with a sharp rap.

He shouldn't worry about what Clara Wells thought. Unfortunately for him, he did, and far too much. He could admit that to himself, here, at night and all alone in the dark. Why, when she gave him one of her condemning and disappointed looks, she made him feel more ashamed than anyone ever had. He had tried to tell himself she was nothing but a naive girl who knew much of books and little of the real world, but it didn't help.

She was a mature young woman with many responsibilities. She was intelligent and shrewd, and indulgent of her aunt and uncle's foibles. Yet she was not so indulgent of *his*. Why?

Because she knew him to be capable of more, and that he was not the wastrel everyone else thought him to be?

That notion pleased and terrified him. It had been so long since he had cared about what anybody thought of him, he wasn't ready to do so again.

And yet he did care what she thought of him. Very much.

He leaned back and closed his eyes. He would find a way to control his wayward emotions. Really, Clara Wells was too naive. Or a great actress. She seemed absolutely unaware of how her intense gaze could work upon a man. To have a woman stare at one so frankly, with no thought of fear or favor... The very uniqueness of it was exciting. Did she *really* not know that?

Who was he trying to deceive? There was no dishonesty in her eyes.

But it didn't matter anyway. Miss Wells was far too bookish and serious, despite Jean Claude's continuing assertion that she was "a little powder keg." Jonas Clark was the type of man who would suit her exactly. Paris told himself he should admit it, accept it and forget her. He shouldn't allow the incredible surges of jealousy he felt when he saw them together. The portrait would be finished eventually, and they would go. All of them.

Now he had work to do, and he should waste no more time. With the best of intentions to concentrate on his business, Paris looked at the top letter from Mycroft and placed his index finger below the salutation. Then, very slowly, his finger moved along the line of writing and his mouth formed the words one by one.

Clara crept down the stairs. Suddenly, she realized she was not alone.

Zeus was padding along behind her, his eyes glowing demonically green in the light of her candle. "Go away, Zeus!" she hissed, thinking that Jupiter might be in the vicinity. If only Lord Mulholland would tie up his dog! He was lax in that regard, too, although he had been most concerned for Jupiter's wounds.

She would *not* think about Paris Mulholland anymore tonight!

Zeus sat and regarded her steadily. "Fine. Stay here, then," Clara whispered with frustration before continuing on her way. A glance back over her shoulder proved that Zeus was obeying her last order.

Then she saw a light shining beneath the study door. Could Lord Mulholland still be awake? What could he be doing so late into the night?

It was, of course, none of her business. She should simply continue on her way to the kitchen.

After all, what *could* be keeping him awake so late? Answering love letters? Probably he had fallen asleep. Perhaps with a candle burning, which would be a dangerous thing.

In the interest of safety—and only that—she crept toward the study cautiously.

She put her hand on the door's handle.

"Enough!" The word was said softly and with a weary sigh, in a voice that could be no other than Lord Mulholland's. Yet how unlike him to sound so despondent!

Her hand that held the candle trembled as she peered inside the room. Lord Mulholland was apparently alone. He stood beside a small table, his hair in disarray as if he had just been aroused from slumber, his shirt open and displaying an astonishing amount of muscular chest above his tight-fitting trousers and a brandy snifter in his long, elegant fingers. His attire was so like that of the Paris Mulholland in her dream that Clara had to smother a gasp, and then try to remain calm.

What was he doing here so late, with that brandy in his hand? A secret drinker?

He started to turn and she quickly blew out the candle, holding her breath and not daring to move.

Then he chuckled.

Was he mad? That didn't seem so farfetched at the moment. Or maybe only drunk, for it was a mocking laugh. "Come, Jupe," he said, and she thought that his elocution didn't sound like that of a drunken man. "Let's go to bed. This will keep 'til morning. And I absolutely will not think about Clara Wells."

He thought about *her?* Lord Paris Mulholland *thought* about her? Paris Mulholland thought about *her?* She wanted to dance, or shout or fly—something to express the incredible joy that filled her.

Then the study went dark.

He mustn't find her here! What would he think?

Moving as quickly as she could, she sidled along the corridor, hoping she could get to the kitchen without being seen.

Something cold touched her hand! She almost screamed, until she realized it was a dog's wet nose. She stood still, not daring to move.

"Come on, Jupe!" Lord Mulholland ordered from the landing of the stairs, or so it sounded. "Is it that damnable cat?"

"Go away!" Clara whispered, and mercifully, the dog went.

Feeling that she had had a narrow escape in more ways than one, yet delighted to think that she, of all women, could interest Lord Mulholland in any way, Clara hurriedly got herself a roll and relighted her candle. She began to return to her room, nibbling on the delicious bread, when she heard noises coming from the room that Aunt Aurora used as her studio. She looked closer and saw that the door was ajar.

Who could be in there? Lord Mulholland? He had gone upstairs. Aunt Aurora? Not likely. She slept heavily, and only woke if she was ill. Uncle Byron? He never disturbed the sanctity of the studio. Jonas Clark? He never asked about the painting, so it didn't seem likely that he would sneak down to look at it in the middle of the night. Tommy Taddington? She could see *him* invading the studio.

With her mouth a hard, grim line, Clara opened the door and marched in. Moonlight poured through the open windows, lighting everything in its silvery glow, and she saw something that filled her with dismay.

It was Jupiter, nuzzling among the canvases. His tail protruded from the pile leaning against the wall.

Perhaps he had found a mouse. Or Zeus! She hurried forward, avoiding the bulky easel that held the drapery-covered portrait of Lord Mulholland. "Jupiter!" she whispered severely. "Come out of there at once! *Jupiter!*"

She set the candle on the floor and crouched down, getting closer. "Here, Jupiter! Come here!" She reached in and grabbed hold of his collar.

Apparently the dog was not appreciative of her efforts, for she had quite a struggle to pull him out, tugging and moving backward at the same time. Intent on getting him out, she forgot the exact placement of the easel and backed right into it. It rocked, then fell over with a crash, mercifully missing the candle.

"You . . . you dog!" she cried softly as she let go of his collar. She hurried to right the toppled easel, and saw Jupiter dash from the room. "You *should* run, you demon," she muttered as she set the portrait back in place, its covering still intact. A quick survey of the edges proved it was undamaged.

She stared at the drapery over the picture, mindful of Aunt Aurora's superstition about anybody seeing her work before it was finished.

But who would know? No one, not even the dog. With sudden decision, she reached out—

"Peeking, Miss Wells?" drawled Lord Mulholland.

She spun around, aware of several things at once. The first was acute embarrassment that she had been caught in an act of overt curiosity. The second was she was in her thin nightdress and only slightly thicker robe. The third was he was smiling knowingly as if he could see right through those garments as well as read her mind. And the fourth—and most dismaying—was that he was not only wearing similar clothing to the ones he had worn in her dream, but that his pose in the doorway was nearly exact, too. She cleared her throat, and tried to keep her voice steady. "I heard a noise. Your dog was in here snooping among the canvases."

"I believe Jupe was not the only one snooping," he remarked. He came inside the room and closed the door behind him, reminding her—as if she needed any additional reminders!—that she was alone with Paris Mulholland in the dead of night, both of them attired in a most inappropriate manner.

"I came to investigate the noise," she replied defensively, crossing her arms over her chest.

He ran his arrogant gaze over her. "You must have very good hearing to have discerned such sounds from your bedroom."

"I was hungry. I got a roll from the kitchen."

He smiled and came closer. "That would explain the crumbs on your lips."

His words and his seductive, low tones were enough to start her blushing. She had to be strong! She couldn't let him know how he was affecting her! That would only—could only—lead to disappointment. She forced herself to speak, and to keep her voice firm and businesslike, which was not at all easy. "I see you, too, were roused from your preparations for bed. I suggest we retire before anyone else from the household arrives."

His smile was devilment incarnate. "Miss Wells, I must profess myself shocked, although I confess I find the prospect of retiring with you rather intriguing."

"That is not what I meant at all!" she spluttered angrily. "I meant we should go to bed. Alone. Separately!"

He laughed softly. "I had no idea the thought of sharing my bed could be met with such horror. Obviously I have wounded your delicate sensibilities, and I humbly beg your pardon."

His words were completely without humility; however, she could think of no effective counter at the moment.

He strolled toward the easel and she moved away with alacrity. "I must also confess that I, too, am curious to see how your aunt is getting on."

"She won't like it if you look."

"*You* were going to." He turned away from the easel and came toward her, his face illuminated by the flickering candle. The devil incarnate indeed! But back away she would not. He would not touch her. He was an English aristocrat. He had been to Oxford. She was a duke's granddaughter.

He touched her. On the cheek. A very delicate touch with his forefinger. "You expect *me* to behave better than you, Miss Wells?" he asked softly, a wry smile playing about his lips.

"Yes, I do," she said, trying to sound determined, all her effort threatening to be undone by the pleasure his touch sent thrilling through her.

"You present me with an interesting dilemma. Most people believe me to be the epitome of wasted profli-

gacy, yet you seem to think me an honorable nobleman. I wonder why, and which you would truly
prefer?''

''I expect you to be honorable all the time,'' she
answered, her pulse throbbing in her ears, her breathing rushed and shallow. She should move away, but
she couldn't. She felt like a moth trapped in the flame
of his eyes. Suddenly, he leaned over and blew out her
candle, trapping her in the darkness.

''That would be your mistake,'' he murmured and
she felt his arms go around her and draw her to him.

Chapter Thirteen

Paris Mulholland kissed her. His lips were firm and sure, confident of the effect he could arouse within her. And with good cause.

She had been kissed before, by young men who expected her to have lax morals because of her guardians' occupations, or by old roués unwilling to admit that their days as great lovers were over. She had quickly and effectively rebuffed their clumsy efforts at seduction.

Never had she been kissed like this, by a man who clearly knew exactly what he was doing. Exactly what she wanted him to do. It was even better than in her dreams.

She felt like potter's clay in his hands. Or melting wax. His tongue pushed gently through her lips to touch hers, setting new flames of desire shooting through her.

"Gracious merciful goodness!" Aunt Aurora cried from the doorway. "What is this?"

Clara gasped and drew back in horror as her aunt charged into the room, ribbons flying, nightcap slightly askew, her face ghastly because of the light shining upward from the candle she held—yet there was not shock or condemnation on her face, but undeniable excitement.

"Aunt Aurora," Clara began, barely resisting the urge to wipe her lips lest some trace of that incredible kiss were visible. Clearly Aunt Aurora had not witnessed that, or she would not look so...so pleased. "I heard a noise and—"

"My dog was here. I heard a bang and came—" Lord Mulholland said simultaneously.

"That's *it!*" Aunt Aurora cried, holding up her hand to silence them dramatically. "I know what it was!"

Clara held her breath as she glanced at Lord Mulholland. She thought he was just as baffled by Aunt Aurora's delighted expression as she was.

"Eros and Psyche!" Aunt Aurora declared.

At the name Eros, Clara blushed hotly. Perhaps she had been hit by one of Eros's arrows. That would be a nice explanation for her momentary lapse of sanity in Lord Mulholland's arms.

"Who?" Lord Mulholland asked coolly, as if he was often discovered in a state of dishabille with a woman in the middle of the night.

He probably was.

"The son of Venus, goddess of love, and his wife," Aunt Aurora explained.

"Mrs. Wells, I fail to see the resemblance between a chubby little archer and myself," his lordship replied loftily.

Had the man no shame, that he could sound so self-confidently arrogant after what had just happened? Or was he that completely selfish? Why, if anyone else discovered them there, her reputation would be destroyed.

"The moment of surprise, the look of desire...
yes, that's it *exactly*. You must let me paint you. I shall
call it, *Eros Discovered*. Oh, it will be a masterpiece.
I just know it!"

"Aunt Aurora!" Clara said sternly. *The look of
desire? Eros Discovered?* It was too much!

Undeterred, Aunt Aurora shoved the candle into
Clara's hand. "Hold that, Clara," she commanded.

"Now, you, come here and lie on the floor!" Aunt
Aurora ordered Lord Mulholland like a general on the
field of battle. Even more surprising, he obeyed, still
smiling as if vastly amused.

"To hear is to obey, sweet lady," the rogue said, lying down. "Am I to be asleep, or—" he looked at
Clara and winked "—dead, perhaps?"

Damn the man! And shouldn't Aunt Aurora be a
little concerned that they were all standing together
less than properly dressed?

"Don't be silly!" Aunt Aurora admonished.
"Asleep, of course. On your stomach."

Lord Mulholland looked suitably sheepish as he
assumed the required position.

Despite Clara's enjoyment of his squelching, she
was now all too certain that her aunt had not just
heard her muse—she had been overwhelmed by it.
Unfortunately, Clara knew from years of personal
experience that there would be no rest or relief until
Aunt Aurora's idea had been pursued. If Clara tried
to leave, Aunt Aurora would make no end of fuss and
noise. Considering the lateness of the hour and her
garments, that would be a disaster. She could see
Reverend Clark's righteous disapproval and Tommy
Taddington's smirk. The best thing to do would be to
cooperate.

"Now, then, Clara," Aunt Aurora continued, apparently completely unaware of her niece's reluctance to participate, "bend over him a little. Yes, like that. Look curious and delighted. Pleasantly surprised."

Aunt Aurora took a few steps back and surveyed them critically. "Eros, you look like a corpse, not the slumbering god of love. Turn on your side. Stop grinning! One arm over your eyes. Clara, you must look like a woman in love."

There was a long moment of silence as Clara stared down at the recumbent lord who looked far too innocent with his eyes closed and seemingly asleep. So he would look to his wife when he lay beside her in bed.

Aghast at this turn of her treacherous mind, Clara didn't know whether to laugh or cry or step on Lord Mulholland.

"No, no, that's not right. My lord, sit up. It should look as if you were sleeping on your back when Psyche woke you. Yes, put your hands behind you to steady yourself. Now, stare up at Clara—"

"With pleasure."

"Be quiet, if you please," Aunt Aurora ordered. "I'm trying to think."

Lord Mulholland did not look so amused now, for his roguish grin turned into a very real frown.

"Cooperate and it will soon be over," Clara whispered through clenched teeth, as much to herself as to him.

Aunt Aurora prowled around them like a cat waiting to be fed. Her brow wrinkled with concentration. "Clara, lean closer. *Closer.*"

Clara thought she was already far too close. She could feel Lord Mulholland's breath on her cheek. She stared at Lord Mulholland's straight and shapely nose, which was unfortunately above his tantalizing lips. But she did not dare meet his eyes.

"Yes—perfect!" Aunt Aurora sighed rapturously. "I simply *must* paint this picture. You will have to pose again. At night. The light is perfect! This shall be my greatest work! I can feel it in my very bones!"

"May I rise now?" Lord Mulholland asked. "This floor is not very comfortable."

"Aunt Aurora, perhaps his lordship would rather not," Clara said, hoping he would refuse. She had no wish to be in this particular position relative to him ever again.

"Oh, but you must!" Aunt Aurora faced the rising lord. "You must, my lord." She raised her arm dramatically as if calling for divine aid. "It would be a crime to art not to pose for this picture!"

"Well," Lord Mulholland said, brushing off his trousers, "far be it from me to be an artistic criminal. I would be delighted to pose."

Clara would rather go to the Old Bailey. "Aunt Aurora," she began, determined to preserve some semblance of dignity before Lord Mulholland, "we cannot pose at night. It wouldn't be proper."

"You would rather do it during the day?" the model for Eros inquired.

"No!" Clara said sharply. The risk of discovery would be even greater.

"If we keep the door closed and unless we make a lot of noise, no one need know we're here," Lord Mulholland said persuasively.

"Don't you ever *sleep?*" Clara demanded.

"What do you mean?" he asked, his expression suddenly suspicious. "Have you been spying on me?"

"Of course not!" Clara cried.

"Oh, dear me, I quite forgot to consider that," Aunt Aurora said, looking only slightly guilty.

"I require very little sleep," Lord Mulholland said, his tone the frostiest Clara had ever heard him employ. "We could rest in the afternoon."

So, he was not going to take the excuse she had offered him. And Aunt Aurora was giving her the pleading look Clara found so hard to resist. As Lord Mulholland had said, as long as they were quiet—and very, very careful—no one need know what they were doing. *She* certainly wouldn't tell anybody, and Aunt Aurora would keep the secret if her painting was at stake.

That left only Lord Mulholland to be trusted with her reputation. She gazed at him steadily, this man whose ostensible character was not at all trustworthy.

"Afraid of a little adventure?" he teased.

She would not be called a coward for anything. "Oh, very well," she conceded grudgingly.

"Wonderful!" Aunt Aurora proclaimed.

Clara tried to read Lord Mulholland's expression, but could not tell if she had made a wise decision or the most imprudent one of her life.

"We shall have to find some cushions for you, my lord," Aunt Aurora continued pensively, the muse once more in command.

"I shall be only too delighted to see that they are provided," he replied with a courteous little bow.

"And sheets or something." Aunt Aurora paused, then went on, still thinking out loud. "Or better still, you should both be nude."

"*What?*" her models demanded simultaneously.

"Nude. Naked. Gloriously naked!"

"You *can't* mean it, Aunt Aurora!" Clara protested. If she did, Aunt Aurora's pleading expression notwithstanding, she would refuse to pose.

"I don't think the Greeks wore any nightclothes," the artist replied matter-of-factly.

"But I can't pose nude! And certainly not with this—any man!" If she had to put up with Aunt Aurora bemoaning the loss of a potential masterpiece for the rest of her life, that would still be preferable to posing nude!

"Surely when it's for such a worthy cause, you can set aside any little scruples," Lord Mulholland remarked calmly.

"Posing naked may be a 'little scruple' to you, my lord," Clara said, "for you probably have no reputation left to ruin. *I,* however, do, and I assure you, it is no 'little scruple' to me!"

"Do you fear no one will want to marry you afterward?" he asked with a mocking smile. "I should rather think the opposite. You might consider this a type of advertisement."

She was too angry to respond, and could only glare at him.

"Come, Clara, there is no need for such an overwrought reaction," said her aunt. "Of course, I was but thinking aloud. I shall do something properly modest, with togas and gowns." Aunt Aurora grew meditative. "That might be even better. Something flowing. White. Trimmed with gold. And Eros with the sheet wrapped about his waist. Thank you, Clara."

Clara was only slightly mollified by the costumes her aunt proposed. They were better than being naked, but not by much. "I think it was time we all went back to our rooms."

"And stayed there," Lord Mulholland added coldly.

"Oh, yes, indeed. I must be fresh in the morning. We shall start *Eros Discovered* tomorrow night, and I promise, I shall only let you lose an hour's sleep," Aunt Aurora said. "Come, children."

Aunt Aurora turned and went out the door. Clara started to follow, but felt Lord Mulholland's detaining hand on her arm and she was forced to stop. "What do *you* want?" she whispered fiercely. "Haven't you caused enough trouble tonight?"

"Was this the first time you have enjoyed nocturnal rambles?" he whispered just as ferociously. "I do not take kindly to being spied upon." Suddenly she saw a side of Paris Mulholland that no one else had ever glimpsed. A primitive, aggressively protective one. Nevertheless, she wasn't afraid. She was simply astounded by the vulnerability his reaction suggested.

"I *wasn't* spying," she asserted. "Tonight, or any other time."

He gazed at her intently for a long moment. Then, just as suddenly, the fierce protectiveness vanished and he let go of her. "Forgive me, Miss Wells," he said contritely. "I get tired when I work late at night."

"You were *working?*" she asked incredulously.

"On my vast social correspondence," he replied carelessly. "Did you not know that no ball or party or hunt can be considered complete without me?"

She needed no reminders of how different their lives were. "Of course. How silly of me to forget," she said with similar nonchalance.

"What is all this talk of Eros and Psyche?" he asked.

"You know the legend," she said.

"No, I don't," he replied, and she saw that he was genuinely puzzled.

"This is neither the time nor the place to tell you the story," she said, glancing toward the door. She should leave here at once, before someone heard them.

"Tell me tomorrow," he said, his seductive voice full of persuasion and his expression almost pleading.

"Oh, very well. Tomorrow." With that, Clara hurried after Aunt Aurora and upstairs, quite happy to get away from the power of his voice and the yearning intensity in his eyes.

She went to bed, and unsuccessfully tried to sleep. Only near the dawn did she finally fall asleep, and then it was to dream of two naked bodies lying on a pile of cushions, their sweat-slicked flesh glowing in the light of a single lamp, and their limbs entwined.

Chapter Fourteen

Having lost so much sleep and endured so much stress, it was no surprise to Clara that she felt tired and peevish all the next morning as she whiled away her time in the morning room, blind to the prettiness of its delicate blue-flowered wallpaper and white muslin draperies, dull in mind and unable to concentrate enough to read. All she seemed capable of doing was brooding upon Lord Mulholland. All her treacherous imagination seemed capable of doing was remembering how he had looked last night, and the incredible sensation of his kiss.

Paris, indeed! Clara had always thought Helen of Troy a weak and selfish woman who had let herself be seduced by a charming prince; if the mythical Paris had been like Paris Mulholland—well, Clara could now sympathize with Helen's decision to leave her husband.

"Ah, there you are, Miss Wells," Mrs. Dibble said. The diminutive housekeeper who, despite her lack of height, seemed to have the energy of ten women, bustled into the room, her silver-gray taffeta skirts rustling like dry leaves in autumn. "Luncheon is being served in the small dining room," she announced, casting a critical eye over the rosewood furnishings and several small ceramic figures on the mantel.

Clara suspected she was looking for dust, and was very glad she wasn't a maid under Mrs. Dibble's command.

"Nothing fancy," Mrs. Dibble continued as she began needlessly adjusting the thin muslin curtains. "A simple buffet. Lord Mulholland prefers that on a weekday, and it's easier for all concerned, I must say, since the maids can attend to other matters. My, my, I believe I shall have to replace these, after all."

The curtains looked fine to Clara, but Mrs. Dibble didn't appear to be the type of woman to allow differences of opinion. No doubt she ruled the household with no interference from the lackadaisical lord.

"It will be a battle convincing his lordship," she said with a sigh, immediately confounding Clara. "He is most particular about this room. It was his dear mother's favorite. Oh, many's the hour she spent in here! 'Martha,' she used to say, 'I wish my bed were in this room, although I'd rather sleep in the garden.'" Mrs. Dibble glanced at Clara as if gauging her reaction and fearing censure. "She didn't mean that, of course—about sleeping in the garden."

"It's so lovely, I can certainly understand why she would be tempted."

"Ah, that's just it exactly, Miss Wells," Mrs. Dibble replied approvingly. "It's a good thing she said it after his lordship's father had passed on, too, because he probably would have let her, although the night air would have been terrible for one of her constitution."

If Lady Mulholland had possessed her son's charm and manners, Clara could understand why her hus-

band would have given in to any demand, however
risky or frivolous.

Mrs. Dibble hurried to the door. "Good morning,
Miss Wells. Enjoy your lunch." She dipped a slight
curtsy and was gone.

With weary steps Clara made her way to the smaller,
more intimate dining room where a sideboard held
several dishes for a buffet luncheon. Reverend Clark
was the first person she saw there, apart from the servants, and his welcoming smile did nothing to lighten
her mood. "Are you ill, Miss Wells?" he inquired solicitously.

"A bit tired, Reverend," she answered. "I was
reading too far into the night, I fear."

"You must take care you do not damage your eyesight," he said, and she noticed that his tone was more
patronizing than Lord Mulholland's had ever been.
Reverend Clark didn't speak to her as if she were
merely a child; he spoke to her as if she were an *ignorant* child.

Before she could respond, Mr. Taddington sauntered in the room, treating them all to the sight of his
mouth gaping in a prodigious yawn. "What's that
about eyesight?" Mr. Taddington asked as he sat at
the long table.

"I was cautioning Miss Wells to take care of hers,"
Reverend Clark replied.

"Indeed, yes," Mr. Taddington agreed, unfolding
his napkin. "Fellow in our office went blind, you
know, staring at all the little numbers for too long. A
great pity, really, because he could add three columns
at the same time. Father pensioned him off hand-
somely, though. He'd been with the company twenty-
five years."

"Perhaps had he been provided with good lighting for twenty-five years, it would have saved his eyesight, which I'm sure no pension can make up for," Clara declared.

"It's one hundred pounds a year," Mr. Taddington protested. "Twice his salary! My father didn't have to give him anything."

"More's the pity," Clara retorted, helping herself to ham and peas. "Even though he gave of his money, this man gave your father what cannot be measured in such cold terms. He will never see the sun shine or the first flowers of spring or his wife's smiling face."

"His wife's been dead these ten years!"

Clara gave up the conversation and sat down at the table. Tommy Taddington would probably never understand the harmful effects of poor working conditions, and she was in no mood to educate him.

This decision was aided in no small part by the arrival of Lord Mulholland, who was accompanied by her aunt and uncle.

Paris Mulholland looked as handsome and rested as always. There was such an atmosphere of repressed excitement around Aunt Aurora that Clara wondered how she had ever thought Aunt Aurora could keep *Eros Discovered* a secret.

To Clara's greater dismay, Lord Mulholland gave her a smile that could only be called secretive. It was the type of look a man might give a lover. Did he *never* think of the consequences of such things?

Fortunately, Reverend Clark was helping himself to kippers and so failed to notice, and Mr. Taddington's attention was apparently fixated upon Uncle Byron's canary yellow cravat.

"Hail, fellow Argonauts tossed about upon the Sea of Life!" Uncle Byron declaimed before making a beeline for the buffet table. "Ah, ambrosia awaits!"

"How goes the portrait?" Mr. Taddington asked.

"Most excellently!" Aunt Aurora nodded so enthusiastically, her turban seemed in danger of landing on the teapot. It looked rather more like a tea cozy than a headdress, Clara thought, determined to be distracted from Lord Mulholland. "Delightful!" her aunt went on. "I have never had a more patient subject. His portrait will be sublime."

Clara let her breath out slowly. Perhaps, just perhaps, Aunt Aurora would be content to paint *Eros* and forgo any discussion of the subject.

"Being required to sit for long periods staring out a window is not as simple as it appears, gentlemen," Lord Mulholland said. His plate now ready, he sat opposite Clara. Just to upset her, she was sure. "Fortunately, I have plenty of delectable memories to keep me company."

I will not blush, Clara told herself. Uselessly. She tried to concentrate on the food before her.

"What shall we do this afternoon?" Mr. Taddington asked. "Riding? A hunt, perhaps?"

"I believe I must beg to be excused," Lord Mulholland replied sadly. "My time is already bespoken. Sadly, this estate does not run itself."

"Oh." Mr. Taddington looked taken aback, as if it were inconceivable that Lord Mulholland had any demands upon his time at all.

Clara recognized the surprise, for she had felt the same way last night. He had told her his occupation was only social correspondence, but when she recalled the small mountain of papers on Lord Mulholland's desk, that hardly seemed likely. *Nobody* could be that popular, and several of the papers were legal-size, as if they were contracts or deeds or similar business papers.

It could be that he preferred to work at night, in the peace and quiet of the slumbering house.

It would also mean that he worked with more diligence on such matters than she would ever have suspected. Indeed, there were many things about Paris Mulholland she would never have suspected, not the least of which was that he was far more intelligent and responsible than he let on.

Why would he keep such attributes a secret? Why did he persist in playing the lighthearted wastrel?

His next remark caught her attention at once. "I want to be finished with most of my financial business before our other guests arrive this afternoon."

Clara swallowed hard and stared down at her Doulton plate. How could she forget Lord Pimblett and his daughters, including the one who was going to be Lord Mulholland's wife?

"The beauteous Helena!" Uncle Byron declared, waving his fork with a flourish and inadvertently adding to Clara's anguish. "Tell me, my lord, do you believe she is the epitome of earthly beauty, as they say she is?"

"Byron!" Aunt Aurora cried, aghast. "You cannot ask him to judge! Remember your Greek!"

"Ah, yes," Reverend Clark said with a superior smile. "The whole trouble with Troy began when Paris was asked to judge which of three goddesses was the most beautiful—Hera, the wife of Zeus, Athene, goddess of wisdom, and Aphrodite, goddess of love.

They all tried to bribe him. In the end, he chose Aphrodite, who had offered him Helen if he did."

"To prove my wisdom, then, I will have to leave it to your judgment," Lord Mulholland replied with a strangely aloof shrug for one speaking about the woman to whom he was soon to be affianced. "Lady Helena is reckoned a great beauty."

This was such a lackluster endorsement, Clara could believe that he did not love Helena Pimblett. She was momentarily pleased, until she recalled that even if Lord Mulholland was not passionately in love with Lady Helena, that did not mean a marriage wouldn't take place. Arranged marriages for reasons of wealth and social position happened all the time, even in these supposedly more enlightened times.

"What hour are you expecting them? It is my intention to visit with the vicar this afternoon," Reverend Clark announced. "We plan to continue our discussion of his sermon."

"You needn't hurry back. I daresay the drawing room before dinner will be an acceptable time to make their acquaintance."

Perhaps she could plead a headache was Clara's first thought after hearing this. Her second was that lack of sleep was making her stupid. She was going to have to meet Lady Helena here eventually, and she might as well get it over with. Besides, she truly did want to see Hester again.

"I'm sure the vicar would welcome your company, Miss Wells," Reverend Clark said with a significant look, "if you would care to join us?"

"No, I thank you for the invitation, but I fear I am too fatigued to be good company this afternoon," she answered honestly.

"Unable to sleep last night?" Lord Mulholland inquired kindly.

She shot him a condemning glance. The man could be a master criminal with that innocent face. "Yes, my lord."

"Well, my dear child, you won't get to sleep by wandering all over the house in your nightclothes," Aunt Aurora said, momentarily ceasing to contemplate the large slice of roast beef before her. "It's a wonder you didn't get a chill."

Would Aunt Aurora never learn to hold her tongue? Clara thought with dismay as the other two gentlemen's heads swiveled in her direction. Clara felt as if Aunt Aurora had just announced she had done an imitation of Lady Godiva's ride in the foyer.

"Were you not warm enough?" Lord Mulholland asked innocently.

Warm? She had never felt so…hot…in her life. And he knew it, too, damn him.

"I meant no criticism of the heating," Aunt Aurora replied gravely.

"I confess I thought it rather overheated," Lord Mulholland commented. "Tropical, almost. A most pleasant sensation, of course, but it was rather difficult to sleep."

When Clara saw the stunned expressions of the other two young men who looked as if they felt they had spent the night in another climactic region entirely, she had a sudden, overwhelming and completely inappropriate desire to laugh. Fortunately, she directed her glance to Lord Mulholland, who slyly winked in the most impertinent manner, as if she were some kind of brazen hussy. His expression sobered her at once.

"Thus she paced the weary night away," Uncle Byron suddenly intoned, thereby proving that his attention had not been totally taken with the bountiful food before him. "Thus she trod the weary night away? Thus she strolled upon the lonely ramparts? No, I like the first much better."

The situation was fast developing all the qualities of a bad dream, Clara thought despairingly, and with none of the sinful pleasures of her real dreams. She rose from the table. "If you will excuse me, I believe I shall go for a walk in the garden."

Clara Wells' bearing was as regal as a queen's, Paris thought as he regretfully watched her go. Perhaps Jean Claude's assertion that she possessed royal blood wasn't so farfetched.

And perhaps he shouldn't have made any references to what had happened last night.

He simply couldn't help himself. The memory of her in his arms and the kiss they had shared was too vivid and delightful. She kept intruding into his mind, and he had wanted to know if she had been as affected.

Unfortunately, he couldn't be sure if she hated him, tolerated him or cared for him. Never in his life had he met such an inscrutable woman. Or one so intelligent, protective and honorable.

If he didn't take care, he might fall in love with her.

He feared it was already too late for his heart to be forced to follow the rules of reason. If his passion could be dominated by his rational mind, he never would have given in to the temptation to kiss her, and would certainly never have agreed to pose for *Eros Discovered*. Nor would he have felt so disappointed when he later realized that Clara's scruples would probably ensure that she never posed with him again, and certainly never in such an intriguing and compromising position.

"Ah, Caliope, divine muse of epic poetry!" Byron Wells cried despondently, reminding Paris that he was not alone, "I am *stuck!*"

"Come, Byron," his wife consoled, "let us take a turn about the garden, too."

The artistic couple departed, and once they were out of sight, Tommy gave Paris a speculative look. "What do you think Lord and Lady Pimblett will make of *them?*"

"I met them at the Pimbletts' town house," Paris said matter-of-factly, and as if he himself hadn't been wondering about their appearance there. The Wells were definitely not the type of people one tended to meet at the Pimbletts'.

"The lovely Helena will be sorry you'll be wasting the mornings posing for your portrait," Tommy continued meaningfully, "unless you intend it to be a present for your bride."

Paris had never been as sorely tempted to punch Tommy in the face as he was at this moment, but the impulse passed quickly. Tommy was only saying in a very unsubtle way what several other people would think. However, Paris had no wish to consider Helena at all. Not now, and not ever.

Nevertheless, he forced an equanimical smile onto his face. "Perhaps I shall make a gift of it."

"Marriage is not a joking matter, Paris," Jonas said reprovingly, as if, Paris thought, he was nearer sixty than thirty. "Now, if you will excuse me, I don't want to be late for the vicar. *Some* of us prefer to spend our time in serious pursuits."

His last words did not make Paris feel guilty. Rather, they made all Paris's frustrations vanish as if by magic. Had not Clara Wells refused an invitation to accompany Jonas? If she cared anything at all for the cleric, she would have accepted.

"If you say so," Paris said, his face grave and his tone teasing. "I seem to recall a studious young fellow who spent several hours composing sonnets to the landlady's daughter."

"I was much younger then," Jonas replied angrily.

"I wonder how the fair Rosamunde is getting along with her husband, the butcher?"

"Goodbye," Jonas snapped, marching from the room, the very epitome of indignation.

"That wasn't very nice, Paris," Tommy chided, trying not to smile. "He really thought he loved her."

"He loved *parts* of her," Paris acknowledged, remembering how Jonas could barely keep from staring at the woman's bountiful bosom. "He's getting too pompous."

"Well, be that as it may," Tommy said, "I'll see if he wants some company on the ride."

Paris contemplated joining them—until he recalled that a certain young lady had said she would enlighten him about Eros and Psyche.

Chapter Fifteen

Clara did not stroll through the beautiful garden this time. Barely noticing the flowers in bloom, she marched about it like an agitated soldier who sees defeat coming.

She kept telling herself she shouldn't be so upset that other guests were arriving. What did it matter if one was considered a great beauty and practically engaged to Paris Mulholland? Clara was intelligent enough to understand that a rich and handsome nobleman would have nothing to do with a poor woman. Well, except perhaps for one thing.

She would not allow herself to be seduced. She wanted a husband and a home and children and a man who valued her and respected her.

She also knew that she had some cause to fear that Aunt Aurora and Uncle Byron would say something embarrassing; however, thanks to Lord Mulholland, that particular situation had so far been avoided. There was no need to suppose he couldn't continue his subtle direction of the social conversation.

In fact, she should be *glad* of the additional company. Surely their arrival would signal the end to any possibility of posing for *Eros Discovered*. Although

Lord Mulholland didn't have nearly as much to lose if discovered in a compromising position as she did, he would not wish his future bride or her family to find him doing something so improper.

Besides, it was just as likely that Lord Mulholland was only leading both herself and her aunt on to make mischief, with no intention of actually posing.

That could explain why he was so agreeable to the notion of posing last night—because he knew the whole discussion was moot.

What a rogue! She should be *delighted* that he was considered engaged to another woman.

She halted abruptly. Lord Mulholland was standing directly in her way on the path. "May I help you, my lord?" she inquired, cursing the rush of excitement she felt when she saw him.

"You were going to tell me the story of Eros and Psyche."

"You said you had business to finish this afternoon."

He waved his hand in the gracefully dismissive gesture she was beginning to know well. It drew her attention to his long slender fingers that she had reason to know were stronger than they looked. "Business can wait a little while. I would far rather sit in the garden and listen to you tell me a story."

Was it any wonder he could seduce women, with such eyes and such a voice? He made it seem as if there could be nothing more important to him than listening to you, she thought helplessly.

"Here is a bench." He took her hand to lead her there, and she was absolutely powerless to resist him. The very touch of his hand on hers, coupled with his steadfast regard and her memory of last night, was enough to make her whole body throb with desire.

Fortunately, the memory of what people would think if they were seen talking together alone and unchaperoned came to her aid. "I can't," she said, balking. "It wouldn't be proper."

He assumed a furtive air and peered at the shrubbery. "No spies about, I think," he whispered. "And this bench is out of sight of the house and servants."

"You may find compromising my reputation amusing, my lord, but I assure you, I do not."

"Forgive me," he said with apparent sincerity. "I fear levity has gotten to be a habit with me. However, I must beg you to tell me the story, because my knowledge of Ovid's *Metamorphoses* is most woefully lacking."

"It would do you no good with Eros and Psyche. He didn't write about them in that work."

"There, you see!" Lord Mulholland said triumphantly, sitting on one end of a stone bench set back among the yews. "I have no desire to have my ignorance so obvious to your good aunt. Surely if you sit at the far end of the bench, no one will think the worse of you. And I shall defend your reputation with my last breath."

"A curious change from last night, my lord, when you seemed determined to ruin it by seducing me."

To her surprise, his expression became one of genuine contrition. "I must beg your forgiveness again, Miss Wells. I won't make any more such mistakes, I promise you."

"Good," she retorted, telling herself she was happy and relieved to think that he wouldn't try to kiss her again.

She also assumed that she had guessed correctly. He did *not* intend to pose with her that night.

She sat on the other end of the bench, fighting her absurd disappointment. "Very well, my lord," she said, "I will tell you the story of Eros, or Cupid, and Psyche, who became his wife. Which is found, incidently, in a group of stories called," she said, looking at him with a mocking grin of her own, *"The Golden Ass."*

He laughed softly. "If you do not take care, Miss Wells, I fear levity might become a habit with you, too."

He settled himself on the bench and gave her his full attention, which she found rather disconcerting. "Now, my Scheherazade, you may begin."

Deciding she had best tell the tale quickly and get it over with, Clara commenced, staring off into the distance so that she wouldn't be so aware of Lord Mulholland's attention.

"Psyche was a princess, the youngest of three daughters of a king, and the most beautiful. She was so beautiful that the king's subjects ceased to worship Aphrodite, the goddess of love and beauty, and turned their adoration to Psyche.

"This did not please Aphrodite, nor, might I add, Psyche."

Clara paused, half expecting the nobleman to ask why Psyche was not flattered, as surely most women would be. When he didn't speak, she risked a glance at him, to find something akin to sympathy in his blue eyes. She looked away quickly, because it occurred to her that Lord Mulholland probably knew a thing or two about being regarded solely as an object of comeliness.

"She was so beautiful that nobody thought to court her," Clara continued, telling herself she had made a ridiculous comparison, as this part of the story clearly illustrated. Why, if all the women interested in marrying Paris Mulholland were to form a line, it would reach from the door of his manor house to the road, some three miles hence.

Regretfully, she could see *herself* at the front of it.

She sensed Lord Mulholland's steadfast gaze, and she resumed her story. "She wanted only a normal life." *Just like me.* "Aphrodite, however, wanted to have revenge on Psyche, so she called for her son, Eros, and told him to make the girl fall in love with a very poor, very ugly man. Then, trusting in her son, she went away.

"Meanwhile, Psyche's father had realized his youngest daughter was unhappy, so he went to the oracle of Apollo and asked the gods what he should do.

"The oracle told him that Psyche was destined to marry a supernatural being whom even the gods feared, one who flew like a dragon. Her father should take her to the top of a mountain and leave her to her fate."

"Rather harsh, I must say," Lord Mulholland noted.

Clara nodded and still did not look at him. "Naturally, her poor parents were distraught by this news. Nevertheless, they felt they could not dispute the words of the oracle, so they dressed Psyche in mourning and took her to the mountain."

Lord Mulholland leaned forward, perplexed. "Didn't she try to run away?"

"Apparently she was pleased that she was going to be married, if nothing else, because her life was so lonely and miserable. She was treated as little more than an object to be venerated, not a woman."

He leaned against the back of the bench. "Upset because no one took the trouble to see beyond her face, eh?" he murmured thoughtfully. It sounded as if *his* way had been more hindered than helped by his physical beauty, Clara thought sympathetically.

He glanced at her far too shrewdly. "Psyche is sitting on top of a mountain. Then what?"

Clara cleared her throat and commanded herself to concentrate on her story. "The west wind lifted her up and took her to a beautiful garden containing a marvelous palace." Clara's gaze roved over the beauty surrounding her and to the great house before her. "She could not resist going inside, and wandering about. It seemed to be quite empty."

"Was it day, or night?" Lord Mulholland asked casually.

"Daylight. Bright daylight," Clara answered quickly, determined that he make no connection between the story and last night. This was just a myth and had no bearing on her life beyond her aunt's desire to paint a picture. "Finally a voice spoke to her and told her that there were invisible servants to serve her, and that everything in the palace belonged to her. That pleased her, until it came time for her to retire. All she could think about was the description the oracle had provided of her husband, and she waited in terror for the creature.

"The voices comforted her, telling her that she shouldn't be afraid of her husband. She would surely love him." Clara lowered her voice and spoke softly, struggling to remain calm and breathe normally. "In the night and in the dark, he came to her bed." *This was only a story*. "She didn't see his face as he..." She hesitated and flushed hotly.

"Yes?" Lord Mulholland prompted. She didn't dare look at his face, afraid to see a familiar devilish gleam in his eyes.

Perhaps he was enjoying her embarrassment. With sudden resolve to show that she was on to his game, she looked boldly at him. "As he made love with her."

Did his gaze *never* falter? Was there no way *he* could be embarrassed? Admitting defeat in the face of his unwavering regard, Clara looked down the garden path. "He left before the sun rose, but before he did, he told her that he loved her dearly and would return each night.

"So, during the day, Psyche lived alone in the great palace, seeing no one and with only voices for company. She grew very lonely, even though her husband came to her every night and made her forget her loneliness in his arms."

"Quite a lover," Lord Mulholland observed approvingly.

Clara shifted on the bench and tried to ignore him. "Nevertheless, Psyche continued to miss her family during the day, and they continued to mourn her loss, thinking that she was dead.

"Finally, Psyche grew so lonely that not even her husband could comfort her. She begged him to let her see her sisters again.

"Her husband finally relented, cautioning her that it might lead to disaster. He particularly warned her to say nothing of her husband, although she was quite free to show her sisters her home and give them anything they wanted from it."

"Generous fellow, but why all the secrecy about his identity?"

"I've never quite understood that part myself," Clara confessed. "I think he knew the sisters would be jealous. As long as they thought Psyche was married to a monster, they wouldn't begrudge her worldly possessions."

"I suppose."

"Or perhaps he was being modest," she said, giving him a sidelong glance.

His only response was a decidedly derisive, and yet still elegant, snort.

"Apparently he understood Psyche's sisters better than she did, because they *were* envious. Not only did she have a palace and everything else she could want, she told them that she was married to a handsome young man."

"She lied?"

Clara felt herself in an uncomfortable position regarding Psyche's character, but she would not change the story to suit her circumstances. "I think she told them what she hoped was true.

"But to continue my story. The sisters were indeed jealous. Giving them all sorts of gifts only added to their gall. They believed that Psyche would even become a goddess. They were so angered by this thought that when they were returned home, they didn't show anyone their gifts. They claimed they hadn't been able to find Psyche. Her poor parents were terribly upset, of course. The sisters didn't care. They only thought of having revenge on Psyche.

"Psyche, however, thought the visit had gone very well, and wanted to have them return. Again, her husband warned her against them. This time, he told her she was carrying his child. If she kept his secret, the baby would be immortal; if she didn't, it wouldn't be.

"Psyche was happier than ever, and she wanted to tell her sisters of this additional good fortune. Besides, she said to her husband, 'Haven't I kept your secret so far?' He was finally persuaded to bring the sisters again."

"Loved not wisely, but too well, poor deluded fellow."

"Well, what was the point of keeping his identity secret anyway?" Clara demanded defensively. "The sisters already guessed he wasn't a mortal. And why couldn't she see him? He didn't have to keep his form a mystery, except to continue to test his wife. Granted she was not very clever not to see her sisters' true nature, but it doesn't sound as if her husband had much sympathy for her loneliness, either."

"Such a passionate defense," Lord Mulholland said. "Should I require a defender, I should hope to have one so sincere!"

Clara flushed hotly. "Well, he was not exactly kind to her."

"Except, I think it is safe to assume, in bed."

"Does being a good lover excuse everything else?"

This time it was Lord Mulholland who looked uncomfortable. "Let us say, for the sake of argument, although I can think of nothing I would rather do than sit in a garden and argue with you, Miss Wells, that both of them are not handling the situation with suitable wisdom."

Clara had the distinct sensation that she was not handling this particular situation with suitable wisdom, or she would simply finish the story and leave him.

With renewed determination to do just that, she continued. ''Her sisters pretended to be upset, and told her that the people who lived nearby had seen her husband. He was a giant *snake* who would surely devour her and her child. The oracle had said she would marry a dragon, hadn't it?

''Psyche wasn't sure what to think or do. Perhaps she had been tricked by her invisible husband. Seeing her confusion, the sisters told her she must find out the truth for herself. They suggested she wait until he slept, then arm herself with a knife, take a lamp to see him by and kill him. That way, she would have his riches, and she could marry someone else, someone human.''

''Most helpful of them, I must say,'' Lord Mulholland said skeptically. ''She believed them, I suppose? You would think the woman would know if she had a snake in her bed or not.''

Clara could not disagree, but she did not wish to engage in a discussion on *that* particular point. ''Anyway, night came, and with it, her loving husband. After he was asleep—''

''Did they make love that night?''

Clara blushed. ''One could assume so, I suppose.''

''My word, she was a brave woman. What if her lover *had* been a snake?''

''I believe she probably knew he wasn't, but couldn't overcome her natural curiosity to see him.''

''How very feminine of her.''

Clara gave him a disgusted look. "How very *normal,* I would say. Wouldn't you want to see to whom you were making love?"

"Absolutely." His roguish smile made her blush yet again, and she felt the warmth all the way through her body. Or maybe it was nothing more than the heat of a summer's afternoon. She hoped.

"Very well, then," she went on waspishly. "She picked up a knife and lit a lamp and looked. What she saw delighted her, for it was a very handsome young man with golden hair, and wings."

"I should think she would have noticed wings, too," Lord Mulholland said gravely.

"I wouldn't know what a woman would notice at such a time," Clara answered primly.

Suddenly he moved swiftly down the bench and took her in his arms. Before she could protest, he said, "This is merely an experiment, Miss Wells. Put your arms around me and see if you don't feel my shoulder blades. In the name of research."

"This is absurd."

"So is that story. I won't let you go until you try."

"You're a beast!"

"On the contrary, I'm very human," he said. He was breathing quickly, too, as she could tell by his chest, at which she was staring so she wouldn't see his mocking eyes.

Powerless to protest, she moved her hands slowly under his arms and upward. She had to inch closer to his body to reach his shoulder blades. "I concur she should have been able to tell about the wings," she managed to admit.

"Perhaps she was too overwhelmed by delightful sensations to take proper notice," Lord Mulholland whispered, his deep voice in her ear, his breath tickling her cheek. Slowly he leaned forward, forcing her back.

"What... what are doing?"

"Lie down."

"I will not!"

"This is research," he admonished.

She refused to be placed in such a compromising position, no matter how exciting. She pushed at his broad chest.

He let her up easily, with a good-natured chuckle. "You disappoint me, Miss Wells."

She scrambled to her feet.

"I think there could be an explanation," he said.

Clara's curiosity made her look at him.

He lay prostrate on the bench, then straightened his arms so that only his hips and legs maintained contact with the surface. "If he was making love to her and he didn't want her to touch his wings, he could raise himself like this." He gave her a quizzical glance. "Don't you agree?"

"I must bow to your superior knowledge, my lord," she said curtly.

He was sitting back on the end of the bench in an instant. "Enough research. Go on with the story."

"I don't think you're really interested in it, my lord, except for certain lascivious aspects. All you need to know further is that when she held the oil lamp above him and saw that he was divinely handsome, a drop of oil fell on his shoulder, waking him. He was upset and angry. I believe this is the moment my aunt wishes to paint. Good day to you, my lord."

With that, she strode down the path toward the trout stream, barely able to restrain herself from breaking into a run because she was so angry at him, for his lewd suggestions.

And worse, with herself. Because she had been filled with the most intense, passionate desire to be beneath him on the bench.

Chapter Sixteen

Late that night, Paris stared at the empty grate in his study and told himself that he should not go to the studio. He had made enough of a fool of himself this afternoon, acting like a clown in the garden, and all because he couldn't bear to be so close to Clara Wells without touching her.

What had happened to all his self-control? Usually he was in complete command of himself in any circumstance. Unfortunately, he was discovering that he certainly was not if Clara Wells was nearby.

Because he was falling in love with her.

There was no point to try to deny it anymore. She touched his heart with her concern for her guardians, compelled his admiration with her intelligence and flamed his desire with her passionate nature.

All for nothing, he thought, the irony of the situation not lost upon him. To think the alleged wastrel was going to be undone by a reputation he did not deserve, but had accepted because it was an easy way through life.

Well, it was too late to correct it now, at least as far as any relationship with Clara was concerned. He would have to accept that.

There was one thing he *could* do, though. He could refuse to pose for *Eros Discovered,* because she was right: she did have a reputation to consider. Any hint of scandal attached to him could be easily brushed off, given his title, wealth and considerable charm, the result of years of cultivation, from the time he discovered that a good-looking, personable fellow could get away with many things others could not.

He kicked the andiron and scowled. Would that his father had not died when he was so young! *He* would have seen that his son was known as a man of integrity.

Such a serious thing as a man's honorable reputation was of little importance to his mother, who had been almost a child herself. She only wished everything to be pleasant and everyone to be happy. Charming and pretty herself, everyone around her aided that fantastical view of the world and saw to it that she heard only what she wanted to hear. Including her son.

He had gotten away by playing the happy-go-lucky wastrel for so long, could he even change if he wanted to?

If the reward was great enough?

Oh, this was all nonsense. Clara would never give in to her aunt's wish to paint that picture of Cupid and Psyche, especially not after his exhibition in the garden. She would find some excuse not to come. And rightly so. They could have no future together.

He heard a noise. From the studio?

What if Clara did come to pose? Would she think him a man incapable of keeping his word in even so small a matter as posing for a painting if he did not arrive?

With a sudden determination that she must not think that, he strode from the room, leaving his jacket tossed over the back of the chair.

The studio was empty. He decided to wait, just in case.

His gaze roved over the room and lighted upon the easel with its covered canvas—his portrait. What harm could there be in a look?

Nevertheless, he went toward it as cautiously as if the easel itself might cry a warning. When he was about to lift the covering, he heard the handle of the door turn.

Swiftly, he jumped back and sat on the gilt chair, trying to look calm and composed.

Aurora Wells bustled into the room, attired in her painting smock and with her arms full of fabric that looked vaguely familiar. Behind her, wearing a dressing gown she held resolutely closed, was Clara, her brown hair unbound and her feet bare.

He couldn't help staring at her. The tightly clutched dressing gown indicated a slim, delightful figure. Even her feet were shapely, peeking out from the bottom of the robe. Her unbound hair reached nearly to her waist. It would be wonderful to bury his hands in it.

Mrs. Wells immediately broke the silence. "Ah, here you are, my lord! Good! I assured Clara you would be. Aren't you sorry you doubted him?" she accused her niece, glancing back over her shoulder at an obviously reluctant Clara before looking at him again. "She said you would probably forget your promise."

So, Clara Wells *did* think as little of him as that.

What else could he expect? This was to be his punishment for allowing the world to see him as nothing more than a wealthy gadabout.

A sense of fatality washed over him. If Clara Wells saw only that, and thought so little of him, there was no point to dissuading her, or anyone else.

He would be the charming wastrel, and if his frivolous banter masked a heavy heart, so be it. "I never forget a promise," he said, sauntering toward her with a roguish gleam in his eye.

Clara could only stare helplessly, totally aware of the blatant sexuality of Paris Mulholland's walk, the promise in his piercing blue eyes and the answering passion stirring within her.

"Where are the cushions?" Aunt Aurora demanded, holding her candle higher, thereby breaking the spell. She was obviously completely oblivious to either Lord Mulholland's approach or Clara's dismay. "I told Witherspoon I needed several—oh, here they are, piled in the corner. How neat of the man! Clara, help me arrange them."

"Where would you like them?" Lord Mulholland asked, mercifully turning away from Clara and picking up a red satin cushion.

"I'll set up the easel," Clara offered, hoping to busy herself so she wouldn't think too much about the situation while, following Aunt Aurora's directions, Lord Mulholland began laying the cushions on the floor nearest the windows.

She carefully lifted the draped portrait of Lord Mulholland. When Aunt Aurora saw what she was doing, she hurried over to help.

"Ladies, please, allow me," his lordship said, briskly moving to take Aunt Aurora's place.

"It's heavy," Clara cautioned, grateful that a stronger person had replaced Aunt Aurora, but wary of being this close to this particular person, even though they were separated by a six-foot canvas.

If only Aunt Aurora would change her mind! Clara had tried to at least postpone posing, only to see her aunt come closer to tears than she had ever remembered. Aunt Aurora was completely convinced that this picture of Eros and Psyche was going to be her greatest work, and said as much. Finally, Clara had relented. Foolishly, perhaps, but she had.

To make matters even worse, Aunt Aurora was making Clara wear something that could only be considered indecent. It was supposed to look like a floor-length Grecian gown and was made out of very thin white fabric. If somebody saw Clara in this garb at this hour, they wouldn't care that her aunt was close by. They would think Clara a woman of the loosest morals, or perhaps surmise she was trying to entice Lord Mulholland into marriage with the basest of means.

She could easily imagine what would happen if Reverend Clark happened to come into the studio. Or Tommy Taddington. Scandal, disaster... Her mind went so far as to envision an article in the *Times* denouncing the lax morals of the younger generation, with her as the prime example.

They maneuvered the canvas to the wall and set it down.

"That one should do very nicely," Aunt Aurora said, indicating a blank canvas, which they lifted into place on her easel.

She was only posing for a picture, Clara reminded herself. Her aunt would be right there. Lord Mulholland would not dare anything improper, and neither would she.

Despite her resolution, Clara very nearly decamped. Only her aunt's admonition to move the easel a little to the left prevented her from following her impulse.

When the cushions were arranged to her aunt's satisfaction, she said, "Now, you lie here, my lord. On your side." He obeyed. "Raised on your elbow, looking toward me. Your other arm is a problem."

"I beg your pardon," he apologized gravely.

Must he be so agreeable? So charming? So roguishly handsome? It wasn't fair!

Aunt Aurora stared at him thoughtfully, one hand on her chin. "Just lay it along your thigh. You know, it's really too bad this isn't going to be a nude."

"I would be most happy to oblige," Lord Mulholland said with his devilish grin. He immediately stood up and removed his shirt, tossing it onto the nearby chair.

"Delightful musculature," Aunt Aurora said approvingly.

"Aunt!" Clara gasped, even though she saw that Aunt Aurora's estimation was not without merit. "This isn't...! You *can't*...! I *won't!*"

"I don't see why not," Aunt Aurora chided. "No one else is here. You've seen plenty of nudes before. This is for *art!*"

Lord Mulholland's hand was on his trouser buttons, and he was looking at her with a seriously speculative expression, as if wondering if she had often been in the same room as naked models.

"You never let me near the studio when you were painting them," Clara protested, wanting to set Lord

Mulholland straight on that particular of her life, as if it could possibly make any difference. Only after the words were out of her mouth did she realize that it almost sounded as if she had been fighting for admittance. She took a deep breath, tried to stay calm and continued. "Nor have I ever been a naked model! Please, Aunt! It is so improper! What will people say?"

"You intend to lead your whole life guided by what other people think?" Lord Mulholland asked. "They are often very wrong."

"As I well know," she replied.

"My darling girl," Aunt Aurora said, speaking in her loftiest tones, "if you were simply disrobing to display your body for an immoral or vain purpose, I would agree. However, *we* are engaged in the highest calling of mankind, seeking to enlighten the dull, humdrum lives of the masses by stirring their souls with the passion expressed in art. How can that be immoral?"

Clara knew her aunt's opinion of such things; she had heard it expressed often enough, yet never had it had such an impact on her as it did at this very moment. "Because you are suggesting that I be *naked* with a man I barely know!" she said with all the frustration she felt.

"Let me understand you. If we were old acquaintances, you would have no such scruple?" Lord Mulholland inquired, his voice questioning and his eyes twinkling merrily. "Perhaps in a few days..." He let his words trail off suggestively.

She wanted to hit him right in the grin.

"*I* would do it, for the sake of art," Aunt Aurora said emphatically.

"I know," Clara all but wailed, feeling trapped and foolish, determined and dismayed.

"Mrs. Wells," Lord Mulholland said, turning to her aunt, "I must confess now that the moment of truth has arrived, I, too, am discovering that I do, in fact, possess a certain modesty. And while it is true no man is a hero to his valet, I would also propose that few men reputed to be irresistible to the female sex can maintain that reputation in the nude. And we do not know for certain that the gods of Olympus and their mates did not wear clothes when they slept. Those palaces might have been terribly drafty. I fear I'm getting goose bumps myself, even as I speak."

Clara could see quite well that he was not. He was standing there half-naked as a satyr and enjoying every minute of her discomfort.

Fortunately, his words had an effect on her aunt, who clearly did not want to lose Lord Mulholland as a model. "Oh, very well," she said with more discourtesy than Clara had ever seen her display before. "Lord Mulholland, if you will recline as before. Clara, drape these about him, please, and then take off your dressing gown."

Clara obeyed, picking up the light muslin fabric and going toward the recumbent Lord Mulholland.

"I haven't been tucked in for a very long time," he said quietly when Clara laid the fabric over his waist.

She yanked it up toward his neck.

"No, no!" Aunt Aurora said. "Just the waist and legs. Drape it—it's supposed to be his bed linen, remember."

Clara once again mutely obeyed, trying not to notice how slender his waist was, or how muscular his thighs.

"Haven't I seen this fabric somewhere?" Lord Mulholland asked, addressing Aunt Aurora. "Isn't it drapes or something?"

"One of the maids found it for me when I described what I needed. I believe it used to hang in the morning room."

"Oh, yes. Mrs. Dibble informed me that they were in poor condition," he said. "I am glad to see that they can have another use."

"That's fine, Clara. Now off with your dressing gown and pick up the lamp."

Clara could feel Lord Mulholland's eyes on her as she removed the outer garment. She might as well have *been* naked, she thought peevishly, as she glanced down at the garment her aunt had fashioned from another of the old curtains. She had joined two together, leaving a hole for Clara's head. After Clara had put that on over her chemise and a single thin petticoat, her aunt had taken an old curtain cord of gold and fashioned a girdle that went around her waist and crossed between her breasts to go over her shoulders, where they crossed again in the back. It did look rather Grecian, and made the most of her slender, not very voluptuous figure.

"Lift the lamp and crouch down, looking at his face."

Clara did as her aunt commanded. His lordship smiled at her.

"That won't do at all!" Aunt Aurora cried suddenly from behind the easel.

Clara was so sure that she was going to chide Lord Mulholland for smiling when he should have been looking dismayed and angry that it took her a moment to understand her aunt when she said, "The petticoat will have to go. The skirt is ruining the whole flow of the gown.''

''But—''

''Just the petticoat,'' Aunt Aurora said. ''Come, wiggle out of it. That's a good girl.''

Clara admitted defeat. She went behind the easel and did as her aunt had directed, then, shooting Lord Mulholland an angry look that dared him to comment, she resumed her position. Aunt Aurora darted forward and adjusted her niece's hair, a lock at a time, it seemed.

''There! Much better!'' Aunt Aurora said, returning to her easel and surveying them critically. ''Hold the lamp a little higher. My lord, you must look upset. In pain from your wound, but more from Psyche's lack of trust. Remember, you knew all along disaster was coming, but you love her anyway. Clara, you must look at his face, not his chest.''

Clara reddened and did as she was told, to see a very different Lord Mulholland gazing at her. The dismay was there in the furrowed brows, surprise in his slightly parted lips and love was there, too, in the softness and sympathy in his eyes. But only for a moment, until the mask of languid levity returned.

''Perfect expression, my dear Clara!'' Aunt Aurora cried. ''Surprise, delight, adoration—perfect! Now neither of you move a muscle for as long as you can bear it.''

Chapter Seventeen

The next evening, Clara stood in the drawing room, alone and silently preparing herself for the ordeal ahead. The Pimbletts had arrived, as Clara had heard, if not witnessed. Indeed, nobody in the house could have missed the commotion, not even someone who had fled to the garret and tried to concentrate on *Tom Jones*.

Too agitated to sit, Clara tried to keep two things in mind as she waited. The first was that she would be glad to meet Hester Pimblett again; the second was that after the portrait was done, her family would be leaving and she would never see Lord Mulholland or his friends again. It didn't matter what any of them thought of her, or her guardians, nor did she care to confirm what she thought she had seen in his eyes last night.

Any tender feelings for her had probably been feigned, for the sake of the picture.

They must have been, for he had never looked at her like that again for the duration of the hour's posing, and he had departed from the studio with a simple wave of his hand.

It was nearly time for dinner. In another few minutes, everyone would assemble here before the meal. She hoped the next person to join her would be Hester, or anybody except Lord Mulholland. She certainly had no wish to be alone with him again.

In the meantime, all she need do is maintain an impersonal, socially acceptable demeanor.

Fortunately, Reverend Clark was the next person to enter the drawing room. "Oh, good evening, Miss Wells," he said with a start when he caught sight of her, running his gaze approvingly over her plain gray gown and simple hairstyle.

Clara subdued her distaste at his condescending approval. She neither sought nor wanted his good opinion; she just didn't want his disapproval.

He looked around, and a guilty flush spread over his features. She surmised he was wondering about the propriety of being unchaperoned with a young lady. She should be pleased he had the proper sensibilities, she knew, and yet his guilty expression only added to her annoyance. She was suddenly struck by a nearly overwhelming desire to say something bawdy and wicked, just to see what he would do. Something relatively harmless, of course. After all, she would never indulge in any kind of improper activity with him, and she was quite sure he would never suggest it.

Lamentably, the same could not be said for Lord Mulholland, who strolled into the room immediately after Reverend Clark.

Clara chewed her lip in consternation and told herself she was glad she was wearing her dull gray dress with its high, tight neckline. She should not be wishing she had on the most fashionable gown money could buy, and have her hair adorned with flowers and pearls, and her arms clad with diamond bracelets.

Indeed, a part of her was happy she was not when he looked at her, his blue eyes twinkling with sly merriment. Better by far that she should dress as she did to remind them both that they were from different worlds.

She was saved from having to speak by the eruption of the Pimbletts into the room.

Lady Pimblett's dress was of a simple cut, but made of a gorgeous pale blue watered silk taffeta and trimmed with expensive lace. She carried her fan and reticule, which surely contained smelling salts, and wore a diamond tiara in her black hair, which Clara could tell owed more to the art of her hairdresser than youth.

As Lady Pimblett reclined gracefully on the sofa, Clara wondered if her ladyship would faint before the evening was over, and recalled Lord Mulholland's bet with more pleasure than she should have.

Lord Pimblett was as blustery and red-faced as she remembered. His thick white hair and side whiskers looked even whiter beside his florid complexion. He gave his host a stiff and formal bow, and Clara thought that no matter how courteous and rich Lord Mulholland was, the older lord did not quite approve of his potential future son-in-law.

Lady Helena, who wore the finest gown money could buy and who had flowers and pearls in her hair, was as beautiful as any mythical daughter of the gods. She also possessed a stately, shapely figure, fashionably pale skin and lovely features that included a fine nose, as well as brilliant and dark eyes beneath her elaborately styled, raven black hair. If anything marred the perfection of the young woman, it was that the expression of her eyes was rather too shrewd and calculating, and that her softly rounded chin threatened to follow the example of her mother's, which was distinctly double. Still, Lady Helena's gown could not have emphasized her beauty more if it had been designed by Aphrodite herself. It was of deep, rich forest green velvet, with gold leaves and vines embroidered about the bodice and hem, and must have taken at least fifty yards of fabric to make. What kind of fool would think she could compete with *her?*

Fortunately, Hester was just as Clara remembered her. Although Hester's hair was a common brown, her complexion unremarkable, her features plain, to Clara's mind, she was the finer lady, for her mien was open and friendly. More, Clara instinctively felt that she might have found a friend and kindred spirit who knew what it was to be overshadowed by more ostentatious relatives. Hester, however, did not seem to begrudge her sisters' beauty.

Last in the parade, for so it appeared to Clara, was Henrietta, the youngest. She, too, was lovely, and she probably would have been the focus of male attention, had it not been for the presence of her elder sister and a distinct immaturity in her giddy manner. If ever Clara had seen anyone who could be said to mince and simper, it was Henrietta Pimblett.

"Paris!" Lady Helena deliberately pushed past Clara and walked toward him with her arm gracefully outstretched, presenting her soft white hand for him to kiss.

He gallantly complied, his lips brushing hers for a brief moment before he let go of her hand. "Helena." He glanced significantly at the others in the room.

Obviously Lady Helena was quite willing to take a cue. "How do you do?" she inquired.

"Very well, thank you," Reverend Clark replied. He looked a little stunned, as if overwhelmed by the sight of so much style and pulchritude.

Clara let a small curtsy be her answer.

"You didn't say you would have other guests," Lord Pimblett remarked ungraciously.

"I shall be sure to alert you in future, and then you may decline my invitation if they are not to your liking," Lord Mulholland said, a flash of temper in his eyes, although his mouth was all smiles.

Apparently, however, Lord Pimblett discerned nothing of his host's rancor, for he looked pleased and flattered by Lord Mulholland's response.

"It had never occurred to me that you would not approve of a minister," Lord Mulholland continued, his tone more lenient.

Reverend Clark's hand touched his collar in silent confirmation of his profession and as if to remind himself of his right to be among the company.

"And I met the Wells at your last ball," their host concluded.

"The Wells? I do not recall the name," Lady Pimblett murmured after her husband directed a sharp glance her way.

Before Lord Mulholland could come to Clara's aid—and why she felt confident he would, she didn't stop to consider—Aunt Aurora breezed into the room. Clara had to suppress an urge to groan aloud. Not only was there that unmistakable scent of the studio about her person, but Aunt Aurora had chosen to wear her brightest, most ruffled, most outrageous gown of yellow and purple stripes. Her hair was topped by a matching turban and several bangles clacked on her arms.

Lord Pimblett stared, Lady Pimblett gasped, Lady Helena's lips curled with derision, Reverend Clark looked dismayed, Hester's eyes widened, Henrietta giggled and Lord Mulholland smiled with true warmth and friendship and tolerance.

Clara loved him for it, even as she sensed she was going to need all the forbearance she could muster.

"Goodness gracious, what a lovely evening!" Aunt Aurora exclaimed, mercifully breaking the silence and destroying the tableau of reactions. "Have you noticed the sunset?" She bustled toward the windows and drew the curtains aside with a flourish. The sudden influx of waning sunlight seemed to strike Lady Pimblett with a wave of nausea, for she moved as swiftly as she could from the weak rays.

"What a view!" Aunt Aurora resumed. "Most picturesque, my lord. I could stay here and paint *forever.*"

Clara forced herself to smile, although she felt anything but amused. What would Lord Mulholland and the Pimbletts think? That her aunt wanted to remain in permanent residence? "You would soon grow bored, Aunt," she said.

"Never!" Aunt Aurora replied emphatically. "You must be Lord Pimblett," she said, ignoring Clara and advancing upon the startled nobleman without waiting to be properly introduced. "I'm so sorry we didn't get introduced at your ball. How delightful to make your acquaintance at last. And the famous Lady Pimblett! We meet again!" Aunt Aurora ran a cursory gaze over the noblewoman, who was fanning herself rapidly. "Alas, time is unkind to us all. But I perceive your beauty lives on in the faces of your daughters. This must be the Lady Helena," she said, pausing in front of the startled Henrietta, who burst into a giggle that had more than a hint of self-conscious pride in it.

"Madam, you are mistaken. *I* am Helena," that worthy damsel replied haughtily.

"Are you *really?*" Aunt Aurora said lightly. "I never should have guessed."

Clara didn't know what to make of her aunt's error, but she wasn't sorry for it when she saw the surprised affront on the face of the beauty as Lady Helena sat beside her mother on the sofa.

Nevertheless, Clara felt far from happy as she waited for her aunt to either make some kind of statement about the legendary Paris and Helen, or ask if any of the Pimbletts wanted their portrait painted. To her surprise, her aunt did neither. She simply went and stood beside Reverend Clark as Uncle Byron swept into the room and paused dramatically, holding something behind his back.

He wore his black evening suit with a scarlet brocade waistcoat and a huge red cravat. It looked as if somebody had slit his throat. "Noble Paris!" he cried. "Do you know what I have found? A prize! Buried treasure! A blessing!"

Lord Mulholland smiled with what looked like genuine interest. "What is it? Have you found a secret room filled with gold doubloons?"

"Better, far better, my man!" From behind his back Uncle Byron drew forth a slim leather book, the binding old and the gilt title nearly worn away. "A most unique epic poem of the rape of the Sabine women.''

"The *what* of the *who?*" Lord Pimblett gasped.

"My dear, I feel faint...." Lady Pimblett panted. "Hester, my salts!"

Hester hurried to revive her mother with the smelling salts, looking as embarrassed as if she had been one of the women chosen to begin the populating of Rome by a gang of wifeless men.

Reverend Clark cleared his throat and adjusted his collar unnecessarily, Henrietta giggled and Clara had no idea what expression was on the face of Paris Mulholland, because she didn't dare to look. If she saw laughter in his face, she wouldn't know what to do.

Then he spoke in a calm, measured voice. "Overreacting a bit, aren't we?"

She could have kissed him, for he was completely right, and she should have realized that, too.

"I most certainly am not," Uncle Byron declared. "This is a long-lost masterpiece! I am *sure* of it."

He gingerly and reverently opened the book. "I found it behind some other books. The cover is the softest of leathers, the pages parchment. It's in iambic pentameter. I am sure it's a missing work by none other than William Shakespeare, the Bard of Avon!"

"How do you know it's Shakespeare?" Clara asked, her curiosity overcoming her sense of impropriety.

"The age, the writing, the style. If it's not Shakespeare, it could be Jonson. Or Marlowe. Or Marvell, perhaps. One of them, at any rate. It's very valuable, I'm sure." He set the book down on one of the tables and held it open at the title page. "See here—*The Rape of the Sabines!*"

Hester Pimblett flinched. Reverend Clark was apparently caught in the dilemma of trying to look intellectually curious and socially disapproving, as well as shielding Henrietta's youthful eyes from the potentially offensive literature.

Clara discreetly cleared her throat. "Perhaps we can read it another time."

Lord Mulholland picked up the volume and leafed through it slowly. "Indeed," he said. "We shall soon be called to dinner. But I do not think we should all touch it. The pages are delicate. Too many hands..." he finished suggestively.

Uncle Byron gasped in horror. "You're absolutely right, my lord! I should have thought of that myself! Egad, the contact with human flesh might be ruinous. I shall take it back to the library myself. And tomorrow you should see about having it authenticated and providing an appropriate glass case!" Uncle Byron carefully took the book from Lord Mulholland and hurried off.

Henrietta giggled. "A nice subject for a book that is, I must say," she simpered sarcastically, batting her eyes at Reverend Clark.

"There are some subjects a *lady* should not hear about," Lord Pimblett said forcefully.

"Nonsense," Clara said just as firmly. "Certainly some parts of history can be shocking, but that doesn't mean we should not be informed."

"But young ladies' fragile minds must be protected," Lord Pimblett declared. Lady Pimblett murmured her assent.

"Protected from what?" Clara demanded. "Knowledge? History?"

"Anything upsetting," Lord Pimblett replied.

"Why?"

"Because, um, because they haven't the comprehension! They cannot be expected to understand! They aren't—"

Clara crossed her arms, trying to control her temper. "If young women cannot comprehend or understand such historical information, perhaps it is because they have never had the opportunity to learn how."

Lord Pimblett glared at her. Clara glared back. She believed she was in the right with all her heart, and no lord was going to tell her otherwise.

Lord Mulholland stepped between them. "Maybe we could persuade Miss Wells to mark out the more sensational aspects, like a female Thomas Bowdler."

"Who ruined Shakespeare?" Clara demanded. "Never. I maintain that there is probably nothing in that volume that Lady Hester need be protected from, and I will certainly not act as a censor for it. Knowledge is not something to be hoarded. It should be dispersed freely."

"A little knowledge is a dangerous thing," Reverend Clark pronounced, and Lord Pimblett nodded his august agreement.

Clara turned on the minister. "Pope said, 'A little *learning* is a dang'rous thing.' This story tells the legend of the founding of Rome. It is not necessarily a lascivious tale." She faced Lord Mulholland. "It is history. And why should women *not* know about the rape of the Sabines?" she asked passionately. "I daresay the story means much more to a woman that it would to a man. And one could say that the whole theme of violation is central to an understanding of the history of Rome. One could argue that, by conquest, they violated the whole of the known world and—"

"Enough!" Lord Mulholland cried in mock horror, lifting up his hands as if warding off a blow. "I cannot bear philosophical arguments on an empty stomach."

Clara colored, realizing she had gotten carried away with her subject. "But you *do* see, don't you," she insisted, albeit in a more reasonable tone, "that a sound judgment cannot be made with only the most simplistic of knowledge? Pope goes on to say, 'Drink deep, or taste not the Pierian spring.'"

"The man had a prodigious thirst."

Henrietta giggled, and even Reverend Clark smiled. Lady Helena looked smug.

"He meant learning. We should all be given the opportunity to drink deep from the fountain of knowledge."

"Tommy!" Lord Mulholland accosted the young man, who stopped in the doorway and stared like a surprised rabbit. "Do you think one should drink deep from the Pierian spring, or only have a sip?"

"You know I hate riddles, Paris," Mr. Taddington said with a frown as he entered the room.

He was attired in the most splendid sartorial excess, and he might almost have looked attractive, if he wasn't staring like a dazed sheep.

Lord Mulholland shrugged and grinned at the women. "Tommy declines to participate in our discussion. Jonas, what do *you* think?"

"I thought you were joking," Tommy Taddington protested in a whine and with a baleful glance at Lady Helena. "And that's not what you asked me at all. It was something about drinking."

Reverend Clark ignored Mr. Taddington, and Paris Mulholland, too, Clara noted. He kept his eyes on the smiling Henrietta as he said with a hint of superiority, "Of course I agree. Everyone should have the opportunity to learn as much as they can. I know Lord Mulholland thinks so, too, despite his flippancy."

Clara remembered the school, and silently concurred with Reverend Clark's observation about Lord Mulholland, wondering why he persisted in hiding his real opinion. Just to keep anyone from feeling offended?

Before she could try to find out, Uncle Byron returned. He walked up to Lord Pimblett and made a flourishing bow, which momentarily distracted the nobleman, and everybody else, from the discussion and any thought of *The Rape of the Sabines.*

"Salutations, my gracious paterfamilias!" he declaimed with his most theatrical manner. "Forgive my rudeness, not waiting to be introduced. I was carried away upon a sea of excitement." His gaze swept over the family, from Lady Pimblett reclining on the sofa with the salts bottle held under her aristocratic nose by the dutiful Hester, to Lady Helena, who was looking statuesque and picturesque, to Henrietta, who smothered a giggle. "I am charmed to meet you and your delightful family."

"And you are?" Lord Pimblett asked coldly.

"Byron Wells, at your service, my lord," Uncle Byron replied with another sweeping bow. "Poet. I see you have already met my delightful wife, Aurora. An artist. She paints."

"Indeed?" Lord Pimblett said stiffly. "My wife also paints. China."

Uncle Byron's chest swelled visibly and his smile was beaming. "*My* wife is currently painting a portrait of Lord Mulholland."

Lady Helena's lovely lip curled ever so slightly. "Is she *that* kind of artist?" she asked in the same tone as one might ask if a woman was *that* kind of prostitute.

"Hester!" Lady Pimblett gasped as if she were expiring on the spot, not inappropriate given the murderous eye her husband turned her way. No doubt he was wondering how such riffraff had ever been allowed under his roof.

Lady Helena turned to Lord Mulholland questioningly. Henrietta smothered another giggle.

Clara was so angry, she forgot to be embarrassed.

Fortunately, Uncle Byron was a most unperceptive man, which unfortunately helped to explain his poetry. He said happily, "Oh, yes! It shall be a masterpiece!"

"I thought I should have myself recorded for posterity," Lord Mulholland said. "Don't you agree?"

Clara was pleased to see that Lady Helena could think of no response to this sally. Then she remembered the last time her aunt had spoken of painting a masterpiece, and looked at her wildly. Although she could dismiss the senior Pimbletts as ignorant snobs, it would nevertheless be humiliating for these people to hear that her aunt intended to paint her niece and Lord Mulholland as Cupid and Psyche. Or anything together.

Surprisingly, her aunt was standing most benignly. She remained blessedly silent as Witherspoon appeared in the drawing room door to announce dinner.

Chapter Eighteen

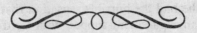

Lord Pimblett assisted his wife to her feet and stepped forward to lead the way to the dining room. Lady Helena rose with startling alacrity and immediately laid claim to Lord Mulholland's arm. Henrietta, obviously following her older sister's example, grabbed Reverend Clark. Mr. Taddington approached Hester, Uncle Byron properly moved to escort his wife and Clara was left alone, at the last.

Lord Mulholland looked at her briefly, then turned to Lady Helena. "I shall be delighted to escort Lady Helena . . . tonight."

Clara's heart leapt, for she was sure that he was not pleased to see her in this socially awkward position. Lady Helena's puzzled, sidelong glance seemed to confirm Clara's guess—but then Lord Mulholland smiled and turned all his attention to his dinner companion.

Clara felt bereft, even as she berated herself for letting her emotions get carried away. Lord Mulholland's remarks in the drawing room might be nothing more than a host's desire to have everything pleasant, not any other kind of desire.

Oh, she was as bad as Aunt Aurora, she thought mournfully as she followed the others into the dining room, which was lit with several tall, white candles that made the candelabra and table silver gleam brightly. She should never have gotten carried away on the subject of education.

She was even more miserable as the dinner progressed. She had the horrible sensation that she was sitting at an engagement supper, with Lord Mulholland and Lady Helena as the bride and groom. Lady Helena sat at Lord Mulholland's right, and spent most of the meal leaning toward him—and giving him quite a show of her soft white bosom, Clara thought vindictively. Lady Pimblett sat silent on his left, and occasional satisfied smiles crossed her patrician face as she regarded the couple.

Tommy Taddington was beside Lady Pimblett, with Lady Hester beside him, then Uncle Byron and finally Clara, who had to endure sitting beside Lord Pimblett, seated at the foot of the table. Opposite Clara sat Aunt Aurora, Henrietta and Reverend Clark, who was beside Lady Helena.

Witherspoon and his battalion of footmen proceeded to serve a sumptuous repast, beginning with soup and proceeding to fish and oysters, then to roast lamb, beef and pork with salad, peas and various other vegetables, until finally sweets and desserts made their appearance. Each course had its own appropriate wine, which Tommy Taddington sampled liberally.

Clara discovered she had little appetite; indeed, she was much more concerned with trying to learn what Lord Mulholland thought of his other guests—particularly the female ones—than with the food.

She could reach no conclusion. He certainly acted as if nothing were amiss, and was his usual charming self.

In general, however, the Pimbletts seemed mortified at having to sit at the same table as Clara's family, and said very little, leaving most of the conversation to Lord Mulholland and Lady Helena, if a series of mutual compliments punctuated by Lady Helena's tinny laugh could be called conversation.

He *must* have been toying with her, Clara concluded bitterly, if he could so pointedly ignore her now. She had been nothing more than a chance to practice his seductive technique. Since another, more worthy woman had arrived, he had tired of his game and ceased to pay any attention to her. Well, she should thank heaven that she had been spared falling irreparably in love with him. Her heart was not broken. Damaged, perhaps, and hurt, but not broken.

She glanced at Paris Mulholland, so at ease among the company, looking as a medieval lord in his hall might have looked, commanding and virile. Yet he was extremely elegant and civilized, as if a veneer of considerable polish had been laid upon centuries of being undisputed lords and masters of their domain.

The dinner finally and mercifully came to an end, and the ladies retired to the drawing room, leaving the men alone.

Clara mentally girded her loins, for she knew being alone with the female Pimbletts was going to be an ordeal. Her aunt, so uncharacteristically silent during the meal, might suddenly gush forth once freed of the dam of male company.

Perhaps she should plead illness, she thought wretchedly. She did feel far from well. However, that would leave Aunt Aurora alone in the lioness's den.

No, she decided, she would not allow herself to feel less than worthy of such company, especially when she recalled Lady Pimblett's silence, Lady Helena's ostentatious flirtation and Henrietta's girlish giggles. Besides, Hester would be there.

Clara might have spared herself much anxiety. The moment the women were alone, the Pimbletts began speaking French, clearly believing that Clara and her aunt would not understand a word. This, of course, was a mistake, for Aunt Aurora and Uncle Byron had lived many years in Europe before Clara came to live with them, and often spoke foreign languages at home among their artistic friends.

Hester alone seemed to appreciate the rudeness of her mother and sisters' conversation, for she glanced nervously about and blushed furiously. Unfortunately, she seemed powerless to remedy the situation.

Before Clara could approach Hester and engage the embarrassed young woman in a general conversation, she realized that Lady Pimblett and her daughters were discussing their host; specifically, his financial situation, which was reportedly excellent. It was quite clear that both those redoubtable ladies considered a marriage between Lady Helena and Lord Mulholland a mere matter of time and settlements.

"You and your daughter speak French most delightfully, Lady Pimblett," Aunt Aurora said in that language with a pleasant smile on her face as she settled herself on a chair near the French doors.

Lady Helena started, scowled and did not even have the grace to look embarrassed. Her mother's fan moved rapidly. "Tell me," Aunt Aurora continued, "do you also speak German?"

"No, we do not," Lady Helena replied coldly in English.

"What a pity!" Aunt Aurora said. "Clara speaks both languages, as well as Italian. She reads and writes Latin and Greek, too." Aunt Aurora turned to her niece and said in rapid German, "I don't believe I've ever encountered a ruder family."

Clara couldn't resist a little sweet revenge, so she answered in German, "That's true, but they would make a pretty family portrait."

Aunt Aurora actually sneered for the briefest of moments. "Them? I would not waste the paint."

"Lady Helena, then. She's quite lovely."

"She has no soul. I have never in my life seen emptier eyes."

"I was expecting you to suggest a picture of Lord Mulholland—Paris—with her, Helena."

"*He* may be a worthy subject, but I would not waste my time with her," Aunt Aurora said with a sniff as she arranged her skirts.

"He has a soul, you would say?" Clara asked.

"Most definitely."

Clara felt absurdly pleased by this revelation on her aunt's part.

The Pimbletts had retreated into stony silence. Clara was sorry for having to hurt Hester's feelings by excluding her from the conversation, and gave her a friendly smile while she approached the young woman and stood beside her, looking out at the garden beyond the terrace. "It's a lovely garden, isn't it?"

"Yes," Hester answered in a soft and gentle voice. She gave Clara an envious look. "Is it true that you know Latin and Greek?"

Clara smiled at the unexpected expression and nodded. Before she could say anything more, however, Lady Helena said with no attempt to mask her contempt, "How very masculine of you."

Clara was relieved that the gentlemen entered the room at that moment. Otherwise, she would surely have made some caustic, impolite reply that would only have made the atmosphere even more unpleasant.

Reverend Clark led the gentlemen. He glanced at Clara, then Henrietta, and to Clara's unmitigated relief, headed straight for the grinning youngest Pimblett.

Lord Pimblett marched in and, yawning, sat beside his wife, who was reclining listlessly on the rest of the sofa. Tommy Taddington hovered uncertainly inside the door, his gaze fixed on Lady Helena.

"Hail, gentle mortals!" Uncle Byron said, coming in just before their host, who followed with a wineglass held lightly between his elegant fingers, an amused smile on his handsome face.

Of them all, only Lord Mulholland appeared to be completely comfortable. Even the usually imperturbable Aunt Aurora was obviously finding the Pimbletts a trial.

"Will you grace us with some music?" Lord Mulholland asked Lady Helena. "That charming little air you played the last time we were together comes to mind."

How easily he flattered the woman's vanity! Her smile was vast and triumphant as she made her way to the instrument and sat gracefully upon the seat. How slyly she glanced at her mother when Lord Mulholland came to stand beside the piano.

And how completely Lord Paris Mulholland fit into this glittering room, at ease among the noble company, Clara thought despondently. Indeed, he seemed to glitter, too, like one of the prisms on the chandelier. While she was like some poor, plain moth drawn closer to the flame of his glimmering personality, despite herself.

Unable to subdue her dismay, she caught Aunt Aurora's eye. To her surprise, her aunt gave her a very warm and understanding smile before turning to the white-haired, red-faced lord seated across from her. "Perhaps you know the Duke of Chesterton, my lord?" she asked archly.

No! Clara wanted to shout. Not here! Not now! The Pimbletts had already passed their ignorant judgment. If they could not appreciate Clara and her guardians for their own merits, why try to impress them by speaking of a connection better forgotten by all concerned? Aunt Aurora *knew* any mention of Clara's grandfather enraged Uncle Byron almost to the point of apoplexy.

Clara contemplated a fast dash from the room, Uncle Byron looked as if he had been shot and Aunt Aurora smiled triumphantly.

It was too late to stop Aunt Aurora, Clara realized dismally. She had launched her javelin. All that remained was to see the damage it might do, and try to keep things from getting out of hand.

"I have seen him in the House of Lords," Lord Pimblett replied. "A most dignified, noble fellow."

"He is an *imbecile!*" Uncle Byron ejaculated.

"He is Clara's grandpapa," Aunt Aurora said brightly, ignoring Uncle Byron's outburst, which had captured the attention of everyone else, including Lady Helena, whose fingers froze over the keys.

"Indeed?" Lord Pimblett said weakly.

"Now that you mention it, there is a distinct resemblance," Lord Mulholland noted.

Clara gave him a startled glance. To tell the truth, she had never seen her maternal grandfather, and only now was it being borne in upon her that perhaps Lord Mulholland had.

Her grandfather was an influential man in the higher social circles. Could it be that Lord Mulholland hoped to advance himself by making a claim to know her? If so, he would be sorely mistaken. He would admit to being acquainted with Clara to his peril. Surely, if he knew the story of her family, he would realize that.

"Oh, yes, in the noble carriage of her head," Lord Mulholland said, "and the flash of fire in her eyes. Miss Wells' eyes are very like his, to speak the truth. My first day in the House of Lords he made a very impassioned speech about taxes." He regarded her steadily. "He looked as angry as I have ever seen *you.*"

His words, even at this distance, struck her with a startling intimacy that was not lost on Lady Helena, for she gave Clara a hostile look.

"The duke is a mutton-headed fool!" Uncle Byron shouted. "If he were here now," he cried, brandishing an imaginary rapier, "I would run him through!" *Thrust!* "He would taste my fatal steel!" *Jab!* "The . . . evil . . . scoundrel!"

"That is harsh, sir," Lord Mulholland calmly observed.

As if she had not been the one to ignite the stagnant conversation, Aunt Aurora immediately and defensively said, "You cannot expect my husband to have any respect for the duke, my lord. After all, the man disinherited his daughter for marrying my husband's brother."

"Disinherited?" Lady Helena asked as if she had never heard of such a fascinating familial relationship in her life and was eager to recommend it to her friends.

Clara felt rooted to the floor, too mortified to move or meet anyone's eye.

"*Completely!*" Uncle Byron bellowed triumphantly. "*Absolutely!* As if anybody wanted to be connected to the old boar anyway!"

At this outburst of impassioned rhetoric, Lady Pimblett swooned. Once more, Hester hurried to her aid.

Aunt Aurora sighed loudly. "Such a love match! Dear Clara's mother, who was the duke's youngest daughter, *adored* Walter. He was her dancing master. They fell in love the moment they saw one another. Walter told us so himself."

"But to marry against her father's wishes and cause such a breach..." Hester volunteered cautiously, falling silent when she realized everyone was looking at her and more importantly, that her mother's supposedly weak grasp on the hand holding the salts had become one so powerful, Lady Pimblett's knuckles were turning white. Nonetheless, Clara was grateful for Hester's kind words, which began to dispel the sense of doom that had momentarily held her in its thrall.

"I daresay it would have been much more prudent to love in secret," Lord Mulholland said lightly.

Lord Mulholland's facetious comment freed her completely. "Prudent, perhaps, but not honorable," Clara said, no longer numbed into silence.

To her surprise, she saw understanding in his penetrating eyes, although a devilish smile still lurked about his lips. He was baiting someone, and she hoped she was not his target. If so, he would have to be disappointed, now that she was on to him.

Lady Pimblett's fan moved as rapidly as a butterfly's wings. Lord Mulholland watched her as one enthralled. If he was trying to distress that statuelike dame, he was succeeding. Maybe he had another bet.

She wished he was trying to disturb Lady Helena, who gave him a quickly speculative glance before turning toward her father with a disapproving frown. The young lady was clearly playing both sides with an eye to the main chance, Clara thought, wondering if Lady Helena would be willing to love in secret and without benefit of marriage. Clara rather thought she might, if the carrot of marriage was dangled before her.

"Oh, poor dear Walter was very honorable about it," Aunt Aurora continued. "When he understood that Elizabeth cared for him as he did for her, he went at once to her father to ask for her hand. Well, Walter never told us exactly what happened, but I take it the duke was rather uncharitable."

"Uncharitable!" Uncle Byron cried. "The man was insulting!" Still holding his imaginary sword, he punctuated his words with stabs through the imaginary duke's heart. "Base *rogue!* Detestable *villain!* I *scorn* to *speak* his *name!*"

"Yes, Byron," Aunt Aurora said calmly. "Sit down, my dear, before you tire yourself out completely. The duke is the one who should be upset. Look at what his foolish pride has cost him—the knowledge of our dear, sweet, intelligent Clara."

Clara couldn't help fidgeting at her aunt's words. "I don't think you need tell everything—" she began.

Aunt Aurora did not hear her niece's protest, or if she did, chose to ignore it. "They ran away and married in Gretna Green, and had fourteen very happy years of marriage, which gave us our darling Clara. Such a tragedy their lives were cut off so soon," Aunt Aurora finished with her voice full of feeling. "A sudden, fatal fever. They died within days of each other."

"That black-hearted, evil, treacherous, ignorant—" Uncle Byron rumbled.

"Yes, my dear. You're absolutely right," Aunt Aurora said. "Come, let us retire to the quiet contemplation of nature in the garden."

With remarkable vigor, Aunt Aurora tugged Uncle Byron, who was still muttering epithets, outside.

"So many years of happiness is worthy of envy," Hester said softly.

"How could they possibly be happy," Lord Pimblett spluttered, "when the duke had disowned them?"

"We cannot begrudge the course of young love when it produces so charming a result," Lord Mulholland said, raising his wineglass in a salute. He quickly turned away. "Lady Helena, you have stopped playing."

Helena looked startled, then she smiled at Lord Mulholland, gave Clara a swift, smug look and began to play a simple melody. Lord Mulholland turned his back to the rest of the room as if engrossed by her music.

Clara hoped the conversation would take a different course since their host had made it so plain he had no further interest in the previous topic, and then peevishly wondered why it had taken him so long to do so.

Her desire was not to be fulfilled, for the apparently undiscerning Henrietta clasped her hands together as if praying for something similar to happen to her and cried rapturously, "Oh, it's so *romantic!* What do *you* think, Reverend Clark?"

Clara's attention was drawn from the couple at the piano when Reverend Clark spoke. "It is indeed a shocking and unwelcome notion that a child should not honor her parents. Perhaps if the duke had not objected so strongly, their ardor would have cooled by itself."

"Never," Clara said decisively.

Lord Mulholland turned and eyed her. She could not tell what he was thinking from his inscrutable expression, nor did she care to. She wished she had never heard of him, or his house or his other guests.

He set down his wineglass. "Do you dance, Miss Wells?"

Chapter Nineteen

Paris watched as Clara Wells's all-too-revealing eyes narrowed suspiciously. Surely she didn't want to sit there and continue to listen to the Pimbletts dissect her history? Or perhaps she relished the chance to let everyone know she was of noble stock. Either way, he was the host here, and he had no desire to participate in further genealogical conversation. He would far rather dance, preferably with the passionate Clara, even if it meant displaying more of his regard for her, which was not the wisest thing to do, given the number of witnesses. However, he had found Helena agonizingly boring all through dinner, and would relish the excuse to be away from her.

Of course, the fact that he would have Clara Wells in his arms was an added inducement, but he tried not to think about that.

"What a wonderful idea!" Henrietta exclaimed before coyly eyeing the other single gentlemen.

"Since her father was a dancing teacher," Helena said with that honeyed venom she was such an expert at expelling, "I am sure she can dance very well. It will be a pleasure to watch her."

As if Clara Wells were a dancing bear or some other poor creature put on display, Paris thought with disgust. He should have known better than to suggest such a thing with Helena Pimblett in the room, who so lacked subtlety that everyone, with the possible exception of the kindhearted Aurora Wells, would hear the insult intended by her words.

"Or perhaps she would prefer to play the instrument?" Helena asked sweetly.

Paris did not have to wonder long what Clara Wells' reaction would be. She stood, chin up, eyes blazing. What was that interesting American saying? Loaded for bear. In this case, it was absolutely appropriate. "I would be delighted to dance," she said, stepping forward.

Helena made no effort to hide her displeasure, and a glance at Lady Pimblett revealed that the worthy dame was completely recovered and not at all pleased, which tickled Paris immensely.

"I believe a waltz would be just the thing," he said gravely before taking his place in front of Clara. He put his arm about her slender waist and took her hand in his. Helena began to play a waltz as if it were a call to arms.

Paris wouldn't have cared if she had played a dirge, for Clara Wells was indeed a most accomplished dancer, light and graceful despite her unrepentant anger that still showed in her expressive face. Moving so near her, where he had ample opportunity to look closely at her, he could see how upset she was by the expression in her hazel eyes and the flush on her silky cheeks.

Poor, beautiful, ambitious Helena! Trying so hard to entice him and instead accomplishing the opposite!

She had never stood much of a chance to win his heart, if she cared about that, or his hand or, more precisely, his wealth, which he suspected was her primary objective. Whatever slim chance there may have been to achieve her goal was completely gone, destroyed by her own small-minded jealousy and pettiness.

Besides, there was nothing intriguing about Helena Pimblett. He had no sense that there were layers of thought and feeling to discover beneath her beautiful exterior, not like this fascinating woman in his arms, who had approached this waltz the way an ancient warrior might have approached single combat.

The dispossessed daughter of a duke and a dancing master. She even had interesting parents. It was really too bad they had died. He would have enjoyed meeting them very much.

"You are holding me too tight," the fascinating Miss Wells whispered between clenched teeth.

"I beg your pardon," he replied, loosening his hold and at the same time extremely aware that there were no whalebone stays beneath his palm.

Perhaps only a thin chemise covered her naked skin and perfect breasts, whose rounded shape was clearly discernible within her modest bodice. How delightful it would be to take the pins from her thick, brown hair and let it fall around her, then to slip the chemise from her shoulders and downward, exposing her pale soft breasts to his eager lips...

Clara gasped and halted abruptly.

"I'm sorry," Paris said, startled and shocked. "I haven't stepped on a partner's foot since I was thirteen."

But then he had never had such distracting visions when he was dancing, either. Usually he was doing his best to be witty and amusing.

"Since you are so preoccupied, my lord," Clara said haughtily, "perhaps we should stop. If you would prefer, I will play and you may dance with someone else."

Helena practically leapt from the piano bench, and Paris knew he was doomed to dance with her.

Perhaps that was for the best, he thought, reluctantly relinquishing his hold on Clara. He had managed not to demonstrate any significant interest in her throughout dinner—although it had taken great self-control.

He was only preparing the way for despair if he showed any affection for Clara Wells. She would never want him, a man who had yet to read an entire book.

He made a gallant bow toward Helena and accepted the inevitable.

It was soon obvious that Clara Wells was a much better dancer than musician.

However, as if to confirm his estimation of the hopelessness of his feelings for her, she continued to play the pianoforte for the rest of the evening, forcing him to dance with Helena, who felt like a barge in his arms after Clara and who leaned much too close as if intending to give him a view of the ample endowments pushed up by her corset. Nevertheless, Paris also managed to dance with Hester, who moved with self-conscious temerity and Henrietta, who flung herself about like some kind of whirling dervish. Paris quickly compelled Tommy and Jonas to take part in the impromptu ball and once even Lord and Lady Pimblett joined in a waltz. That was, he noticed, after Clara Wells made it quite clear that she had no intention of dancing again, with anyone.

After nearly two hours, Paris had had enough. "I must rest," he said, slumping into a chair. "I am not used to so much exercise. Witherspoon, bring some wine."

Clara Wells rose. "Since you are all fatigued, I am surely no longer of use, so I must beg leave to be excused." She moved swiftly and majestically toward the door. "Good night!"

She was gone before Paris could protest.

"*What* an extraordinary creature!" Helena said scornfully. "Paris, really! Whatever were you thinking to invite such people here?"

"I wanted to have my portrait done," he replied placidly, not caring for Helena's tone, but not willing to give her further reason for jealousy by displaying too strong a response. Indeed, he wanted nothing more than to leave the room, but that would only give cause for speculation.

Lord Pimblett fastened a choleric gaze on his wife. "How did you come to make their acquaintance?" he demanded.

"I met Mrs. Wells at the British Museum," Lady Pimblett answered, her voice a cross between a whine and a sigh. "She mentioned *something* about painting and a niece and the Duke of Chesterton." Lady Pimblett cleared her throat delicately. "I had heard that the duke had recently offered his, um, protection to a young lady whose family were artists. I assumed..." She didn't finish, but shrugged her elegant white shoulders and looked around helplessly, as if anybody else would also have invited the relatives of the duke's latest mistress to their party, and how could she possibly be to blame for this social blunder?

If Paris had ever doubted that the Pimbletts were all too interested in social climbing, this would have ended those doubts at once. As it was, it merely confirmed his unflattering view of the elder Pimbletts.

"I was pleased to make their acquaintance. I find the aunt and uncle amusing," he drawled with one of his most meaningless smiles that nevertheless seemed to convey a great deal of meaning to the others.

"Did you ever see anything like that gown?" Helena asked with a sneering smile.

"Can Miss Wells really read Latin and Greek?" Hester asked wistfully.

"I've never asked her," Paris answered truthfully. "It wouldn't surprise me."

"You read Latin and Greek, I'm sure," Henrietta said to the staid Jonas, giggling.

"Indeed," he replied. "However, despite what Miss Wells thinks, I do not believe young ladies should be exposed to the texts of certain works. They are too...explicit."

"How so?" Henrietta asked eagerly.

Jonas flushed beet red. "Ovid, for example, deals with subjects that are not fit for women."

"What subjects?" Helena asked with a hungry gleam in her eye.

Paris could guess what subjects Jonas was referring to by the way the reverend gentleman blushed. "Why, my dear!" he drawled, looking at Helena. "I never took you for a scholar."

"I have better things to do than study musty old books!" Helena huffed.

Paris could not think of one constructive thing Helena did, except perhaps stand as a model of current fashion trends. He could never imagine *her* taking charge of the family purse the way Clara Wells did.

Lord Pimblett gave another prodigious yawn. "I quite agree with Reverend Clark that Latin and Greek are unfit subjects for ladies. Now I believe it's time to retire," he announced. "Come, wife, come, girls."

Helena looked as if she were going to protest, but apparently thought better of it when Paris did not demur.

The Pimbletts withdrew, leaving Tommy, Jonas and Paris alone in the drawing room. Paris couldn't help heaving a relieved sigh. He felt as if somebody had removed a pair of excruciatingly tight boots. "How about some brandy, gentlemen?"

"Excellent suggestion!" Tommy said, and one of the footmen was dispatched to the study to fetch it. "I quite envy you, old man!"

"What for?" Paris asked, sitting down on a sofa and throwing one leg over the arm.

"The beautiful Lady Helena. She's madly in love with you."

"Or my money," he replied.

Jonas's face assumed a forbidding expression Paris recognized and he waited for the condemnation that was not long in coming. Indeed, Jonas spoke before the brandy was in his hand. "Are you toying with Lady Helena's affections?" he demanded.

"Not at all," Paris answered. "If Helena wants to delude herself into believing she is in love with me, I can do nothing to prevent it."

"Then you shouldn't have danced with her," Jonas said.

"*You* danced with her, too," Paris pointed out. "Should I accuse you of toying with her affections?"

"You know I would do no such thing."

"Whereas I *would*. Jonas, you wound me!"

"Well, Paris," Tommy said as he eyed the golden brown brandy speculatively, "you've been know to do such things before."

"Ah, I knew my terrible past would catch up with me one day!" Paris cried, throwing his arm over his face melodramatically. "Alas! I have toyed with the affections of women and now must suffer." He peeked out from under his arm with a wry grin. "Lady Helena will not sustain a broken heart over me, gentlemen, I am quite certain. She would soon find a richer man upon which to bestow her charms."

"I do not like your accusation," Tommy said with a sudden show of temper. "She couldn't be so mercenary!"

"Oh, no?" Paris replied skeptically. "I daresay she would not exert herself to entice me if I were stone broke."

"I say!" Tommy protested. "That's a terrible thing to say, after you've been leading her on! Why don't you stick to seducing Miss Wells and leave Lady Helena out of it!"

Paris put both feet on the floor and glared at his friend. "*What* did you say?"

Tommy blanched. "It—it looked like you were trying to seduce her," he stammered. "You were holding her very close and making eyes at her... well, it looked that way." He appealed to Jonas. "Didn't it? That's why she stopped dancing with him."

"Given your reputation, I thought she was very wise to offer to play the piano," Jonas said.

Paris fought to calm himself. Getting angry at Tommy would avail nothing. He would do better to curb any manifestations of regard for Miss Wells. He was being far too obvious.

"Gad, men!" he said carelessly. "You make it sound as if I might ravish her on the floor."

The sudden image of himself making love with Clara Wells on the drawing room floor burst into his brain with startling vividness.

Damn! What was happening to him? He didn't want to seduce Clara Wells. He didn't want to tempt her to his bed for one night of bliss. He wanted to make her love him, for a long time. Say, the rest of their lives.

He wanted her to be his wife, more than anything he had ever wanted. This unforeseen notion shocked him, delighted him and upset him. "Good night, gentlemen," he said abruptly, striding from the room without caring what they thought. He had to be alone, somewhere where he could restore the balance of his thoughts and emotions.

He ran up the stairs. It was earlier than he usually retired, so Jean Claude would still be in the servants' hall awaiting a summons.

Paris marched along the corridor, ignored the sight of the door to Clara's bedroom and threw open the door of his own bedchamber, to encounter a triumphantly beaming Jean Claude.

"Did I not say so?" the valet crowed as Paris entered.

"What are you talking about?" Paris asked, feigning ignorance, but not troubling to hide his annoyance at finding his valet already there.

"The little duchess! I *knew* she was of noble blood."

"You said *royal* blood," Paris reminded him as he closed the door firmly. "And how do you know about her past?"

Jean Claude waved both his hands in excited dismissal. "Servants know everything. But that is not important."

Paris pulled off his jacket, tossed it on the bed and loosened his cravat. "You're right. It's not important."

Jean Claude stood in the middle of the large room and placed his hands on his thin hips. "Am I speaking with a turnip? A cabbage? Now there is no reason you cannot marry her!"

"Who?"

"The niece!" Jean Claude cried, picking up the discarded jacket and shaking it out. "Miss Wells, of course, you foolish Englishman."

Paris whirled on his valet. "I don't care to be insulted by my servant," he snarled. "Get out."

Jean Claude's eyes widened as he stood frozen with shock.

Paris was immediately contrite. He had never lost his temper with the volatile Jean Claude before, and he regretted doing so now. "Forgive me, Jean. I'm just tired."

"Very well," Jean Claude said with extreme dignity. "Do you wish me to stay?"

"No, I'll finish myself," his master replied wearily, although he had no intention of changing his clothes. It would be some time before he could retire, for he had pages of correspondence from Mycroft to read that he had neglected for far too long. That Clara

Wells's presence had rendered unimportant for too long.

"Good night, my lord."

"Good night."

Outside in the corridor, however, Jean Claude's formal manner disappeared. He grinned and rubbed his hands together gleefully like a demented genie. "Ah, *l'amour!*"

Chapter Twenty

"Zeus?" Clara called softly, peering under her bed. She did not see a familiar dark shape, and sighed with exasperation.

So much for the faint hope that she had been sitting here listening for him the past three hours while he was under the bed all the time. He should be here, and he would make the devil's own noise if he was locked outside the house.

She had realized when she had first come upstairs that Zeus wasn't in her room, but she had no desire to go back downstairs searching for him, not when Lord Mulholland and the others were yet there. She had decided to wait for Zeus to come scratching at the door.

She was still waiting, although she had heard her guardians retire, then the Pimbletts, then rapid footfalls that sounded like those of Lord Mulholland going past her door, followed momentarily by those of the other two gentlemen. Servants had come and gone, and all had been silent for what seemed an age. It was probably no more than half an hour.

She got to her feet, glad she had dismissed the maid and not yet undressed. She would have to go downstairs and call Zeus as quietly as possible, and hope she didn't disturb anyone.

Especially a certain young lord whose very glance was enough to render her incompetent, and whose almost-fiancée was sleeping a few rooms away.

Cautiously Clara opened her door and surveyed the corridor. Nothing disturbed the silence, so she tiptoed to the staircase and made her way downstairs.

She opened the large front door. ''Zeus! Here, puss, puss, puss!'' After waiting another few moments, she tried again. With no luck.

Perhaps the kitchen door would be a better place. She turned to go along the corridor, then stopped abruptly.

A light shone out from the study door. Lord Mulholland must be there. Again. Danger of fire or not, this time she would stay as far away from the study as possible, she thought as she tiptoed along the hall close to the far wall.

Despite her resolve, she simply couldn't resist the urge to peek inside.

The study was empty, shrouded in shadows and lit only by a single candle.

Disappointment filled her, even though she should be glad he was not there. She should be relieved that she would not confront him again, alone. At night. In the shadows.

She let her gaze rove over the only room in the house Mrs. Dibble had told her she must not enter and then went to the door, her curiosity getting the better of her. It had an aura of comfortable masculinity about it. That was not surprising, because for all Lord Mulholland's style and grace, there was no hint of the dandy about him.

She regarded the piles of papers on Lord Mulholland's large mahogany desk. His business was certainly none of hers. And yet he had been awake so late and so often, poring over these papers. She often suspected that he came to the studio directly from this room, and many times he seemed fatigued. Could he be in some kind of financial difficulty? It seemed impossible.

If he were, how could a man like Lord Mulholland cope with such woes? He had lived all his life in luxury; to do without would be a terrible blow. He would find it difficult but, she thought, a man like him, with all his personal attributes, would triumph over such predicaments, and surely his many friends would come to his aid. He would not suffer long.

And what of them? He had yet to pay his aunt her full fee. Should she not be far more concerned about that, than envisioning Paris Mulholland destitute and in need of her—anybody's—help?

She should find out if he was in trouble. For her guardians' sake, and her own. She would hate to learn that she had endured these days without the compensation that she would not have to worry about money for the next few months.

She went toward the desk, trying to read the topmost paper, which was upside down to her.

"Aren't you going a little far afield in your quest for knowledge?" a voice drawled from the door. "Or are you practicing for Japanese again?"

With a guilty start, Clara stared at Lord Mulholland as he came into the room. "Find anything of interest?" he inquired coolly. Nevertheless, she could see real anger in his blue eyes as he looked at her. He pushed the door shut, the click of the latch sounding loud in the stillness.

Had she really thought there was nothing to fear except seduction when it came to Lord Mulholland? she thought wildly as she moved back until she felt the hard solidity of the desk. She must have been blind. Even though he still wore his evening clothes, menace emanated from him as another man might exude the scent of bay rum.

"I—I wasn't prying into your personal affairs," she stammered quickly. She straightened her shoulders. "I was afraid the wax from the candle was going to drip onto your papers."

It was a lie, yet apparently he was convinced, for the menace disappeared, to be replaced by his usual mocking smile. "But why are you skulking about my house at this time of night, my curious Psyche?" Slowly he pulled off his cravat and loosened the collar of his shirt.

She swallowed hard. "Zeus is still outside. I was going to call him in. Now if you will pardon me, I will get Zeus and return to my room."

"Not so fast, Miss Wells." Lord Mulholland sauntered around the desk like a leopard on the prowl. She turned on her heel, keeping her eyes on him as he sat in his chair, regarding her steadily with his all-too-shrewd eyes as if he were some kind of judge. She took a few steps backward. "Since my private sanctuary has been violated, I must insist upon a punishment."

"*What?*"

"A simple thing, really," he said with a wave of his hand. "Mycroft writes the most incredibly dull correspondence. Going through his letters makes my head ache. I would like you to read this one to me." He picked up the paper on the top of the pile.

"Are you not concerned I shall invade the privacy of your business matters?" she asked, torn between the need to get away from this sinfully tempting man and her curiosity about his financial affairs.

"Oh, there's nothing so vital in that, I'm sure. Besides, I'm quite certain I can trust to your discretion. I wouldn't want to have to send you packing before your charming aunt has finished her task."

"You should have been a blackmailer," Clara noted. He probably could have made a fortune at it if he had chosen vulnerable women, seduced them and then demanded money for his secrecy.

He laughed softly. "I really must protest this characterization of me as a potential criminal. I assure you, my morals are quite as good as anybody's."

"I'm sure they are as good as *some* people's," she replied, very aware of the intimacy of the shadowy darkness. "Very well. I will do as you ask. Give me the letter, my lord."

"Come and fetch it."

Scowling at his command, even though his tone was persuasive rather than authoritative, she came forward and tugged it swiftly from his grasp.

He smiled mockingly. "Please, have a seat, Miss Wells. This will likely take some time."

"Then perhaps tomorrow would be better," she said.

"I need to know the contents tonight. Don't worry. You are safer here than in the studio."

Safer from what, Clara thought angrily as she sat in the proffered chair. She certainly wasn't safer here than when she was with her aunt, even from her own tumultuous emotions, if not from him. However, she had said she would read it, and the letter might reveal if he was in financial difficulties.

She began to read the letter, which had to do with investments abroad, annuities at home and rents and expenditures. Judging by this, there was nothing wrong with Lord Mulholland's finances. Indeed, his businesses seemed to be thriving. Everything sounded quite complicated, but Lord Mulholland's occasional nods and intense expression told her that he fully comprehended the letter's contents, if she did not.

"Thank you," he said when she reached the closing. "Have you ever considered a career upon the stage, Miss Wells?"

"Certainly not!" The stage was one of the most immoral professions in the world. She, of all people, would never engage in such a career.

"With that lovely voice of yours, you would do very well."

She blinked, conscious of his scrutiny, and the fact that they were alone. "Am I excused, my lord?" she asked, commanding her voice to remain steady.

He ran his gaze over her. "That dress is quite the ugliest creation of its type I've ever seen. Are you attempting to cure yourself of vanity or something of that sort that you feel it necessary to disguise your natural attributes?"

"Are these insults intended as further punishment for my stupid decision to enter your inner sanctum, my lord?" she demanded, standing quickly and finding herself startlingly close to tears at his criticism—of her dress, of all silly things. "If so, I believe I have been punished enough."

She started toward the door, but he was in front of her before she reached it. "Granted I did not use the most delightful choice of words, Miss Wells, but I didn't mean to upset you. I think you have a lovely voice, and you're a very pretty woman."

There. He had said what he had been longing to say for days, to put into words something of the feelings she inspired in him.

Unfortunately, to Paris's great and genuine surprise, Clara reared back as if he had physically struck her, and her eyes were full of angry tears. "I knew you were a man of low principles," she declared, "but I must say I am not pleased to discover that you are cruel, too!"

"Cruel?" he asked, incredulous, moving to block the door. Of all the reactions he had expected, this had not been one of them.

"It is cruel to treat me like a simpleton," she said, pushing past him and fumbling with the latch. "My voice may not be unpleasant, but it is meanspirited to tell me I am pretty when I know full well I am not. Do you think I am that witless, or that desperate for your attentions that I would leave behind sense for empty flattery?"

"I was giving you sincere compliments. I do think you're pretty. If I were trying to merely flatter you, I would have said you were beautiful."

"Thank you for confirming that you do not think me attractive, my lord," she muttered, finally succeeding in opening the door. *"Good night!"*

She marched into the hall. "Zeus!" she declared, her voice low and irate. "Here you are! I will lock you inside if you do this again!"

Paris watched as she scooped up the large animal who had been sitting in the corridor and strode away without so much as a backward glance.

Then he closed the door and cursed. Surely now he had all the answers he needed about Clara Wells and her feelings for him.

She thought him despicable and capable of just about anything.

What else could he have expected?

Clara stared down at the beautiful china plate and lovely meal before her and tried not to notice anything going on around her, difficult though it was.

At this evening's dinner, Lord Pimblett persisted in talking about several people the Wells had never met, and never would. Jonas Clark was duly impressed, and occasionally interjected a fond wish to be introduced to such august individuals. Clara thought the young man would make archbishop before he died, he seemed so interested in the elite and so determined to advance himself.

Tommy Taddington was more interested in the food than the talk, although he sometimes paused long enough to cast baleful glances at Lord Pimblett's eldest daughter.

Aunt Aurora and Uncle Byron ate more than they talked, and Clara knew from the looks that passed between them that they considered Lord Pimblett a long-winded, ignorant fellow not worthy of their attention.

Henrietta watched everything with avid, curious eyes, and Clara had the distinct impression that this visit would be the subject of innumerable letters to several female friends.

Lady Helena looked as satisfied as it was possible for a vain, spoiled young woman to look as she spoke to, and only to, their host.

Paris Mulholland's expressions seemed a little more strained than usual, as well they might if he were seriously contemplating marriage with Helena Pimblett, who was so obviously shallow and mercenary. Even if he was a thoughtless scoundrel and even if he treated everyone as his personal plaything, Clara couldn't help feeling that he deserved better than Helena Pimblett. Surely he could see that.

Or did Lady Helena's family connections outweigh her personal defects? Did he even possess any serious thoughts about so important a step as marriage?

Maybe not. Nevertheless, every time the two lords lifted a wineglass, Clara feared an engagement announcement was about to be made. Instead, they merely drank.

Her dread did not end with the finish of the meal, either. When the ladies retired to the drawing room, she still had the awful feeling that *something* of significance was about to be said.

However, Lady Helena and her mother merely sat and looked decorative, with no word of an engagement between them. More surprisingly, Aunt Aurora pleaded fatigue and retired before the men arrived, leaving Clara with no ally except perhaps Hester, who industriously embroidered a lace handkerchief. Henrietta fussed with a vase of flowers, destroying a lovely arrangement.

Clara went to the tall windows that overlooked the garden and the terrace. It was a pretty prospect in the light of dusk. The woman who was mistress of this house and possessed that garden would be very lucky.

She lifted a rose from a nearby vase, but its beautiful scent brought no comfort as she strolled outside onto the terrace.

As the light waned, the glow from the windows of the house provided a different kind of illumination, casting strange shadows from the balustrade, and in the garden, which would never be hers.

She must not hope. She must not want. She must remember that the mistress of the house would be the wife of Paris Mulholland. Even if he were not the man she feared him to be, but was the man she knew he *could* be, surely she had enough proof of his lack of regard last night, when he had treated her like a naughty child. He had purposefully humiliated her. If he cared for her in the slightest, he wouldn't have done that. He would have kissed her.

"Ah, Lord Mulholland!" Lady Helena cried, and Clara glanced over her shoulder to see the gentlemen enter the room.

Their host strolled toward the fireplace and leaned against the mantel. Reverend Clark went to stand beside Henrietta, who blushed and giggled, and Mr. Taddington wandered over to the general vicinity of Lady Pimblett and her eldest daughter. Uncle Byron was not with them, nor was Lord Pimblett.

Why not go inside? She knew how he thought of her, as nothing more than a thing to be trifled with. As for what the Pimbletts thought of her, their opinion simply didn't matter as long as they knew her to be a woman of honor.

"Your uncle has gone back to the book he found," Lord Mulholland said to her when she returned, looking at her with an expression she didn't care to decipher. "He seems quite convinced that there must be a clue to the author somewhere in the lines. His lordship has pleaded a slight stomach upset, and begged to be excused.''

Clara had her own ideas about Lord Pimblett begging anything; however, she did not bemoan the absence of the blustery lord and her enthusiastic uncle. It would make it all the easier for her to claim fatigue and retire early, too.

''I was hoping to entice you into a game of whist,'' Lady Helena purred to Lord Mulholland, obviously not a bit concerned about her father's indisposition.

''I am sorry to disappoint you, Lady Helena,'' his lordship replied, ''but I was hoping to persuade Miss Wells to continue the story of Cupid and Psyche this evening. Scheherazade was interrupted once, and I have been anxious to hear the rest of the tale.''

Despite her sincere belief that she was proof against him, Clara flushed, remembering all too well the last time he had called her that name.

Lady Helena looked decidedly disgruntled.

''Perhaps we can play later?'' Lord Mulholland offered softly in that seductive voice to which no living woman could possibly be impervious.

''Of course, if you would like,'' Lady Helena replied somewhat breathlessly.

He must know what he was doing, a disgruntled Clara thought. A man of his worldliness would be very aware of how he affected women, and although Clara didn't like Lady Helena, she condemned him for not being fair to her, either. Clearly Lady Helena had great expectations of him, yet several times now Clara had found reason to doubt his attachment to her. If he had no intention of asking for Lady Helena's hand, he should tell her so.

Perhaps, in one sense, Clara realized with dismay, she had been flattering herself to think that he was toying with her alone. She may not have had even that slight distinction from other females.

Lady Helena lost some of Clara's sympathy when she said with smug, triumphant satisfaction, "I should like to hear Miss Wells' version of the story." She made it sound as if Clara were sure to be incompetent.

A flash of anger conquered Clara's feeling of dismay. Had these two physically fine specimens decided they alone had feelings worthy of consideration? Their rank, wealth and looks did not give them the right to pass judgment or use people however they would. "Perhaps the other ladies and gentlemen would rather do something else?" she suggested coldly.

"I can think of almost nothing that would give me more pleasure," Lord Mulholland said. His gaze swept over everyone in the room.

Clara knew he had the power of sexual attraction—she had felt the magnetism of his masculinity often enough—but never before had she witnessed the full dominating force of Paris Mulholland's personality. He was silently daring anyone to disagree with him. Nobody did. Nobody could have. Not even she.

"Please begin, Miss Wells," he said, as his gaze came to rest upon her.

Chapter Twenty-One

In the instant their eyes met, everything changed. Clara had been determined not to acquiesce to his request, but now there was no way she could refuse, because his forcefulness disappeared as suddenly as it had manifested itself, to be replaced by a wistful, yearning expression only a totally heartless creature could ignore.

Had a more perplexing, confoundedly attractive man ever existed?

"Oh, indeed. We should give Miss Wells the chance to show us the benefits of reading Latin and Greek," Lady Helena said scornfully, breaking the spell of Lord Mulholland's intimate regard.

The kind and gentle Hester smiled her encouragement, and young Henrietta was already blushing and giggling as if she had heard a particular kind of limerick. Reverend Clark was apparently not sure whether he should approve of the proposal or not.

Clara told herself that while she did not have beauty or other socially desirable attributes, and although she might be nothing more to Lord Mulholland than an amusement to pass the time, she was different from every woman here because of her learning, and if that was all she possessed to distinguish herself, she would use it.

However, she would not become Scheherazade by embellishing the tale. She would repeat the bare academic facts of the story. "I have already told you half of the myth, Lord Mulholland," she said, giving him the briefest of glances. "If everyone here is familiar with the story, I could start where I finished."

"I know who Cupid is," Tommy Taddington announced, "but I must say I've never heard of this other fellow. Who was he, some poor chap hit by one of the fat little creature's arrows?"

"Psyche was Cupid's wife," Clara explained.

"Oh, I say, really?" Mr. Taddington exclaimed, blushing. "I'd heard that about the ancient Greeks, but I never believed it."

"Psyche was a beautiful woman."

"Isn't that rather odd? I mean, that's marrying pretty young, isn't it?"

"The god Cupid was a young adult, not a child," Clara replied. "He was very handsome, with golden hair and wings." She recalled a certain demonstration of a winged embrace and hesitated.

Henrietta giggled even more, and Mr. Taddington fell into a demoralized silence. Lady Helena glanced sharply at the fair and handsome Lord Mulholland. "A god, indeed," she murmured.

Apparently Lord Mulholland didn't hear her. "Start from the beginning anyway," he coaxed. "You tell a story so well, I shall enjoy rehearing it."

His tone was beguiling and so intimate, it was easy to forget they were not alone, and that he was only trifling with her, until Clara caught sight of the frowning Reverend Clark out of the corner of her eye.

"Perhaps you would care to tell the tale," she offered, addressing the young minister.

"No, I would not," he said firmly, and he flushed to the tips of his ears. He said no more, and Clara noted that while he seemed mortified, he did not leave the room. He sat beside Henrietta.

It occurred to Clara that for a man such as Reverend Clark who wanted a student as well as a wife, Henrietta Pimblett might be the perfect choice. She was giddy and vain, yet not hopelessly silly or flirtatious. With Reverend Clark for an older, wiser and patient husband, she could improve. And with a jolly, pretty wife, so might Reverend Clark.

To turn the current of her thoughts away from potential marriages and suitable partners, she began again to tell of Cupid and Psyche, quickly repeating the tale as far as she had gotten in the garden. She soon became aware that Lady Pimblett and Helena were completely and utterly bored, because they took no pains to hide their state, yawning and exchanging weary glances. She suspected only the silence of the others kept them from whispering criticism.

When she reached the part about the lamp and the oil, she noticed that Lord Mulholland leaned forward a little more eagerly, and she tried to ignore his obvious interest.

"Cupid did not speak at first," she continued. "He flew to the top of a tree, and from his perch berated Psyche for disobeying him. He told her that he had disregarded his mother to marry her. Hadn't he warned her against trying to find out who he was, and about her sisters? Her sisters would suffer for what they had done. Then, before he flew off, he said, quite vainly, that she would suffer by being apart from him."

"So she would, if she loved him," Henrietta simpered, looking at Reverend Clark in such a way that Clara was sure the youngest Pimblett was already planning a double wedding.

"A man in love sometimes says odd things," Lord Mulholland noted quietly.

Clara tried to focus on the story. "After Eros left her—"

"Who the devil's Eros?" Mr. Taddington demanded.

"That's another name for Cupid," Clara explained, cursing the slip of her tongue that reminded her of the portrait Aunt Aurora was painting—and that Lord Mulholland no doubt enjoyed posing for because she was uncomfortable doing so, the infuriating man. "Anyway, Psyche tried to follow him, to no avail. Then she attempted to drown herself, but the stream wouldn't let her."

"The stream wouldn't *let* her?" Hester asked.

"Too shallow a location, I daresay," Lord Mulholland remarked. "She seems rather lacking in discernment, our poor Psyche."

Clara glanced at him sharply. Was that intended for her? His eyes told her nothing.

"Perhaps she realized the sin of attempting to destroy herself," Reverend Clark said.

"Maybe the water was too cold," Mr. Taddington offered. "I fell in a stream while I was fishing on our Scottish estate once. By God, I thought I'd—"

"Scottish estate?" Lady Helena inquired with far more interest than she had demonstrated in the story.

"Yes. About five thousand acres. Massive stone house. Bunch of sullen tenants—everything one would expect."

Lady Helena looked at the portly young man with new respect. A sense of relief intruded upon Clara, which she immediately tried to subdue.

"Miss Wells, please continue," Lord Mulholland said.

"Whatever the reason," Clara said, reminded that she was merely the entertainment here and nothing else, "she did not die. She kept trying to find her husband again. Sadly, it was hopeless, for he had fled to the house of his mother, the goddess Venus.

"Eventually, Psyche reached the home of her eldest sister, whose treachery she did not forgive or forget. She told her sister what had truly happened, and that her husband was not a monster, but the god Cupid himself." She could not help darting a glance at Lord Mulholland, whose gaze was still fixed upon her in a most disconcerting manner. She cleared her throat. "Having finally come to comprehend her sisters' envy, Psyche told her that when Cupid had deserted her, he said he would have her sister for his wife instead."

"What the devil was she up to?" Tommy Taddington cried.

"Revenge, I should think," Lord Mulholland observed.

"Her sister is about to learn a lesson," Henrietta said, without a giggle, and there was personal satisfaction in her tone.

Clara could believe Henrietta had spent some time imagining a few lessons for her own elder sister.

"We must remember these tales come down to us from long before the time of our Savior," Reverend Clark reminded them, "who taught us that forgiveness is the way of love."

He said it with a slight smile, and Clara thought he was a wiser and a better man than she might have given him credit for.

Henrietta gazed at the clergyman with awe and great respect, while Lady Helena continued to regard Mr. Taddington thoughtfully.

"What happened next?" Hester asked, with both dread and curiosity.

"Her sister was so pleased and excited by Psyche's words that she left at once, without even offering Psyche any help at all. She went to the top of a tall mountain and opened her arms wide." Clara's voice rose and she spread her arms like the mythical sister. "'Cupid!' she called out. 'Catch me and take me for your wife.' She jumped from the mountain, expecting the wind to carry her to the god, but she fell upon the rocks and was killed."

"Oh, my," Hester whispered.

"A vivid imagination seems to run in that family," Lord Mulholland remarked. "One would think she would wait until she saw the fellow or felt him, or the wind, or *something* instead of just diving off a mountain."

Clara nodded. "Nevertheless, Psyche went to her other sister and told her the same thing, with the same result."

"Poetic retribution," Reverend Clark murmured. "Yet I believe it did not ease Psyche's suffering."

"No, it did not," Clara concurred. "She was still sad and miserable and alone. She kept wandering, and because she was with child, her journey grew more difficult all the time."

"Where the devil was Eros?" Lord Mulholland asked suddenly. "Surely it didn't take him that long to recover from a slight burn."

"He was sulking in his mother's house and nursing his wound," Clara replied. "He hadn't told his mother what had happened and—"

Lady Pimblett suddenly straightened. "Keeping secrets from his mother?" she demanded sharply. "Terrible child! First he disobeys, then keeps secrets. I hope she punishes him."

"She did, when she found out about his wife," Clara said.

"Who told her?" Tommy Taddington demanded. "I'd lay good money on the sisters, but they were killed, weren't they? Or were they only turned into a plant or something?"

"Oh, they were quite dead. It was a sea gull who told Venus about her son. Like you, Lady Pimblett, she was appalled. She returned to her house and locked her son inside. Then she decided to punish Psyche, hating her all the more.

"Venus went to the other gods and goddesses and complained about her son. The other Olympians were secretly quite delighted to see that, for once, Cupid was suffering for love. And they wanted very much to help Psyche. However, they did not dare to let Venus see this.

"Meanwhile, Psyche decided to seek out her husband's mother to ask her forgiveness."

"Poor Psyche," Hester said sympathetically. "It was not her fault she was beautiful."

"Beauty alone is not something to be ashamed of," Lady Helena said with some spirit. "She should not have bragged about her husband, although—" she glanced coyly at Lord Mulholland "— surely she was just too happy to think clearly."

Clara's optimistic hope that Lady Helena was reconsidering the target of her affections diminished considerably. "*I* think Psyche wanted to see her husband again, and suspected he would be there," she said. "Perhaps she wished that once he saw how she suffered and that it was nearly time for their child to be born, he would relent. Or perhaps she simply couldn't bear to think he didn't love her as much as she loved him."

"A terrible state," Lord Mulholland said softly.

There was such genuine sympathy in his voice that Clara had to look at him, only to see a mask of inscrutability that increased her frustration. What was she thinking? she silently berated herself. That he would suddenly fall on his knees and declare his passionate love for her?

"At any rate," she went on, her voice stronger, "she misjudged her mother-in-law as much as she had her sisters.

"When Venus saw her and realized who she was, she was furiously angry. She also claimed that she would certainly not be pleased to be called a grandmother."

Lady Pimblett looked sympathetic for the first time since Clara had begun the story.

"She claimed that Psyche might make a farmer a good enough wife, and gave her the task of separating seeds and beans from a great pile. Ants took pity on Psyche and did the job.

"Venus returned and saw that it was finished. She couldn't believe that Psyche had succeeded without help, which was indeed true. However, Venus was convinced Cupid had helped her, which I think means that he must have shown or said *something* to his mother about his love for his wife."

"Or maybe he was just lying about brooding and being melancholy," Lord Mulholland said with a heavy sigh and mocking eyes. "Classic signs of a young man in love."

"Symptoms you are familiar with, my lord?" Lady Helena asked archly.

"Oh, absolutely. Once I didn't eat for nearly a whole day when I fancied myself in love. Went about with my cravat tied in the most appallingly sloppy manner, too. Her name was Eliza, I think. No, Elizabeth. Emily?"

"And since then, my lord?" Lady Helena queried. "Any return of such symptoms?"

"None whatsoever," he replied lightly.

Lady Helena's disapproval of his answer would have been amusing, if Clara hadn't felt disappointed, too, and yet there was something in his eyes that made her feel he was not being completely truthful.

Oh, what could it matter? Even if he did care for her, nothing could ever come of it. He would never want to marry a girl of her background, and she would never allow any other liaison but a legal one, so what was there to do but try to endure this visit and be glad when it was over?

She cleared her throat. "Venus set her other tasks, too, and in these Psyche was secretly helped by the gods. Her last task was to take a small box and go to

Hades and bring back some of the Queen of Hell's beauty.

"Why didn't Venus go herself, if she wanted to be the most beautiful?" Mr. Taddington demanded pedantically.

"Nobody wants to go to He...Had...down there," Hester protested.

"Even the gods feared the land of the dead, when there was no promise of resurrection," Reverend Clark noted.

"Obviously the goddess didn't think the poor girl would come back," Lord Mulholland said. "Which doesn't explain how her son was supposed to deal with the fact that his mother was responsible for his wife's demise. Venus sounds as blind as Psyche, in some respects."

"I have to concur," Clara said, reluctantly agreeing with his perception. "Venus was so vain and so selfish, she couldn't see what she was doing. Fortunately, Psyche had advice and help again, and she got some of the beauty. Unfortunately, on her way back to her mother-in-law's, she was tempted by the thought of what was in the box, and by her desire to be appealing to her husband. She opened the box...." Clara paused dramatically and looked around the room.

Tommy Taddington was listening with his eyes wide and his mouth open. Hester looked worried. Lady Pimblett was actually paying attention, her fan motionless. If a smile could look about to burst into a giggle, that would have described Henrietta's expression. Reverend Clark had an admiring look on his face, directed at Henrietta.

When Clara gaze encountered Lord Mulholland's, she faltered, dreading to notice anything in his eyes.

"The box appeared empty," she said, continuing her story. "But immediately a deep and deathlike sleep overcame her, and she fell to the ground.

"By this time, though, Cupid realized how much he missed his wife, so he managed to escape from his mother's house. He found Psyche and—"

"Woke her with a kiss!" Henrietta cried triumphantly.

Clara shook her head. "After he wiped the deadly sleep from her, he woke her by pricking her with one of his arrows."

Henrietta frowned with disappointment. Mr. Taddington squirmed.

"Ensuring that *she* still loved him, after all she'd been through, I should think," Lord Mulholland proposed.

"Exactly—and a wise idea," Clara agreed. "Although he apparently found it necessary to remind her that once again her curiosity had caused her dilemma."

"Not a very clever fellow—but his love was genuine," Lord Mulholland remarked quietly. "For that, I should think he might be forgiven much."

Time seemed to pause for the briefest of moments as he looked at her.

"What happened to the beauty?" Lady Helena asked.

Clara forced herself to continue the tale. "Cupid told Psyche to return to his mother with the beauty and he would go to Jupiter for assistance, which he did. Jupiter and the other Olympians acknowledged that it would be better for everybody if Cupid had a wife to keep him at home rather than flying about making mischief with his arrows, so Jupiter decided to make Psyche immortal.''

"And they lived happily ever after," Henrietta finished, clapping her hands with delight.

"Yes. The storyteller says Venus danced at their wedding," Clara said.

"What about the baby?" Hester asked. "Was it all right?"

Clara felt herself blush. "The child of Psyche and Eros was Pleasure."

"How appropriate," Lord Mulholland said softly.

"I would like to think Venus changed her mind about Psyche when Psyche faced all the tasks she set her. It must have proven to Venus that Psyche's love for her son was genuine and strong, don't you think?" Hester asked hesitantly.

"It should have been the man who had the tasks," Lady Helena said decisively.

"I think so, too," Mr. Taddington immediately agreed.

"So you would suffer for a lady's love?" Lord Mulholland asked Mr. Taddington, as if truly curious. "I should rather think you would pay others to perform the Herculean tasks, wouldn't you?"

"Of course, if I could," Mr. Taddington replied. "That's what money's for. That's why men try so hard to get it."

Lady Helena nodded in agreement, and so did her mother.

"Suppose you lost all your money, and you were still in love," Clara proposed. "Would you not try to win a lady's hand based solely on your own merit?"

That confounded the industrialist's son. "I don't have anything much else than money to recommend me, I think."

Clara was sorry for asking the question, but it was Lady Helena who spoke first. "I should think you would never have to confront such a preposterous idea, Mr. Taddington. Why, people will always need clothing, so there must always be mills to spin the cloth, and I understand your father's company is enormous and makes a huge profit every year."

"It does," Mr. Taddington confirmed, and Lady Helena darted a smug glance at Clara, who decided it would not be appropriate to point out that wars, trade barriers, changing fashions and changing methods all might cause disruption of cloth manufacture.

"Miss Wells places great importance on individual merit, I think," Lord Mulholland said.

Once again, Clara was frustrated in her efforts to understand if he was serious, or only making a joke.

He really was an unbearable man. Neither his wealth nor his charm nor his handsome face gave him the right to make sport with other people.

It was time someone told him so, with no prevaricating.

Someone who had nothing to lose.

Someone who didn't matter to him in the least.

Someone like her.

Chapter Twenty-Two

"Not so angry, please, my lord," Mrs. Wells commanded. "You are dismayed, more than angry. Disappointed. Wistful, perhaps, yet always in love."

Paris Mulholland struggled to maintain the required expression while Clara ignored him, as she had ignored him all too often of late.

It was not easy.

Indeed, although he had found himself in several interesting situations in his lifetime, Paris had never experienced anything quite so frustrating as being wrapped in an old curtain and staring into the beautiful eyes of the woman with whom he was most certainly and regrettably in love while quite unable to move a muscle, not just because of the presence of her relative, but also because he was supposed to be acting for the sake of a picture. He didn't know whether he should groan with anguish, or laugh with scorn at his feelings of impotence.

Ever since the Pimbletts had arrived, Paris had been as close to hell as he ever hoped to find himself. He wanted Clara Wells more than he had ever wanted a woman, yet never had one been so far from his reach.

And the only person he could hold accountable was himself, with his wastrel reputation as a clever wit of no great depth, a handsome man capable of seduction and not much more. For years he had found that beneficial, because it meant no one expected him to be an intellectual. Unfortunately, his reputation surely marked him as the opposite of what Clara Wells craved in a husband.

He very much wanted her to know that there was more to him than that, but his pride would not allow him to drop his mask, lest he also feel compelled to confess his astonishing ignorance. Besides, would she even believe that a man who had gone to Oxford could barely read and had found studying such a constant struggle that, while he had sincerely mourned his mother's death, he was secretly delighted to have an excuse to be spared any further education?

What did she really think of him? Did she even like him? Or was she as indifferent to him as she seemed to be?

He had been driven to discover the nature of her feelings for him the other evening, when he had compelled her to finish the story of Cupid and Psyche. She hadn't wanted to, but he would have said or done almost anything to get her to stay in the drawing room. Sadly, he had been unable to reach any conclusions.

Every night after that when they had posed, he had been tempted to try to find out again, and every night he gave up without making a serious attempt. For one thing, he was afraid that the truth would break his heart. For another, he had discovered that however ridiculous a figure Aurora Wells cut in the drawing room, in the artist's studio she was seriousness personified and dedicated to her work. Gad, how many other older women did he know who would suggest that their niece pose nude, especially with a man of his reputation, because it seemed necessary for the work?

He could see where Clara got her passionate fortitude. Life would never, ever be boring with a resolute, outspoken wife like Clara.

But that could never be. Too many differences, real or perceived, stood between them. He had been forced to content himself with these few moments of intimacy, as bizarre as the situation was.

Nevertheless, he was just as concerned as Clara about the propriety of it, and the danger of discovery. Not for his sake; he could pass it off as an amusing lark with no harm to his reputation. However, Clara's position was another matter entirely. If the Pimbletts found out about this, she would have little hope of a reconciliation with her grandfather or acceptance into the higher social circles, unless she was willing to be treated as some kind of interesting freak. She would not be willing, he was sure, and only the stupidest of fools would imagine that a woman like Clara would come running to his arms for comfort.

He could also easily understand why she wished to remain free of any taint of wrongdoing. She considered her honor and her life as valuable as anyone else's, as well she should, and she had much to forfeit with its loss.

He should have refused to pose with her. Then she might view him in a more noble light. If only the temptation to be with her under any circumstances was not so strong!

He could only hope that eventually she would see beyond his face to the true measure of the man beneath, even if there could never be anything more between them.

Clara stood up abruptly. "I'm sorry, Aunt Aurora, but I'm getting a cramp. May we finish for tonight?"

"I, too, am tired," Paris said, rising.

"Oh, very well," Aunt Aurora said with a sigh. "I've got the preliminary work done. I assure you, children, it's going to be lovely! *Eros Discovered* will be in the National Gallery someday!"

"I hope not," Clara muttered under her breath. She wanted there to be no reminder of this painful time, nor did she have any wish to see her face displayed in any gallery, not even if she bore a resemblance to the Duke of Wellington.

"Interesting way to go down in posterity," Lord Mulholland said, pulling on his shirt. "As a chap who fell in love when he wasn't supposed to."

Very well for him to be so jovial, Clara thought. It didn't matter if Lord Paris Mulholland was displayed in a state of undress. It obviously delighted his vanity.

She should have put a stop to the posing days ago, after she had finished the tale of Cupid and Psyche. She had known then, finally and unequivocally, what kind of selfish, inconsiderate cad she was dealing with. She should have confronted him, then, too, as she had wanted to. She would have, if it hadn't been for Aunt Aurora's fervent belief that this was to be her masterpiece.

Upon further reflection, Clara had decided that once she knew the kind of man he was, she could cope with his frivolous treatment. Unfortunately, this was not proving to be a successful strategy. She simply couldn't stay angry enough. He was too kind, too charming and too accommodating to her aunt's every whim.

"Paris Mulholland, the Eros of his day," he mused, starting to pick up the cushions and pile them where Witherspoon had left them. "Maybe I should have a bow and arrows at my feet."

"Excellent suggestion!" Aunt Aurora cried. "Do you have any?"

Clara threw some of the cushions to the corner. "What kind of Paris would he be without his bow and arrows?" she asked sarcastically.

"What do you mean?" Lord Mulholland inquired, apparently genuinely puzzled.

"Paris was good for two things," Clara replied as she reached for her dressing gown and put it on, something she should have done immediately and she couldn't think why she hadn't. "Seducing women, and archery. He was the one who shot Achilles in the ankle."

"Really?" Lord Mulholland looked as pleased as if he had loosed the fatal dart at the sulky hero personally.

"Most of the time, however," she continued mercilessly, "he stayed in the bedchamber with Helen. Perhaps you'll be lucky and find a Helen in your bed."

"Gad, I hope not!" Lord Mulholland muttered, looking down as he buttoned up his shirt.

It almost sounded as if he *had* found a Helen in his bed in the past.

Clara thought that wasn't impossible. There could be no denying that he was a physically tempting specimen, if that was all one was interested in, and Clara wouldn't put much faith in Lady Helena's morals, not with those greedy, lustful eyes and the way she pressed against Lord Mulholland when they danced.

But no. Lady Helena was not after mere physical pleasure. She wanted the estate and the title and the money as much as the man, if not more. Surely she wouldn't risk that by offering him her body without any formal agreement.

"Come now, children, off to bed," Aunt Aurora chided as if they were both no more than ten years old.

Paris Mulholland was certainly no child, any more than she was.

"Come, Clara, no lingering!"

"Sleep well, Psyche," he murmured, giving her a smile that reminded her of how appealing he could be.

Clara scurried from the room. She had never passed a more stressful time than these past few days, and Lord Mulholland's smiles only added to her dismay.

It was agony to pose with him and not touch him, to hear him speak to Lady Helena and believe that she would never hear him whisper words of love in her ear, to dream every night of being in his arms only to wake to the harsh reality of her hopeless passion. To be the recipient of his attention and smiles, and find herself wanting him more every moment.

She could never be his wife, and wishing would not make it so, she reminded herself bitterly.

Tomorrow. Tomorrow she would tell him that he must stop playing with her emotions. If he refused to pose anymore, then so be it. She simply could not continue to sacrifice her peace of mind for a painting—masterpiece or not.

The next afternoon, Paris rubbed his temples as he tried to decipher one of Mycroft's interminable reports, or rather, he should have been, instead of staring at it unseeing. It was nearly time to dress for dinner, but all his powers of concentration seemed to have deserted him, ever since Clara Wells had arrived at Mulholland House.

He simply had to drive her from his thoughts, at least for a little while.

The handle of his study door turned. His heart seemed to miss a beat as he wondered if it was Clara at the door.

He hoped it was Clara. It would be so much more pleasant to have her read the correspondence, and not just because he liked her voice. When she had read the other letter, he had been able to concentrate totally on Mycroft's meaning, rather than unraveling each one of the man's actual words. The contents had seemed infinitely clearer, and a decision so much easier to reach. Indeed, he had been extremely tempted to ask Clara to help him again, and would have, had it not meant revealing his terrible ignorance.

Unfortunately, Helena Pimblett slyly slipped into the room and closed the door softly. She was already dressed for dinner in a very low-cut gown of rich burgundy silk trimmed with Valenciennes lace. She regarded him with a seductive smile and secretive air, and he was filled with anger that she had violated the sanctity of his study.

"Here you are," she whispered. "Still at work over nasty account books and legal documents?"

"How kind of you to seek me out," he replied, fully cognizant of the real reason she was here, which was rather too obvious. He had been pursued too many times not to recognize the blatant signs, and he felt sure Helena thought he hadn't been paying sufficient attention to her. How could he, when he only wanted to be near Clara?

He rose from his chair courteously, a meaningless smile on his face. "Unfortunately, we have no chaperon."

She smiled with what he supposed she thought was alluring guile, but which instead resembled only cold calculation. "It doesn't matter, does it?"

"For your sake, it does," he replied, going toward the door. He had no wish to be found alone with Helena Pimblett. He would not put it past her to try to compel him to marry her if they were found alone together, and sadly, any trouble the Pimbletts might make on that score would not blow over quickly.

Her skirts blocked his way. "It is so sweet of you to be concerned about me," she murmured with a predatory gleam in her eyes. "I do not think anyone will find us here."

He beat a hasty retreat toward his desk. "I do have a few things to finish before dinner, Helena, so I must ask you to excuse me."

Her skirts whispered like the chorus in a Greek drama as she moved to sit on the chair opposite. "I shall watch you work. It will be a pleasure."

He gave her his most brilliant smile. "You will be far too distracting, I assure you. I shall probably make all kind of errors and wind up penniless, and it will be your fault."

"Paris," she chided with her horrible false laugh, "you are so amusing. As if you could ever be penniless!"

He was feeling so desperate to have her gone, he almost told her he was. Only the rational realization that she probably knew exactly what he was worth prevented him.

Maybe this was fate. Karma. Kismet. A jest of the gods. Paris, the seducer, destroyed by Helena. It would be amusing if he weren't so upset at the thought.

"I really think you should leave, Helena," he said.

He saw that she was startled by his tone. Her eyes narrowed suspiciously even as he gave her another smile. "I simply cannot concentrate with such a beautiful woman in the room."

"I am happy to think I'm more interesting than papers and figures," she said, making absolutely no effort to get up.

Something moved on the terrace. Paris turned quickly, and caught sight of a cat's tail as it disappeared from view. Was Zeus going toward his mistress? Was Clara Wells out there? What would she think if she saw Helena in his study? Had she already looked in the windows?

If so, there was nothing he could do about it now. "It's nearly time for dinner," he said, standing. "I see that you are already dressed, and most delightfully, too, but I fear I had better make haste before my valet arrives to chastise me. Jean Claude has quite a fearsome tongue. Nor would I want to give any cause for embarrassment."

"Embarrassment?"

"I daresay your father would look rather askance if you were discovered here, with me."

"You would do the honorable thing, I'm sure," she said, standing and smoothing down her skirt with a slow, languid caress.

Meaning he would offer to marry her? For that? "I wouldn't trust to the honor of a man named Paris, my dear Helena," he said lightly. "To do so would surely be disastrous."

He saw indecision and slight panic in her calculating eyes. "But you always say you are named after the city, not the mythical person," she said.

"Indeed. However, need I remind you that I'm said to be a wastrel with no serious scruples at all. Including moral ones, I believe. *I* would not suffer overmuch from the taint of disgrace."

Helena finally seemed to perceive that he might not consider it necessary to marry to avoid scandal. She reddened and went toward the door, pausing to look back at him once more, perhaps to see if he was serious.

"I would make sure no one is passing in the hall," he whispered cautiously.

Her expression was one of barely controlled anger. "I thank you, my lord, for your gallant concern. Of course, *I* have a reputation to lose. Other women might not have such fears, and perhaps would not care if they were found alone with you or not. I would beware women of loose morals, especially when they are under the same roof. There are some scandals not even the charming Paris Mulholland can overcome."

Was this some kind of threat? he wondered with sudden dread. Did she know something about *Eros Discovered?* Or was Helena only fishing for answers to vague suspicions?

He had better take care, for Clara's sake. He smiled and looked suitably surprised. "Oh, I shall watch out for predatory, immoral females, my dear Helena, if I find any. Fortunately, the only women here are the servants, and your family. Oh, yes—" he pulled a face of distaste ''—and the studious Miss Wells and her aunt. Hardly the type to entice a fellow like me.''

Helena's expression changed from frowning suspicion to one of smiling triumph before she carefully opened the door, peered down the hall and left the room. Paris sighed with relief before checking the terrace and making certain no young lady lingered there.

Then he frowned. There could be no more prevaricating. He had to stop posing for *Eros Discovered,* for Clara's sake.

Although he saw the necessity for that decision, the thought was far from pleasing. And he wondered if he had the strength to do it.

Chapter Twenty-Three

Clara rose from her seat beside her bedroom window where she had waited since leaving the company after dinner. She had not changed, and her Grecian costume still lay upon the bed. Outside, the night was quiet and tranquil. No illumination shone on the terrace, lawns or garden from upper windows. Everyone had retired. Everyone, she thought, except Lord Mulholland, whose light step had not passed by her door.

She was determined to confront Paris Mulholland tonight, for she had not done so yet. That afternoon, she had planned to speak with him privately, and had approached his study when she knew him to be there, only to catch a glimpse of Helena Pimblett through the terrace doors.

So, no one was allowed inside Paris Mulholland's study? No one except young women, it seemed, especially young women whose affections he trifled with. Clara had been filled with anger. And dismay, and jealousy. She had been so upset, she had not been able to enter and confront him. Not with Helena there, and not even if Helena might prove to be as much a victim of Paris Mulholland's charm as she. Clara had decided to delay until she was in better control of her emotions.

Until she could be sure she wouldn't cry.

She was ready now. Everyone had retired. The house was quiet and he was probably alone in his study. She would speak with him at once, before her aunt appeared to start work on the painting.

She would tell Paris Mulholland exactly what she thought of him.

Once again she made her cautious way down the stairs. This time, she carried no light, and she had no thought for Zeus or Jupiter, or even the fear of discovery. All her effort went into preparing for the confrontation and to the determination not to weaken.

Yes, he was there. She took a deep breath, straightened her shoulders and marched into the room.

He saw her at once and that mocking little smile appeared on his face.

"Do you think I don't know what you are doing?" she demanded without preamble.

"Good evening to you, too, Miss Wells," he replied. It was only then that she noticed how disheveled his hair was, and that his eyes were bloodshot.

"Are you drunk?" she asked indignantly.

"No." Paris rose slowly and went over to a side table, where he poured himself a brandy, trying to buy himself more time to think and to calm himself. "It's a tempting thought, though," he continued with his back to her. "Care to join me?"

"Certainly not."

Oh, dear God, she sounded as if she loathed him. Why? What did she think he had done? Whatever he was guilty of in her eyes, surely it was not deserving of such contempt.

He took a deep breath and willed himself to be strong as he turned to face her. "Is it time to pose?" He raised one eyebrow speculatively before he downed his drink in one gulp.

"No. I came here to talk to you."

"Chastise me, I think would be a better term, judging by your tone. Of what crime do you wish to accuse me?"

"What gives you the right to use people like toys for your amusement?" she charged.

He hid his dismay at her allegation as best he could. "Is that what you believe I have been doing?"

"Yes. With me, and every other woman you have ever met."

"Not 'people,' then. Just women."

"That is bad enough, don't you think?"

Good heavens, if he had wanted to play games with her, he would have made it "Race to the Bed," with him as the prize.

However, she clearly believed that he was evil incarnate, when the only game he had truly been playing had been The Merry Fool in an effort to hide his hopeless regard for her.

He threw himself in his chair and gestured for her to sit opposite him, an invitation she declined. "My dear Miss Wells, you quite take my breath away," he said, managing to sound unconcerned with very great effort. "I think you had better explain yourself. I believe the last time we spoke in this room, you accused me of being unprincipled, cruel and meanspirited. Apparently you have since reevaluated your opinions and I am also a heartless user of women. My, my, is there no end to my evil?"

"I am not so ignorant that I do not see your manipulation—Paris." She made a snake's hiss of his name, which struck him to the core.

"Am I wounding you—Paris? I hope so," she said, and then her voice faltered. "For you have wounded me."

He saw pain and anguish as well as anger in her face. He got up and came around the desk, wanting very much to touch her, yet afraid to. "I didn't mean to hurt you," he said quietly, gazing at her and willing her to believe him. "I'm not toying with you."

She regarded him with frank skepticism. "Would you have me believe that you don't know how you affect me—or any woman?" she demanded.

"Yes," he answered honestly.

"You are not stupid, my lord," she countered. "No matter how much you enjoy pretending otherwise."

"Enjoy?" he retorted. "You think I *enjoy* being ignorant?"

"Oh, come now, my lord!" she cried, moving away from him. "There is no point in playing the charming wastrel anymore. That's why I've come here, to tell you to stop and to insist that we cease posing. I refuse to be used as an object for your amusement."

She understood so little! He supposed he could take pleasure in having succeeded in covering his flaw so well, but as Clara stood before him, her eyes shining with passionate intensity, he knew his ignorance and wasted youth had cost him everything. He strode quickly to the window, his back to her once again as he felt hot tears sting his eyes. He would not have her see that for all the world.

"Do you feel omnipotent, watching us all make idiots of ourselves by falling in love with you?"

"No!" he growled.

"Why did you ask me to read that letter the other night?" she continued boldly. "Wasn't it to make me feel like a child forced to stand in the corner when it's been naughty?"

"No!" Oh, God, did she think him petty, too? He marched to the side table and grabbed the brandy bottle.

"Wasn't it because you enjoy exercising your power over women?"

"No!" He poured himself another drink. A large one.

"Didn't you want to humiliate me even more?"

"God, no!" He downed his brandy neat. "A hundred times, no!"

"Then why did you make me read that letter?" she demanded again.

"I asked you because I couldn't read it myself!"

He saw her shock and surprise, and cursed himself for a fool. But the truth was out, and there was no point to hide it. "Are you happy now, Psyche?" he demanded, glaring at her. "You can blackmail *me,* if you like. The wealthy, the handsome, the charming Lord Mulholland, who can read no better than a child of six! Think of the shame you can cause me! Rest assured, you are safe from me, with such a weapon at your command."

She met his angry gaze steadfastly. No pity. Thank God no condescending pity came into those eyes of hers. Instead, surprise and curiosity. Not unexpected and not necessarily good, but better by far than pity.

"How is it that you cannot?" she asked. "You have been to school. Why, you have been to *Oxford!*"

"I can read if I go very slowly," he said, trying to make light of his problem once again. He casually leaned back against the table. "And then, Paris Mulholland is such a charming, humorous fellow with bags of money, he charmed and laughed and paid his way through school. As for Oxford, I'm sorry to disappoint you, Miss Wells, but very little study goes on among the upper classes at that academic institution. So you see, my dear Psyche, my shallow charm is nothing but a screen to hide my woeful lack."

She was doing quite a study now, apparently, for she looked at him as one fascinated, and not by his looks.

"I would prefer it if you forget what you have learned, except for those opportune moments when you are afraid I am toying with you. Then, like any good warrior, you may draw your weapon and wield it."

"How did such a thing happen?" she asked quietly, taking a seat unbidden, apparently no longer concerned about the propriety of being alone, unchaperoned, with a man. No longer angry, either. Thank God.

"I fell behind in school, and never gave it any thought until it was too late." He smiled sardonically, still attempting to hide the pain of his lack. "Even a wastrel has his pride, Miss Wells. Rather than admit my ignorance, I—"

"Hid it well by playing the clown," she finished for him. "A clever strategy, my lord. Does Mr. Mycroft know?"

He felt as if she were probing his emotions like a surgeon searching for a bullet in his flesh. "No. He merely thinks he has an indecisive employer who takes far too long to make up his wayward mind."

"I shall be happy to help you improve your reading," Clara offered.

"I am too old a dog to learn any new tricks." He wanted a wife, not a teacher. "You will have me believing that you care about my welfare."

Her steadfast gaze did not falter. "I do, my lord. Very much."

He suddenly recalled something else she had said, something he had been too upset to question at the time. "What did you mean when you accused me of making women fall in love?" he asked, sensing something good might rise, phoenixlike, from the ashes of this confrontation.

She colored, and only now did her gaze falter. "Lady Helena obviously thinks you are going to marry her."

"I have *never* in my life given Helena any serious cause to believe that. If she does, she has only herself to blame for leaping to conclusions."

"She was alone with you, in your study. This afternoon."

"If you must be curious, Psyche, ask for the answers and do not sneak about," he chided gently. "There was indeed an attempt at seduction going on, but not by me—and I heartily assure you, with no hope of success."

She rose and came toward him, her gaze searching his face. "Do you really like my voice?" she asked quietly.

"Yes, I do. I was not toying with Helena, and certainly not with you, Clara," he continued softly. "I have been trying to leave you alone."

"Why do you want to leave me alone?" she asked, a vulnerability and tenderness in her eyes that touched him deeply.

"Because I am not worthy of your...esteem," he whispered, hope and shame warring within him as he waited, motionless, wanting so desperately to touch her.

She smiled and he thrilled to see it. "I think I am the best judge of that, my lord."

"Then you do not hate me?"

"No, my lord."

"You like me?"

She nodded shyly. "More than that, I must confess, my lord."

He didn't have to hear anything more. He pulled her into his arms and kissed her passionately, letting his lips speak in another way of the love he felt for her.

She returned his kiss with equal passion, pressing against him, holding him as ardently as he had ever dared to dream.

Happy beyond measure, thrilled beyond hope, Paris felt the current of desire flowing between them like a raging sea.

He never wanted the kiss to end, the moment to cease, the harsh realities of life to intrude.

But something was licking his hand. In his mind, Paris knew it was Jupiter, and as he reluctantly pulled back, his heart condemned the demon dog for robbing him of even a few moments in Clara's arms. "Jupe!" he said harshly. "Get away!"

He pointed at the door, which the dog had somehow nudged open, to see the large, languid shape of Zeus amble past. With a bark of warning, then the baying of the chase, Jupe lunged for the cat, who hissed and disappeared like an evil spirit. Jupiter was after it, barking wildly and careening out of the door.

Paris couldn't have done a more thorough job of making noise if he had tried. Clara gasped and rushed out into the hall. He hurried after and caught a glimpse of her skirt disappearing through the door of the studio.

He went as quickly and quietly as he could, in case by some miracle nobody had been roused by the racket. He paused on the threshold as his eyes adjusted to the dimness.

What the devil did it matter if anyone found them together? he thought suddenly. What would be the worst that could happen? They would be forced to marry. The worst? The idea was so extremely wonderful that he was tempted to knock something over to rouse everyone.

"I think they've gone outside," he heard Clara say from the vicinity of the easel. "The terrace door was open. I closed it."

He heard the anxiety in her voice, and he tried to think of a way to make her relax. "I don't hear anyone," he said.

"No," she answered warily.

"Maybe they thought Jupiter was outside."

"I hope so," his love said fervently, glancing at the door.

"Since we are here, and alone, what do you say we take a look at my portrait?" he suggested in a conspiratorial whisper as he shut the door and went closer, hoping to relieve some of the tension, and incidentally share a few more private moments with her.

"Aunt Aurora wouldn't like it."

"We know the penalty for curiosity can be severe," he said mischievously. "But I'm paying for the portrait, after all. I think I have every right to look. Besides, no one need know, and even if it's hideous, I won't say a word to the artist. Come, now," he finished in his most persuasive tones, "aren't you just a little curious to see if she's captured my delightful face upon the canvas? Aren't you anxious for a little harmless adventure on a moonlit night?"

She laughed softly, and Paris had never heard anything so delightful, except for Clara's admission that she more than liked him.

She began to tiptoe toward the covered easel, as curious as Psyche. "It was your idea to look at this," she whispered, chiding him. "Aren't you going to come here?"

He joined her quickly as she lifted up the covering; however, his attention was not on the painting. It was on Clara. If Cupid had awakened to see upon his wife's face such a compelling expression of excitement, curiosity and anxiety, he never would have left her in anger. He would have taken her in his arms and pressed heated kisses to her lips, her cheeks, her neck...

As he proceeded to do.

Moaning softly, Clara leaned against him. The contact of her body with his was electrifying, and he turned her face upward, seeking her warm, moist lips.

When she broke the kiss several moments later, she said, the merest hint of panic in her panting words, "Paris, somebody might—"

"I don't care," he growled, caressing her back and holding her against him, letting his tongue lightly trail along the soft skin of the curve of her jaw.

"The painting—"

He glanced at it over her shoulder. Then straightened and stared. "My God, do I truly look like the Duke of Wellington—and that smug and self-satisfied?"

Clara twisted to look at it and laughed rather breathlessly. "No. Everyone my aunt paints looks like the Duke of Wellington."

"Well, I'm vastly relieved, I must say." He glanced at the other canvas. "Then Eros and Psyche will look like the dear duke, as well?"

She nodded as she put the drapery back into place, a smile playing about her lips, her eyes aglow with glee, and he simply could not restrain himself. He took her by the shoulders and pulled her to him, kissing her again with all the fervor he felt.

With a low moan, Clara gave herself up to the full force of her emotions, letting herself be carried away on the sea of uncontrolled desire. For so long, it seemed, she had been fighting the currents of yearning, trying to deny the emotions he aroused within her and the passionate need. Now there was no reason to fight anymore.

He loved her, and she loved him. They belonged together, always.

His hands caressed her, increasing her yearning in a thousand subtle ways until she could have refused him nothing.

Then she became dimly and most regrettably aware that the room was getting brighter. Someone was coming inside! She moved away abruptly and faced the opening door.

"I am *so* delighted you both are here!" Aunt Aurora cried happily as she came into the room, attired in her painting smock and holding up a candle.

Clara stepped away from Paris as swiftly as she could without drawing attention to their previous proximity. She dared not risk looking at him, knowing that she was already blushing from her ears to her toes.

"Clara, where's your costume?" Aunt Aurora demanded, heading for her easel and pots of paint. "Oh, never mind. I was thinking of concentrating on the flesh tones of your faces tonight."

"I, um, believe you mentioned that," Clara lied, afraid to so much as glance at Paris, whom she could hear strolling behind her to the corner where the cushions had been piled. How could she bear posing with him now and not touch him, knowing how they felt about each other?

Aunt Aurora eyed her critically. Did her joy show on her face?

What if it did? she thought happily.

"Take your place, Clara, and you, too, if you please, my lord."

Clara obeyed, picking up the candle holder she had used when posing before. She lit the candle by touching the wick to the flame of Aunt Aurora's before turning, prepared to kneel beside the already recumbent—and bare-chested—Paris. "She said flesh tones," he remarked with a twinkle in his eye.

How could he be so calm? she wondered. She felt as if a steam engine's pistons were pumping in her chest. "Of our faces," she replied, trying not to smile.

"Remember, children," Aunt Aurora chided, *"Eros Discovered!"*

Eros discovered indeed! Clara thought helplessly, trying desperately to still the urge to kiss Paris, or to touch him in any way. He seemed well aware of her predicament, too, the rogue. The handsome, lovable, delightful rogue. Then she noticed that he was breathing heavily, too, and her mind imagined what would happen if Aunt Aurora were suddenly to disappear.

"Good heavens!" a male voice suddenly cried in alarm. "What is the meaning of this?"

The Reverend Jonas Clark strode into the room, on his stern visage an expression of appalled outrage and complete condemnation.

Chapter Twenty-Four

Clara got up awkwardly and Paris rose hurriedly, albeit with his usual consummate grace.

"I am painting a picture and Lord Mulholland and Clara are posing," Aunt Aurora replied grandly. "Now if you don't mind, I must ask you to leave. I do not allow spectators in my studio when I work."

Paris watched as Jonas marched toward the easel. What had been a delightfully revealing evening was now completely destroyed, ruined by both Mrs. Wells and Jonas's unexpected arrivals. A swift glance at Clara's pale face and Paris surmised she was feeling much the same sentiment. But now that he knew she loved him, he could easily see the humor in the situation.

Jonas reached the easel and stared at the painting there as if it were drawn with human blood, his mouth open and his eyes astonished.

"Jonas, please, it's nothing serious," Paris said, drawing on his shirt in a leisurely manner.

Jonas addressed Aurora Wells as if they were alone in the room. "Do you mean to tell me, madam," the reverend gentleman said, "that you allow your niece to pose for such immoral works?"

"Immoral? How can you say such a thing?" Aurora Wells demanded vigorously. "There is nothing immoral about two beautiful human bodies."

Clara gasped, and suddenly Paris felt a horrible sense of foreboding. He hurried toward the easel and looked at the painting.

Eros and Psyche were completely and obviously nude, and they were obviously Clara and himself.

His first reaction was an instinctive thrill. Did Clara really look like that beneath her plain, simple bodice and wide skirts? Were her breasts that perfect, her legs that long and slender, her waist so slim? A quick, hungry, primitive desire moved him to regard the living woman, and he was suddenly very sure her aunt had painted as close to the reality as possible.

Just as she had somehow managed to depict his body with rather astonishing accuracy. It was enough to make him wonder if she had bribed Jean Claude for details, or watched him through a keyhole.

"But they are *naked!*" Jonas exclaimed.

"Oh, Aunt!" Clara cried, covering her face with her hands. "How could you! You said we would have clothes on!"

Her very real distress pulled Paris from his reverie, while Aurora Wells contrived to look both sheepish and defiant. "I tried, my dear, truly, but I simply couldn't reconcile myself to the notion that the ancient Greeks wore nightclothes!"

Paris suddenly felt an overwhelming and surely inappropriate desire to laugh, until he realized that Clara was very close to tears. This was obviously a catastrophe to her.

"If that was the case, you should not have painted the picture at all!" Jonas admonished.

"Jonas," Paris said, once more in control of his wayward sense of humor as well as his ardent desire, "lower your voice. We don't need to rouse the whole household."

Unfortunately, the words had no sooner passed Paris's lips than Byron Wells charged into the studio, a poker in his upraised hand.

"Ring the alarum bell!" he bellowed. "Call out the guard!"

The older man took in the scene for an instant, then stared at the painting on the easel. "Aurora, my nymph, my queen!" he cried happily. "Finished already?"

"Aunt, cover it!" Clara ordered, no longer near tears, but conspicuously angry. "Reverend Clark, I—"

"Hide this excellent work of art?" Byron demanded, going closer to study it. "The effect of the light on the cushions, my dear—astonishing. Absolutely astonishing. Even better than your study of apples."

Jonas assumed his most patronizing air. "This is a most unfortunate business, Mrs. Wells, and I am shocked—*shocked!*—that you do not comprehend the terrible impropriety of this...this...*pornography*. I fear you have forgotten your obligations as a guardian. I think you have been most negligent in your duty and responsibility to the young person in your care, if not *harmful*."

Mr. and Mrs. Wells regarded him as if he were speaking gibberish.

Clara spoke first, and firmly. "I think it is you who have forgotten yourself, Reverend Clark. We did not ask for your approval, either of the posing or the picture. Nor did we request your critical opinion. If you do not like it, you may leave the room." She pointed imperiously at the door.

Brava, Clara! Paris wanted to shout.

"Shall I serve sherry, my lord?" Witherspoon intoned from the doorway. "Or tea?"

Everyone turned to look. The voluble Mrs. Dibble, Mrs. Macurdy the cook and a bevy of housemaids and footmen in their nightclothes crowded around the opening.

"*Alors!* Make way!" Jean Claude commanded, pushing his way through the crowd. Upon gaining access, he paused, adjusted his scarlet nightcap, straightened his scarlet satin robe and strode forward. *"Mon Dieu!"* he cried when he saw the picture.

"Exactly," Paris muttered. "Witherspoon, see that everyone returns to their rooms."

Then Paris saw Helena bearing down on them like a particularly enraged goddess. Behind her, as if she were a handmaiden, trotted Henrietta, who was attempting to peek at the picture over her sister's shoulder.

"What is going on?" Helena demanded, marching into the room as if she had every right to do so. She halted and gasped when she saw the picture, then looked from it to Paris and back again, her face growing redder and redder.

Henrietta stared at the picture and giggled.

"We are posing for a painting," Clara said defiantly, although her arms were now wrapped around her body defensively.

"Is *that* what you call it?" Helena asked with a curling lip.

"I say, is the house on fire?" a sleepy Tommy Taddington, wearing a long nightshirt, a wrinkled nightcap and with his eyes but half-open, called out in the hallway.

"No!" Paris shouted in response. "Go back to bed."

Regardless of Paris's exasperated order, Tommy forced his way into the studio. He blinked and looked around as if he had somehow wandered into a foreign country. "What the devil is—?" He spotted the picture. "Oh, my sainted aunt! It's *you!*" he cried, glancing at Paris. He peered at the picture, then, with wide eyes, regarded Clara. "And *you!* What are you supposed to be doing?"

"Of course it's us" was Clara's ungrammatical retort. "What do you expect, when we were the models?" She moved to stand beside her aunt, as if they were the Spartans holding the pass at Thermopylae. She glanced at the picture, then looked at it fully for the first time.

Paris was in the position she recognized, as was she, and they were both naked, but there was nothing lascivious about the work. They looked like two surprised young lovers, the man startled and upset, filled with loving dismay, the young woman thrilled and yet remorseful. Aunt Aurora had caught the necessary expressions exactly. The flesh tones, too, were perfect, and the proportions exact. The cushions, the shadows—it could have been anytime, anywhere.

"Aunt Aurora!" Clara gasped. "It's marvelous! It *is* your best work yet!"

"Well, this is a most pleasant gathering of the demos," Uncle Byron said jauntily. "An impromptu showing, as it were. Perhaps sherry would be just the thing, my lord, wouldn't you agree?''

"Your wife has seen fit to render your niece naked!" Reverend Clark declared, clearly determined to remind them all that a crime had taken place.

"That's not my niece," Uncle Byron said serenely.

Everyone stared at him.

"That's Psyche. With her husband, Eros."

"This is no time for mincing particulars, sir!" Reverend Clark said hotly. "You should be ashamed. And you, too!" he fired at Mrs. Wells.

"Come, now, Jonas," Paris said in his most conciliatory tone. "It's only a painting."

"*Only* a painting!" Clara and her aunt protested in one voice.

"It's a masterpiece! I'm proud to have been a model for it!" Clara went on, her eyes gleaming with angry passion.

"I daresay you are," Helena noted with a scornful smirk.

Henrietta giggled, until Clara faced the younger woman angrily. "Just what do you mean by that?"

"Please, everyone, let us remain calm," Paris said, feeling the situation was getting completely out of hand.

Witherspoon entered, bearing a tray with a decanter and sherry glasses. "I shall serve, my lord," he announced before proceeding to pour.

"Never mind sherry! Go back to bed," Paris said impatiently.

Witherspoon raised an eyebrow.

Lord Pimblett, wearing a robe of surprising pattern, came puffing into the studio, followed by his wife and the ever-faithful Hester carrying smelling salts.

"What is going on here?" he demanded. "What is the meaning of waking responsible people in the middle of the night with all this noise?" He glared at his two daughters. "Why aren't you in bed?"

Then he noticed the large canvas that was still the focus of Tommy Taddington's attention, in spite of the recent arrivals.

Lord Pimblett marched toward it. "Is all this fuss about a painting?" He started, then stared. "My God! Lord Mulholland, what have you been doing?"

"Posing," Paris replied patiently, while secretly wishing all these tiresome people to perdition.

Lord Pimblett ran his gaze over Clara. "I must say this is a scandalous piece of business," he declared before returning his attention to the painting.

There it was at last, Clara thought with a sense of hopelessness. Scandal. As fine a painting as *Eros Discovered* was, it would mean disgrace, at least for the models.

"It is a piece of *art,*" Uncle Byron corrected.

Lord Pimblett ignored him.

Reverend Clark stood with his arms folded against his chest, a deep frown on his face. "I knew you were impulsive and thoughtless, Paris, but I must say I didn't think you were capable of something like this," he said, shaking his head disapprovingly.

"What exactly have I done that warrants such censure?" Paris asked, exasperation creeping in his voice. "I lay on some cushions without a shirt on. You would think Miss Wells and I were in flagrante delicto, the way you're carrying on, and I assure you there was nothing like that happening. For heaven's sake, Jonas, Mrs. Wells was here."

"Yes!" Clara affirmed strongly. "I must say I don't like your insinuations, Reverend Clark, although I am not overly concerned with your judgment. My aunt is an artist. We were her models. Nothing immoral occurred, and I was always dressed."

"My poor confused young man," Uncle Byron said sympathetically. "Society is sadly all too ready to misunderstand the artistic sensibility."

"Indeed," Aunt Aurora agreed with enthusiasm and no hint whatsoever of shame. "Great artists have often been ostracized, reviled and scorned." She gestured dramatically. "We cast aside such trivialities as approval. We are prepared to accept the slings and arrows of the world as we answer to our muse."

"Yes, my dear, my own!" Byron cried, clasping his hands over his heart. "There is no more sacred calling!"

Reverend Clark frowned even more. "I would say the church is a more sacred calling."

"Art can be spiritual," Aunt Aurora argued. "For instance, look at this picture." Reverend Clark seemed to obey in spite of himself. "No, at their faces. Have you ever seen a more divine representation of love? The emotion in all its two parts, Psyche, the mind, recognizing Eros, the body, and finding not a monster, but love? Surely you don't believe, Reverend Clark, that the human body is monstrous?"

"I will not stand here in the middle of the night and quibble over artistic merit," Reverend Clark said firmly. "I still cannot accept, madam, that you have chosen to paint your niece naked, and I think, upon rational reflection, you will agree it was a mistake."

Paris stepped in between them and held up his hands placatingly. "I quite agree the middle of the night is no time for this discussion. It's late. Let us all go to bed."

"*I* think she was right to do so," Clara declared, determined that Reverend Clark and the other critics not have the final word. "The way she's painted them, they are naked and *vulnerable*. No clothes to mask themselves, or their feelings."

Reverend Clark ignored her. "I'm very sorry for you, Paris," he said mournfully.

"Why?"

"Because Miss Wells is quite ruined, as you well know, and you may be tainted, too. News such as this unfortunately flies fast."

"There will be no scandal," Paris said lightly, suddenly determined to end the interminable talking and gawking. "I shall do the honorable thing." He made a formal bow. "I am going to marry Miss Wells."

"*What?*" Clara exclaimed together with Jonas Clark.

She stared at Paris, a war between dismay and happiness waging in her. Happiness because the thought of being Paris's wife filled her with delight and desire; dismay to think that he was being forced into the marriage because of the threat of scandal.

Paris's only answer was a mocking, infuriatingly complacent smile, as if this whole situation were some tremendous joke enacted for his amusement.

Lady Helena blanched, and Henrietta giggled. Hester looked pleased, until called upon by a swooning mother. Tommy Taddington appeared stunned, and Jean Claude did an impromptu jig. Aunt Aurora smiled and dabbed at her eyes with a paint-splattered rag.

"I shall compose a wedding ode!" Uncle Byron cried. "I must have paper and pen!" He rushed out of the room, apparently in a white heat of inspiration.

"I had heard, Lord Mulholland, that you were a man lacking in principle," Lord Pimblett announced in his stuffiest, stiffest manner, "but I had no idea you were *stupid* as well as immoral. Come, daughters. We will leave this house tomorrow. Helena, I bless my lucky stars that we discovered just what kind of fellow this man is before you married him!" With his back as straight as Uncle Byron's poker, the affronted nobleman stalked toward the door.

"Girls!" he bellowed when they lingered for a last look at the picture. Lady Helena tossed her head disdainfully and marched past Clara and her aunt with the same stiff back as her father. Henrietta covered her mouth to smother another titter and trotted after them. Hester smiled wanly and helped her mother from the gilt chair. Lady Pimblett couldn't have needed more assistance if she was suddenly afflicted with paralysis.

Tommy Taddington watched them go, then glanced at those remaining and hurriedly followed.

Jean Claude sidled closer to Clara. *"Très magnifique, mademoiselle,"* he said with a knowing wink before he walked jauntily out the door.

"I understand your honorable intention—" Reverend Clark began, still clearly far from convinced as to Paris's stated intent, when Clara interrupted him by marching straight at Paris and standing before him with her arms akimbo and a fiery expression in her eyes.

"There is no need for you to extricate me from this alleged scandal," she declared. "I do not want you to marry me out of pity, or a misplaced sense of duty. I would far rather have the basest things said about me than *that*. So I reject your solution, my lord, and if there are those—'' she directed a venomous glance at the Reverend Clark ''—who would spread rumors, then I must accept my fate. I bid you all good night.''

With that, she swept past Reverend Clark, past her uncle, past her aunt and out of the room. Once in the corridor, she choked back sobs as she ran up the stairs, seeking the sanctuary of her bedroom, away from Paris and everyone else.

Once there, she sank down onto a chair and covered her face with her hands. They couldn't marry now. Everyone would think she had trapped Paris deliberately! They would look at him with sympathy and her with scorn, if they bothered to look at her at all.

She never should have come here. She should have stayed in London, alone and lonely, but safe! She should have persuaded her aunt to refuse the commission. She should have *never* agreed to pose for *Eros Discovered*.

She should not have fallen in love. Then, perhaps, she would be able to deal with this situation rationally. Instead, all she could do was sit here in a morass of tangled, unwelcome emotions.

There was a soft knock at the door and Aunt Aurora entered unbidden. ''Clara?'' she whispered tentatively as she closed the door softly. She spotted her niece in the chair. ''Clara, my dear, dry your tears.''

''Please leave me,'' she said, wiping her eyes with the hem of her sleeve.

Aunt Aurora wrung her hands and came toward her hesitantly. ''I'm sorry this has happened this way,'' she said, standing before her, ''but there is no need for such a reaction. Lord Mulholland wants to marry you. Why don't you do so?''

''I will not marry a man simply to avoid slander,'' Clara replied bitterly. ''After all, I should be used to gossip and rumors by now.''

Clara immediately regretted her words when she saw the guilty and sorrowful expression on her aunt's face. ''I realize that since you came to live with Byron and myself, your life has been rather... unusual,'' Aunt Aurora said mournfully, ''but we've always had your best interests at heart. We do love you, as if you were the child we never had.''

''I know!'' Clara cried, rising to embrace her aunt fervently. ''I know you love me.''

Her aunt's voice was full of misery. ''We only want your happiness. When I saw you with Lord Mulholland, I thought... You are the best, most worthy girl in the world, and you deserve everything poor, dear Byron and I cannot give you, and that your dolt of a grandfather continues to deny you. If you were to marry Paris Mulholland...''

''Aunt!'' Clara exclaimed, putting her hands on Aunt Aurora's plump shoulders and drawing back to examine her face in the moonlight as a sudden and completely unexpected notion burst into her mind. ''Aunt, what are you trying to say?''

Clara would have thought it impossible for her aunt to look so miserably contrite. ''You *planned* this?'' she demanded, aghast. ''You *wanted* a scandal? To force Paris Mulholland to marry me, so that my grandfather would acknowledge me?''

''I never wanted a scandal,'' Aunt Aurora was swift to protest. ''I just thought of posing together as a way to... as a method of...''

"You wanted us to be *together?*" she said.

"Only when I was sure you cared for each other!" Aunt Aurora professed. "When I saw the way you looked at him that night, when I came upon you in the studio—you've never looked at any young man like that, not even Davy Franks who modeled for Apollo and had quite the most astonishing form *I* ever saw."

"I didn't 'look' at Lord Mulholland in any particular way, except a kind of bemused pity," Clara claimed, even though she knew in her heart that this was a bold-faced lie. Had her feelings been so blatantly obvious? It sounded so...so like Lady Helena!

"But, my dear," Aunt Aurora went on softly, "it was the way he looked at you that convinced me you both needed a little assistance."

"I thought you considered my grandfather an imbecile," Clara said. "Why should you care if he acknowledges me or not? I don't."

"Because he is an imbecile with wealth and social standing, things you deserve."

Of all the things her aunt had done, all the embarrassment she had caused Clara over the years, this was the worst. That she could plot to entrap Clara and Paris Mulholland in marriage! Did Paris see what had been done? Did he guess? Would he think she had been privy to the plan?

"Oh, Aunt," Clara said wearily. "Perhaps you meant well, but...leave me now, please."

She feared if she did not send Aunt Aurora from the room, she would say something that she would regret later. "We can talk in the morning."

Mercifully, Aunt Aurora didn't object. She turned and walked toward the door. She paused on the threshold. "I'm sorry, my dear." Then her usual optimism asserted itself. "I hope you won't be stubborn about this."

When she was gone, Clara stared at the back of the door. "Oh, Aunt Aurora, how could you!" she murmured.

Chapter Twenty-Five

His gaze fastened keenly on the staircase, Paris stood in the doorway of his study the next morning, leaning against the frame in his usual negligent way, but with his lips turned down in a deep frown and his brows lowered in a most unusually worried expression as he waited for Clara. He wanted and needed to explain his sudden announcement last night, and he had vowed to do so the moment he saw her.

He was disheartened to think that she didn't believe his offer had been a sincere one, that she thought he had proposed marriage only as some kind of easy answer to the situation, despite his very real love for her. She must learn that she was completely, utterly wrong. He wanted her for his wife more than he had ever wanted anything, and if she refused, he would be desolate.

A rustle of fabric alerted him to the arrival of a female at the top of the stairs. He moved back into his study when he realized it was Hester and Henrietta coming down for breakfast. He was relieved that Helena wasn't with them, although he supposed he should get the inevitable unpleasantness of meeting her after last night over with. Still, he wouldn't mind if that was somewhat delayed.

Finally, Clara appeared at the top of the stairs.

She wore her plainest, most severe gown, with her hair pulled back tight from her pale face. Her eyes were red-rimmed and puffy, from tears, he suspected, and lack of sleep. He, too, had slept very little, remembering both the delight and dismay occasioned by the events in the studio. As Clara came down the steps, with her back straight and her expression determined, she looked like a saint going to her martyrdom.

He waited until she was abreast of the study door, then called out her name. She started. "What do you want?" she demanded in a whisper.

"Come inside. I *must* speak with you!"

She didn't move. "Hasn't being alone with you caused me enough trouble already?"

"Please!" he pleaded.

Paris Mulholland had never begged for anything in his life, but he would have lain down on a bed of nails and let an elephant walk over him if that would have persuaded Clara Wells to speak with him this morning.

She regarded him steadily for a long moment, then joined him in the study, closing the door behind her.

"Forgive me for acting like a silly fool last night," he said at once.

"When was that, my lord?" she asked with abominable frigidity. "When you said you would marry me?"

"No! Well, yes. I shouldn't have sounded so cavalier, as if I took your acceptance for granted." He looked at her, hoping she would understand that the words he spoke now came from his heart. "I want to marry you." His gaze faltered under the steadfast scrutiny of her unyielding eyes. "If you will have me."

"No, I won't," Clara replied slowly. "Not if you make this offer only out of necessity, so that your name will not be tainted with scandal, or because of some misguided notion of chivalry."

Now it was *her* gaze that faltered, as a charming flush spread upon her cheeks. "Not if you do not truly love me and want me to be your wife."

"I do!" he cried fervently. "Clara, I've never wanted anything more in my entire life. I've never loved anyone as I do you. I love you with all my heart!" He went down on his knee and took her hand in his. "Clara, please, will you do me the honor of becoming my wife?"

There was a sparkle of happiness as her lips twitched at the corners and her blush deepened. "This is not a joke, my lord?" she asked.

"Believe me, I have never been more serious about anything in my entire life."

Her smile broadened and he saw her answer in her shining hazel eyes.

Feeling giddy with happiness, he raised the back of his hand to his forehead melodramatically and gestured toward the garden. "Alas, if you say you care nothing for me, fair maiden, I shall drown myself in yonder fish pond."

"The fish pond is only a foot deep," she noted.

He rose slowly to his feet, the merry devilment in his eyes replaced by something far stronger. "Then you must say you love me, Clara, because I shall love you as long as I live."

Clara lowered her head and spoke very, very softly. "I can't help it, Lord Mulholland. I love you."

He laughed, a burst of unbridled joy. "Not the most flattering of admissions," he said cheerfully. "But I have had enough flattery." He pulled her into his arms for a breathtaking embrace. "Clara, Clara, you've made me the happiest man in the world!"

She was laughing, too, or at least she was until he smothered her laughter with a long, lingering, passionate kiss.

The sound of loud clearing of a masculine throat interrupted them. "I beg your pardon, my lord," Witherspoon said in his most dignified voice as he ran a censorious eye over the couple, "breakfast is being served in the dining room."

Paris bounded toward the butler and shook his hand enthusiastically. "Congratulate me, Witherspoon! Miss Wells and I are getting married!"

"Indeed?" the unflappable family retainer replied, cocking his head to one side, and with a glimmer of delight in his eyes.

"Indeed!" his master responded heartily.

"I suppose we shall become used to the smell of oils eventually, my lord," Witherspoon said with a forlornly dramatic sigh that would have done credit to Uncle Byron himself as the butler turned to go out. His face brightened with a broad smile when he pulled the door closed.

"Oh, Aunt Aurora!" Clara gasped, remembering last night. "She planned it all, you know. The painting and everything. But she thought we were already...that you and I...well, you know...when she suggested we pose." She chewed her lip and eyed him intently. "You're sure you're not marrying me to save my damaged honor, or something equally ludicrous?"

"You must love me," he declared gravely, "if you think I have so much chivalry, and of course it does credit to your discernment, but I should, in all justice, ask you if you truly believe Lord Paris Mulholland is sensitive to criticism of any kind, let alone enough to marry someone he does not love with his whole heart?"

"Your reputation is not a dishonorable one."

"Only a foolish one," he agreed, giving her a light kiss. "To think Aunt Aurora guessed so quickly and so rightly. I never would have suspected she was so shrewd."

Clara flushed in an enchantingly guilty way. "There is something else. Aunt Aurora thinks that if you marry me, my grandfather will acknowledge me."

"What do you think?"

"I don't care if he does, or not. He didn't help me when I was orphaned, and I do not need or want anything from him now. But when I think of everything Aunt Aurora and Uncle Byron have done for me..."

"And *me*," Paris said firmly. "Why, if your aunt had not accosted me about a portrait, think what I would have missed. I shall have to insist that they live with us. Of course, I shall also have a proper studio built, somewhere at the far end of the estate, perhaps, so she can work undisturbed."

"And not disturb us? You *are* wicked, Lord Mulholland."

He grinned. "I must say it's quite a delight to think of myself related to that wonderful woman and her delightfully eccentric spouse.'' He sat on a nearby chair and tugged Clara onto his lap. He reached up and pulled out a hairpin. ''I've been wanting to do this since the first time I saw you.'' He pulled out two more, then paused thoughtfully. ''I think that was when I started to fall in love with you, that very first night at the Pimbletts'. You were so very discouraging.''

''I was rude,'' Clara confessed.

''So was I, teasing you like that.''

''How was I, a stranger, to know you were teasing?''

''Because I was so utterly charming about it.''

The last pin came out and Clara's hair fell about her shoulders. He lifted a strand and pressed it to his lips. ''I think . . . I think we should go to breakfast,'' she murmured, half fearing that if they didn't leave the room, they would soon be in a truly scandalous situation.

He let go of her hair and shook his head, suddenly serious. ''Not until I apologize properly for my behavior last night, even though 'all's well that ends well.' ''

She started to tell him no explanation was necessary—indeed, she had acted like an overwrought fool herself—but he held one finger in front of her lips. ''I was angry and upset, what with your aunt coming into the room at that particular time.

''It's this damnable habit I've got into, Clara, of acting the charming fool. The more upset I am, the worse I seem to get. You'll have to help me change.''

''I love you precisely as you are,'' she said, running her finger over his lips. ''I know you have a serious side. I know about the village school, I believe your church attendance is exemplary and I suspect you provide the bread for those poor souls visiting the House of Correction. You're not nearly as irresponsible as you pretend, my lord.''

"Egad! Have I no secrets from this woman?" he cried in mock horror.

"One or two," she replied mischievously. "I don't really know how you look . . ." She eyed him significantly.

"Naked?"

She nodded.

"You Jezebel! I intend to retain my honor and my dignity until the wedding night!''

She giggled and he frowned. "I am going to have to stop playing the silly merry gadabout," he remarked. "Or else my wife will never take me seriously."

"I do, my lord," Clara said, seeing his very real distress. "I assure you, I do."

" 'My lord'? Paris, if you please."

"Paris," she said shyly. She smiled and wound her finger in his cravat. "Even after we kissed, I was afraid to believe what my heart was telling me about you."

"When you left, and I saw what a stupid mistake I'd made, and at the most important juncture of my life, Clara," Paris said, "I wanted to howl."

"We've both been foolish," Clara said, rising regretfully.

"By trying to make light of the whole situation, I might have lost you."

"Since we are being so bluntly honest with each other," Clara said gravely, "I must confess that I think it would not have been so easy for me to forget you."

"Thank God!" Paris said fervently, taking her hand. "I hope to see that you never even think of such an outrageous thing for the rest of your life."

"Lady Helena will be disappointed," Clara said archly as they went to the door.

"Set your mind at rest, my darling—and ask your aunt if she doesn't think something else is afoot there," Paris said with a roguish grin and a wink as he drew her hand through his arm and led her to the dining room.

Despite her happiness, Clara would sooner have faced a gallery full of prim and pretentious art critics than the group assembled in Paris's dining room that morning, and when they first entered, she thought her fears not amiss. Lord Pimblett looked as if he had slept with his lips turned down and his brow furrowed. Lady Helena's mouth couldn't have looked more pinched if she had eaten lemons for breakfast. She was seated beside Tommy Taddington, who was all condescension and pity. Lady Pimblett was nearly immobile, apparently from shocked sensibility.

The Reverend Clark, standing at another window with his back to the light, frowned. Hester smiled sympathetically, and Henrietta, ever true to form, giggled, albeit nervously. Even she was not blind to the tension in the room.

Uncle Byron stood looking out another window in the same attitude as Lord Nelson might have used on the bridge of the *Victory* before the Battle of Trafalgar. Aunt Aurora stood beside him, but she was watching the door, and her face broke into a delighted and relieved smile the moment she saw her niece and Paris enter the room.

"Good morning, all," Paris said so casually that Clara wondered if he was *completely* impervious to other people's opinion. "Lovely morning, isn't it?"

He waited, clearly relishing the attention. "I must demand that you all wish me joy," he continued. "Miss Wells has consented to be my wife."

"Oh, my *dear!*" Aunt Aurora cried happily, rushing forward to embrace her niece.

"Hail, Hymen's handmaiden!" Uncle Byron declared. Then he halted and looked worried. "That's as far as I've gotten on the wedding ode. But not to worry, children! It shall be ready when required."

Reverend Clark stepped forward. "Paris, don't you think you're being a bit rash?" he asked not unkindly, his concern for his friend apparently outweighing social necessity.

"Not at all," Paris replied merrily. "Indeed, I owe you my thanks. If you hadn't come upon us in that compromising position last night, I might never have had the nerve to ask Clara to marry me."

"Lord Mulholland!" Lord Pimblett blustered sternly, rising from his chair. "Do you mean to tell me that you are breaking your engagement with my daughter to wed this . . . this . . . *bohemian?*"

"No, I don't mean to tell you that, my lord," came the nonchalant reply. Paris went to stand beside Clara, and his hand touched hers. "I have never been engaged to your daughter, and I assure you, I never *had* any intention of being engaged to her." Paris fastened his gaze onto the blushing Lady Helena. "Isn't that right?"

"Papa," the young lady said hurriedly, with a glance at Tommy Taddington, "I may have *implied* that we were engaged. I had, at one point, thought it was so. I *hoped* it was so." Her expression grew more bold. "However, after that *shocking* scene last night, I must say I am relieved I was not. I do not think Lord Mulholland is a man I would want for my husband." She gave the rich Tommy Taddington a meaningful look.

"This is a most scandalous, outrageous business!" Lord Pimblett declared. "You, sir, are unfit for the House of Lords. I thought you were just another one of these dilettante young men who would grow into a sense of responsibility when you married—"

"Sounds terrible, like growing a third eye," Clara whispered irreverently to Paris, who had to struggle to maintain a straight face.

"—but now I find you are completely lacking in moral fiber, sir. Our country's going to the dogs, sir— the *dogs!* when a young man like you takes up with a strumpet like this and then has the unmitigated gall to make the liaison legitimate!"

"Shut your mouth, Pimblett," Paris said quietly.

The Pimblett women gasped en masse and the startled lord stared, speechless.

"Need I remind you that you are speaking of my future wife?" Paris said.

Lady Pimblett glanced at her husband, then her eldest daughter and Paris Mulholland's rich friend. "Edgar," she said, sitting up with surprising vigor, "obviously you have let your emotions run away with you. I'm sure Lord Mulholland has every right to pose with the Duke of Chesterton's granddaughter, since they are to be wed.

"And although I must chastise Lord Mulholland for keeping this happy news so secret," the redoubtable lady continued, "I am pleased we are able to be the first to offer our congratulations. I trust, my dear young man, that you won't hold my husband's impassioned words against us."

Lord Pimblett went limp and collapsed in the nearest chair, like a bagpipe with a leak.

Paris squeezed Clara's hand. He truly hadn't felt a single qualm about what the world would say about him; nevertheless, he was relieved for Clara's sake that Lady Pimblett was running true to form. A woman of her ilk would never knowingly destroy a valuable social connection.

"I believe we should allow the happy couple to make some plans, now that their engagement is no longer a secret," Lady Pimblett said. She glanced at Aunt Aurora as she rose without a hint of frailty. "I shall be delighted to recommend a suitable dressmaker."

And incidently tell everyone you did so, Paris thought with amusement. "Good morning, Lady Pimblett."

Lady Pimblett laid a talonlike hand on her husband's arm. "Come along, Edgar. Fresh air will cool that hot head of yours." She led her deflated husband outside.

Lady Helena likewise rose. "I hope you will be very happy," she said with less scorn than Paris had anticipated before she followed her parents.

"Very happy," Tommy echoed as he trotted after her, and Paris knew he had his explanation for Helena's subdued reaction.

"Girls!" Lady Pimblett called from the terrace.

Hester smiled with happiness and true friendship before she joined the others outside. Henrietta eyed the couple curiously, but a second summons from the seemingly invigorated Lady Pimblett spared them another giggle.

"An admirable woman," Byron declared, going to join his wife. His arm crept around her plump waist. "Sadly, no artistic sensibility. I shudder to think of the china she has ruined!"

An apologetic Reverend Clark came toward Paris and Clara. "I have to have faith that you know what you're doing," he said.

"We do," the happy couple replied simultaneously.

"It just doesn't seem right," he murmured doubtfully.

"Under other circumstances you would probably be absolutely correct," Paris assured him. "However, these are very special circumstances."

Reverend Clark finally smiled as he offered his hand to Paris, who shook it warmly. "I hope I shall be invited to the wedding."

"I was planning on asking you to marry us," Paris said, and Clara smiled her agreement.

"With pleasure," Jonas said happily.

"Even though I might not feel truly wed, having a friend perform the ceremony," Paris said pensively as Jonas sauntered onto the terrace.

"I shall have to make sure you *know* you are," Clara replied mischievously. "Every day. And every night," she finished in a whisper only he could hear.

"To think they call me licentious!" her future husband declared quietly as Clara went to her aunt and kissed her cheek. She also pressed a light kiss on her kindhearted uncle.

"I am so happy!" she said, gazing at them lovingly with tears in her eyes and a smile on her lips.

"As you deserve to be, my dear," Aunt Aurora replied, dabbing at her eyes with the dangling end of her turban. "If only your dear parents could be with us today!"

Uncle Byron cleared his throat loudly. "Yes, my dear. However, let us not slide into the Slough of Despond on this joyous occasion."

Clara wiped her eyes and glanced out the window, then hurried to one with a better view of the garden, beckoning for Paris to join her. "Look!" she said softly.

Lady Pimblett marched along the path, busily gesturing at her husband, whose head hung down like that of a child being scolded. The elder and younger Pimblett girls were seated on a bench near the roses. Tommy Taddington sat bashfully beside Helena, who apparently was graciously condescending to listen to him. Jonas Clark strolled up to Henrietta and sat beside her, bestowing a tender smile upon the young lady. In the distance, Hester made her solitary, graceful way along the yew path.

Closer to the house, Jupiter lay sleeping in the sun, and beside him, curled up and content, was Zeus.

"Ours is not the only unusual match," Clara said with a smile as Paris slipped his arm around her. She leaned her head against his shoulder. "Look, Aunt, Uncle, there's a subject for a picture."

Aunt Aurora smiled at the sight of the happy young couple standing arm in arm in front of the beautiful garden in the bright morning sun. They looked as if they stood on the threshold of Paradise.

She wiped another tear from her eye as she grasped her husband's hand and whispered, "Indeed. Quite a picture."

*   *   *   *   *

Author Note

During the summer of 1995, my family and I were incarcerated in the House of Correction, Folkingham, Lincolnshire.

No, we hadn't broken the law. We had rented the prison gatehouse from The Landmark Trust of Great Britain, a charity devoted to preserving interesting historical buildings and making them useful again. There was a moat, too, for the House of Correction was built on the site of a Norman castle. All in all, a perfect holiday spot for a romance writer, especially one whose ancestors originally came from that area.

We also visited nearby Belton House, a manor used in a television adaptation of Jane Austen's *Pride and Prejudice,* which recently aired on television and where members of my family were employed. Belton House was the prototype for Mulholland House, with several changes to suit my own story.

I had a wonderful time with Paris and Clara, so much so that I've decided to stay in Victorian England for a while—and I couldn't leave Hester all alone, could I? She's about to meet the Dark Duke, a man considered to be a black-hearted scoundrel, and whose life is full of secrets. It will take a perceptive, quietly determined young woman to discover the truth.

Look for Hester's story in the spring of 1997.

HARLEQUIN®

Scandals

A passionate story of romance, where bold, daring characters set out to defy their world of propriety and strict social codes.

"Scandals—a story that will make your heart race and your pulse pound. Spectacular!"
—Suzanne Forster

"Devon is daring, dangerous and altogether delicious."
—Amanda Quick

Don't miss this wonderful full-length novel from Regency favorite Georgina Devon.

Available in December, wherever Harlequin books are sold.

1997
Reader's Engagement Book
A calendar of important dates
and anniversaries for readers to use!

Informative and entertaining—with notable
dates and trivia highlighted throughout the year.

Handy, convenient, pocketbook size to help you
keep track of your own personal important dates.

Added bonus—contains $5.00 worth of coupons
for upcoming Harlequin and Silhouette books.
This calendar more than pays for itself!

 Available beginning in November at
your favorite retail outlet.

The collection of the year!
NEW YORK TIMES BESTSELLING AUTHORS

Linda Lael Miller
Wild About Harry

Janet Dailey
Sweet Promise

Elizabeth Lowell
Reckless Love

Penny Jordan
Love's Choices

and featuring
Nora Roberts
The Calhoun Women

This special trade-size edition features four of the wildly popular titles in the Calhoun miniseries together in one volume—a true collector's item!

Pick up these great authors and a chance to win a weekend for two in New York City at the Marriott Marquis Hotel on Broadway! We'll pay for your flight, your hotel—even a Broadway show!

Available in December at your favorite retail outlet.

NEW YORK
Marriott®
MARQUIS

◆ HARLEQUIN® ❦ *Silhouette®*

Weddings by DeWilde

Since the turn of the century the elegant and fashionable
DeWilde stores have helped brides around the world
turn the fantasy of their "Special Day" into reality. But now the
store and three generations of family are torn apart by the
separation of Grace and Jeffrey DeWilde. Family members
face new challenges and loves in this fast-paced, glamorous,
internationally set series. For weddings and romance, glamour
and fun-filled entertainment, enter the world of DeWildes....

**Watch for *WILDE MAN*,
by Daphne Clair
Coming to you in January, 1997**

The sophisticated image and spotless reputation of DeWilde's
Sydney store was being destroyed by tacky T-shirts and
unmentionable souvenirs! And Maxine Sterling was not going
to let swaggering DeWilde Cutter get away with it! He'd have
to take his gorgeous looks and puzzling name and find
another business. And she was certainly *not* going to fall in
love with a man whose life-style symbolized everything
she'd fought so hard to escape!

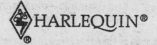

HARLEQUIN®

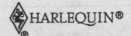
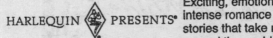

FREE VALENTINE'S BROOCH!
$9.95 U.S. retail value

This Valentine's Day Harlequin brings you
all the essentials—romance, chocolate
and jewelry—in:

VALENTINE *Delights*

Matchmaking chocolate-shop owner Papa Valentine
dispenses sinful desserts, mouth-watering
chocolates…and advice to the lovelorn, in this
collection of three delightfully romantic stories
by Meryl Sawyer, Kate Hoffmann and Gina Wilkins.

As our special Valentine's Day gift to you, each copy
of *Valentine Delights* will have a beautiful, filigreed,
heart-shaped brooch attached to the cover.

Make this your most delicious Valentine's Day
ever with *Valentine Delights!*

Available in February wherever
Harlequin books are sold.

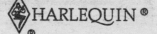

HARLEQUIN ®

Harlequin® Historical

If you're a serious fan of historical romance,
then you're in luck!

Harlequin Historicals brings you
stories by bestselling authors, rising new stars
and talented first-timers.

Ruth Langan & Theresa Michaels
Mary McBride & Cheryl St. John
Margaret Moore & Merline Lovelace
Julie Tetel & Nina Beaumont
Susan Amarillas & Ana Seymour
Deborah Simmons & Linda Castle
Cassandra Austin & Emily French
Miranda Jarrett & Suzanne Barclay
DeLoras Scott & Laurie Grant…

You'll never run out of favorites.

Harlequin Historicals…they're too good to miss!

HH-GEN